'A perfect literary thriller. A moving, gripping story told in beautiful prose. The twists keep coming until the very last page. I loved this book' Erin Kelly

'Whip-smart, lushly written and truly page-turning. I loved *Exquisite*, from the misleading simplicity of the premise and right down through all the dark depths of the she said/she said narrative. Sarah Stovell is a thrilling talent' Holly Seddon

'*Exquisite* is a powerful and assured debut thriller. Slickly claustrophobic and delicately wrought, this arch story of obsession and forbidden love taken to the extreme will have you squirming in your seat even as you're driven to turn the next page. A must-read for 2017' Sarah Pinborough

'Sarah Stovell writes beautifully. In her latest novel she combines that skill with a thrilling dramatic narrative. Exquisite in every way' Essie Fox

'Beautifully written and perfectly twisted, I was sucked deeply into the intertwined worlds of Alice and Bo and found myself reading through my fingers, compelled yet terrified at what the outcome might be … And that ending. Just wow. There could not be a better title for this book' S J I Holliday

'I bloody loved it. So clever, so beautifully written, such brilliant characterisation and THAT ENDING! This book is going to be MASSIVE! It has all the special little things that make it stand out from other psychological thrillers and it had my tummy in knots. I'm going to be shouting about this one for a long time. Definitely in my top reads for 2017' Lisa Hall

'Addictive, terrifying and beautifully written, *Exquisite* is up there with the best psychological thrillers I've ever read. Fucking awesome' Chris Whitaker

'Beautifully written, atmospheric and sexy, *Exquisite* is a satisfying psychological thriller with real class' Cass Green

'The best novel about obsession that I have read in a decade. Beautiful, beautiful writing with two extraordinarily divisive characters. I'm book hungover … pure brilliance. *Exquisite* is going to be HUGE' Liz Loves Books

'A highly addictive, sophisticated and very twisted psychological thriller. The reader is exposed to the workings of the darkest of minds, and each page presents a question, although the answers are not always apparent. The development of the intense and, at times, very disturbing relationship that grows between Bo and Alice is so finely done, with some spectacular characterisation and surprising twists. Sarah Stovell is hugely talented, and *Exquisite* is an absolute triumph' Random Things Through My Letterbox

'Beautifully written prose – put me right inside the heads of these two unreliable narrators … the tension gradually escalated until these two intelligent women became pitted against one another, with more than a hint of *Fatal Attraction*. I found it very difficult to know who to believe, who was telling the truth and who was telling lies. This unforgettable, outstanding psychological thriller should be on everyone's "to buy" list!' Off-the-Shelf Books

'An epically taut page-turner … intense and thought-provoking. *Exquisite* was an utter delight to read' The Quiet Knitter

EXQUISITE

ABOUT THE AUTHOR

Sarah Stovell was born in 1977 and spent most of her life in the Home Counties before a season working in a remote North Yorkshire youth hostel made her realise she was a northerner at heart. She now lives in Northumberland with her partner and two children and is a lecturer in Creative Writing at Lincoln University. Her debut psychological thriller, *Exquisite*, is set in the Lake District.

Exquisite

SARAH STOVELL

Orenda Books
16 Carson Road
West Dulwich
London SE21 8HU
www.orendabooks.co.uk

First published by Orenda Books 2017

A catalogue record for this book is available from the British Library.

ISBN 978-1-910633-74-8
eISBN 978-1-910633-75-5

Typeset in Garamond by MacGuru Ltd
Printed and bound by CPI Group (UK) Ltd, Croydon CRO 4YY

SALES & DISTRIBUTION

In the UK and elsewhere in Europe:
Turnaround Publisher Services
Unit 3, Olympia Trading Estate
Coburg Road
Wood Green
London
N22 6TZ
www.turnaround-uk.com

In USA/Canada:
Trafalgar Square Publishing
Independent Publishers Group
814 North Franklin Street
Chicago, IL 60610
USA
www.ipgbook.com

In Australia and New Zealand:
Affirm Press
28 Thistlethwaite Street
South Melbourne VIC 3205
Australia
www.affirmpress.com.au

For details of other territories, please contact *info@orendabooks.co.uk*

To Guitty

Thank you.

Her Majesty's Prison for Women
Yorkshire

It's better out here, where the roses still bloom. Inside, nothing can bloom at all. There's not enough light, for one thing, and for another, the flowers can sense everyone's misery, and they wilt in half a day.

The wardens think me fanciful when I say things like this, but they think me fanciful, anyway, on account of the fact that I live mostly in my mind and not in the here and now. But the here and now is a dreadful place; I'm grateful that my mind can take me out of it. Most people here don't have that luxury. It's why they ended up in prison in the first place – because they used fists and boots to make their feelings clear instead of words.

I am not like them. I am not like anyone else here. I am a model prisoner. That's why they let me work in the gardens instead of inside. The gardens aren't part of the prison, of course. They're the governor's gardens – for the governor and her husband and children to enjoy. Prisoners aren't allowed gardens. We only have only a courtyard, where our clothes are hung out to dry on good days, although there aren't many good days, because the sun hardly reaches us.

But here in the garden it's better. Because I am a model prisoner who will slog away at whatever they set me to, and because it makes no difference to them whether I'm scrubbing floors or planting flowers, they let me choose my job. So any time I'm not in my cell, I choose to be outside. I tell them I have a greater chance of being rehabilitated if they keep me outside – my hands in the earth, my eyes fixed on the sky, feeling cold rain on my skin – and they listen to me, on account of my being brighter and less trouble than most prisoners.

Today's roses are white. White roses always remind me of her. I still remember that bunch of white roses and the gold twigs covered with berries. The berries seeped and could have been poisonous, but they'd looked just right, spread among the roses like that, tender and translucent as newly-hatched jellyfish.

She would love these roses, if I could send them to her. White roses for eternal love. The meaning wouldn't be lost on her. She was sensitive to symbolic meanings. And perhaps then she would forgive me.

Part One

MEETING

1

Bo

In the mountains, daylight still falled. The frost raged and wind rang like steel through the ice. It was winter up there, but the gentle beat of spring ripened the valley below. Light fell on the church and stone cottages; it greened the trees and warmed the silent lake. Two seasons always claimed this far-flung nook of earth.

It was my favourite time of day – the trek back through the fells after dropping my girls at school. Our home stood two miles outside the village, but from the moment we moved here I was insistent the girls walk to school, whatever the weather. That was the purpose of a Lake District childhood, to my mind: to know the slow movement of the seasons; to breathe beneath clean skies and hear the ice-cold motion of a stream; to run wild until the landscape wore their shoes out.

I thought they'd fight me harder than they did. In Oxford, they'd refused to walk anywhere. Maggie, especially, complained of the cold, the ice, the dark; the cars that passed too quickly through the rainy streets and shocked her legs with spray. But here, walking became something new and exciting. It had been September when we moved, two years ago now, in time for the new school year. The girls had watched with awe as summer's green faded and the burnished light of autumn emerged in the foliage. They liked running out in the morning mist, watching it dissolve to reveal the ochre flush of the fells. They filled their pockets with conkers and fir cones, took them home, scattered them over their bedroom floors, said they were making a bed for the hedgehog they planned to adopt over winter.

I watched them, deeply satisfied. I'd long held a theory – Gus scoffed at the hippiness of it, but so what? – that humans were homesick for the outdoors. This strange urge to shut themselves away from the elements, locked up in houses, cars, offices, thinking they were protected from the wind and the rain and the cancerous sun … it was rotting their very hearts, making them sick. They didn't know the cure was simple: Get outside. Walk. Breathe. Live.

Moving here had been good for everyone, though we'd done it mainly because of my work. At the time, I was researching the murky lives of the women surrounding the Romantic Poets – the women who'd willingly tended to sensational but sick men who had abandoned domestic life and hurt themselves with sonnets.

'I need to be in Grasmere to do this,' I'd told Gus.

He suggested a holiday, but I needed more than that. 'A year at least,' I said. 'Maybe two.'

'We can't uproot the girls for a year or two. If we need to move, we move forever, or not at all.'

It was exactly the response I'd wanted. I'd mastered this particular skill over the years: sowing the seed of half my desire, then letting him grab and plant the rest. That way, he'd always think of it as a joint decision; or, better still, his own idea.

Gus was already retired when we moved. There were twenty-two years between us and he was ready, I thought, and he agreed, for a more peaceful life. A secluded world away from the fog of the city, the grey sky that fell into the dull Thames, the shoppers and the crowds.

'There'll be crowds in the Lake District,' he said. 'You can't get away from the tourists. Even in January, they'll be there.'

What he said was only partly true. Tourists always filled the valleys. They hung around the lakes and towns, took their children to Peter Rabbit World, rowed across Windermere and ate cream teas in lakeside gardens. They paid a duty call to Dove Cottage, and came away reminded of why they'd hated Wordsworth at school. But few of them really left the vales. They didn't see Helvellyn silenced by snow, or the high mountain tarns lying dark beneath the rocky edges of the fells. For most of the year, our home stood unseen.

I rounded a curve in the mountain path and the cottage came into view: limewashed walls, slate roof and a rose trellis, the branches knocking against the lattice in the breeze – so different from the four-storey town house we'd owned in Oxford.

The door was unlocked. I opened it and stepped into the old, quarry-brick hall that took me through to the kitchen. Gus sat in the rocking chair by the woodburner, reading the *Westmorland Gazette*: all the news about stolen sheep, a campaign to save the post office and the decision to close a crumbling footpath in Buttermere. He took no notice of the national news these days. He said the only way to survive what was going on in the world – climate change, a refugee crisis, the Tory reign of terror – was to live in ignorance of it. He never used to be like this. There was a time when he'd read a paper every day on his commute to Paddington, watch the evening news at seven and again at ten, always making sure his opinions were informed. But his mind seemed empty now. It left too much space for dangerous, depressive pondering, and I had to take care around him.

He didn't look up as I walked in. Somehow, over the years, our everyday language had slipped away. We didn't bother anymore with 'Hello' or 'How was your day?' We'd become like furniture to each other: necessary for an easy life, but really just part of our surroundings – noticed only if visitors arrived.

I didn't mind this; not really. There was something hugely comfortable about the way we lived – free to do our own thing, but bound together by companionship, by a life we'd shared for so long now, we could each hardly imagine the house without the other. Besides, I didn't have enough leftover energy to mind. The girls were what mattered. Their needs were huge. I'd always been aware, even when they were tiny and single nights had gone on forever, that this time was fleeting. So I'd put everything I had into it. And although I craved more time for my work – a day, just one day! – I knew, always, that nothing would ever be this important again. There would never be anything in my future more meaningful than the care of my children – the two girls who wore out the very marrow in my bones and pushed me to the limits of my well-being, but made everything wonderful.

I spooned coffee into the espresso maker and set it on the stove to heat, then whipped milk in the Aeroccino. (I'd had to stop using those coloured capsules when Gus went through his environmental crisis. I pointed out that they were recyclable, but he said that was most likely nonsense invented by Nestlé, and that we were just wasting more miles having them transported back to the factory to be tossed into landfill. My husband's principles were admirable, but they did make him hard work to live with at times.)

The smell of brewing coffee rose and mingled with the smell from the bread machine; even though I knew I was at risk of becoming a bourgeois stereotype, I loved it. I wanted this to be the defining smell of my house: warm and comforting, a home people would always be happy to come back to.

I carried the coffee to my study – a small room off the kitchen that had once, a hundred years ago, or so, been the common parlour – and sat at my desk. It was covered in piles: a pile of pages from my manuscript; a pile of books about Samuel Taylor Coleridge's women; and a pile of submissions from aspiring authors who wanted me to offer them a place on the course I was running the following month. My heart sagged as I looked at them. I had to select six from more than a hundred. All of them needed sifting into piles: *definitely not; maybe; definitely yes.* The *definitely not* pile was always disheartening – always so much bigger than the *definitely yes* pile. But in that *yes* pile might be the stirrings of something, some raw talent for me to grab hold of and grow. I longed to discover a voice of the future.

I read four – three *definitely no* and one *maybe* – before the phone interrupted me. It was my biggest failing, this inability to ignore the ringing of the landline or the incoming ping of an email or Facebook alert. It robbed me of so much time. I probably lost two books a decade to frivolous chatting.

It was my mother. Her tone today was injured: she hadn't heard from me for months; she was seventy-five years old; she needed help with her shopping; she'd gone eight days without talking to another human being, and even then it had only been the postman, who made it clear he couldn't wait to get away; she was feeling ill; she was lonely; she was afraid at night, here in her wagon, where anyone could get in; she was feeling, truth be told, abandoned ever since I'd taken the children and moved to the far north of the country.

I tuned her out. I knew my friends had similar problems with their parents. Old age, they said; people became difficult in old age. But my mother had always been like this – demanding that everyone make her their sun, putting her at the centre of their lives, rotating around her, letting her shine but having no vital light of their own. If they didn't do this, it meant they didn't love her enough.

Eventually, I said, 'We'll be down in the summer.'

But my mother went on. I tuned her out again, holding the phone slightly away from my ear. I'd done a good job so far, I reminded myself, of not being like her; of not passing down to my own children this awful, hereditary madness. I was good. I was putting it all right.

The phone call ended. I hadn't been prepared for it, and for a while I sat exhausted, resting my forehead in my hands. There was no flare of the old anger, though; that was long gone. But I couldn't entirely escape the guilt about how I really felt: My aging mother was upset, and I, frankly, did not give a shit.

I returned to the pile of submissions on my desk. They were the usual, predictable stories about car crashes, murders, drugs raids and homosexuals coming out before they were ready and then killing themselves. I hadn't known the world had room in it for this much crap.

But then, there was one. *Last Words.* It was arresting. I read it to the end.

Last Words

The Japanese always burn their dead. Afterwards, the bones are taken out of the furnace and the entire family gathers round and picks them up with chopsticks. They put the bone of their choice into a jar, take it home with them and bury it. It seems a strangely sinister ritual to me. I think it's the chopsticks that do it. They make the whole thing hover a bit too close to cannibalism for my liking. I imagine myself having to gather up my mother's bones with a knife and fork. The idea makes me want to vomit, though I'm sure she herself would relish all the latent symbolism in the image. I have, after all, been wantonly drinking her blood since the day I was born.

My mother is dying. She has cancer, of course, and no will to live. I haven't seen her since I was sixteen and she went off and married Husband Four (the psychopath), leaving me on my own with Husband Three (the drunk) and the occasional weekend visit to Husband One (the father). Husband Two (the good one) died in a car accident when I was six.

My family is the stuff of tragedy, or it would be if the lack of noble emotion hadn't reduced us all to the level of soap opera. Divorce is the family sport. My mother is current champion, though this, like all records, could change at any moment.

It won't be me who inherits her title, though. I don't go near anyone.

I've always been hiding from my mother. Early on, I learnt how to make myself invisible. I kept quiet and endured her. Her fist in my face was just ice.

All in all, it was good when she left. She was gone, and I was free to stop hoping that from beneath the violence would spring the fairy tale, dressed in floral skirts and smelling of fabric softener. They all said she'd regret it. I used to picture her as the years rocked by: alone in her big house, weeping tears of blood.

Three years ago, I found her on Facebook. Emma Butterworth. Still his surname, but that didn't mean it had lasted. I clicked on her every week, without becoming her friend, and knew from a distance whenever she changed her profile picture. I scrolled through her list of friends for anyone I remembered. There was no one. My mother did not hold on to people.

Once, her profile picture changed to one of me and her when I was a baby. She was gazing at me with a devotion not seen since the Nativity. 'I miss her' she'd written. Below it, a few comments: 'Sorry you're having a bad day, Emma.' 'Be kind to yourself.' 'Let go of guilt.' 'You did your best.'

A support group, full of supporters. I didn't click on her again but I didn't block her, either.

And that's how they found me. A message appeared in my inbox from a woman called Liz Elegant: 'Dear Alice. Your mother has asked me to get in touch with you. I know it has been a long time since you two had any contact, but Emma is in hospital and approaching the end of her life. Please get in touch if you would like the hospital address.'

I left it three days then sent a message.

Now I'm here, in the waiting area. There's a window that looks over the road to the park. Families, small and intact, hang around the swings in the sun. I glance out at them, then away. In all my old dreams of family, I didn't know how hard it would be: the uphill slog to domestic fulfilment. I used to think it would happen simply because I deserved it. I'd had my fill, my spill, my broken homes, my bag on my back and nowhere to go. Someone would hand me a future. A golden apple, wet with love.

Instead, I lay down on the floor for them. I unwrapped my skin and let them dance on my flesh with hobnailed boots. Pints of my blood still keep them strong.

I know now. The world has no need for more of my genes.

The door to her room has been closed since I got here. I've had no reason to wait. I've just been getting ready.

I cross the corridor, knock lightly and go in.

'Emma,' I say, and I do not flinch at the sight of her, beaten on the bed.

Slowly, she turns her head. She looks at me for a long time. I take the seat beside her.

'Alice,' she says.

I say nothing.

She reaches for my hand. I let her clasp it in the bones of her own.

Her voice is a whisper, hard as sandpaper. 'Thank you.'

I am silent.

'Put it right,' she says, and her grip tightens on my hand. 'Forgive me now, and put it right.'

A golden apple, wet with love. I take my hand away. Sweat glints on my palm, like poison.

I put the pages down. This was autobiography, clearly – something I usually had no time for, but I could forgive this one. Its author must still be floundering in youth, hadn't yet found a theme bigger than her mother that she could harness. And she was in pain, too. Oh, the words were brutal, the language sharply controlled, but I caught the vulnerability beneath: the longing; that endless, endless longing for the elusive love of the mother.

I fired up my laptop and typed an email to the centre administrator of the country house where the course was being held.

Subject: *Students selected for Advanced Fiction, taught by Bo Luxton.*

I typed the first name, then highlighted it and put it in bold, to indicate that I thought the student worthy of financial assistance.

Alice Dark.

2
Alice

I rose to the surface of sleep. Before I'd even opened my eyes, I was aware of that old slump of my brain, my charred throat, the pain. I glanced at the clock. 12:36 pm. Another day moving on without me.

Next to me, Jake slept on, the unwashed lump of him taking up too much space on the mattress. That mattress was a symbol of all our failures, I thought. We weren't even mature enough to sleep more than six inches off the floor. What hope was there for either of us ever forging a path through the brutal world of the arts?

I stood up, manoeuvring through scattered ashtrays, pouches of tobacco and last night's empty lager bottles to the shower room. I could hear the sounds of Chris and his girlfriend shagging in the room next door. God, no one in this house had a job. They moved through time as if it were endless, their days not numbered. All anyone did was sleep, smoke, drink, fuck and talk about how great they would be one day.

But this was what had attracted me to Jake in the first place: his brazen rejection of mainstream life; his refusal to conform. He'd told me when we met that he was a painter. It was his only passion; he couldn't bear to do anything else. And he'd found a way to make a living from it – hauling his triptychs of colourful, geometric patterns down to the Lanes every Saturday and waiting for young professionals from London to come and buy them. That's what Brighton was to these people: a place where you bought original artwork from unknown, impoverished painters standing on street corners. One day, when the artist won the Turner Prize, this early work would be rare and valuable, and dinner guests would envy the purchaser their gift for spotting genuine, embryonic talent.

In reality, that was all horseshit, and Jake knew it. His marketable work was rubbish. He knocked it out over a couple of hours on a Friday night, in between roll-ups and glugs of Special Brew, and I would have to listen to him lamenting the poor taste of a public who hung this crap in their homes, while the other stuff – the real stuff; the good stuff that he laboured over – went unnoticed.

When I met him the previous October, Jake had just finished a serious painting. He was going to spend a year putting an exhibition together; an agent had seen a piece of his work and been excited about it, but he didn't have enough of a collection yet for her to sign him up.

I said, 'Oh, but that's brilliant. You must do it.'

He smiled shyly at me from behind his pint. 'Yeah,' he said. 'Yeah.'

Jake was just what I needed, I thought then. A man who'd turned his back on conventional expectations and was carving his own, alternative way to success. It was something I had to do, too. I'd been trapped in my admin job for so long, I could actually feel my personality being eroded by spreadsheets and extensive Word documents – each ten thousand words long, and not a single word interesting.

I knew where I was headed if I kept this up. It was a one-way street to blankness – the endless treadmill of boredom that sucked everything out of you until your eyes clouded over and the spark of intelligence left your face, and you spent your days longing for five o'clock and your evenings watching people behaving badly on television because they were desperate, so desperate not to live tiny, insignificant lives like yours that they would actually do this: They would actually suck someone's cock in front of the nation because they had to be remembered for something, and it was better to be remembered for sucking someone's cock on Channel 4 than nothing at all … And I knew, as clearly as I knew night from day, that this life would destroy me, and I couldn't live it.

University had spoiled me. I knew conventional wisdom said that university was meant to prepare me for the workplace, but instead I'd spent three glorious years at York, doing whatever I wanted: a module in Shakespeare, a module in the Romantics, and even, for fun, the odd module in writing stories or novels. I hadn't really understood that, afterwards, unless I'd somehow achieved greatness in something by the age of twenty-one, I'd have to abandon everything I loved (because no one paid anyone to sit around reading books) and grind away at a living which was, in all honesty, barely a living at all.

It had been hard, then, to keep up with the things I loved. The energy dripped out of me and I had nothing left to give to my passions, and although I'd impressed my tutors at college, there were no grants available for someone whose only recommendation was a first-class degree and a love of the written word. Everyone had a first-class degree and a love of the written word. The people handing out grants wanted something more than that, though they couldn't tell you what it was. It was something indefinable. Magic.

But it wasn't magic, I knew that. It was only magic to those who didn't do it. For me, writing was a craft that came slowly, each word on the page some sort of mini birth. A labour. I missed it.

About two weeks after meeting Jake, I took action. I stopped going to work. I didn't even hand in my notice, just woke up one morning and decided not to go. Then I turned my phone off, sat at my table – which wasn't really a table, just a tea chest with a zebra-striped cover over it – and wrote. I did this for three days. All that came out was a load of thinly veiled angst about my mother, but it was a start: eight hundred words, there on the screen. Impulsively, I sent it off to the New Writers' Foundation, an organisation that ran week-long courses for aspiring authors in big, old houses across the country: Devon, Yorkshire, Derbyshire, Northumberland. I was asking a lot, I knew. The course I wanted to do was a select one: Advanced Fiction. You had to be good, or at least reasonably good, to be allowed on it. Also, it cost £650. I filled in a form for a fee waiver.

The course was in May. It was late April now and I still hadn't heard back. I assumed I hadn't made the cut.

I stepped out of the shower, wrapped myself in a towel – damp, slightly smelly – and went back to the bedroom to get dressed. Jake was still asleep, so I made a lot of noise in an attempt to rouse him. He was meant to be at the Job Centre at one-fifteen or he'd be sanctioned and have his benefits stopped. It was the one thing he had to do, this fortnightly twenty-minute restriction on his freedom, and he only ever managed it by the skin of his teeth.

Jake fell into the category of 'long-term unemployed'. Once, when I'd ended up going with him to sign on, I'd seen a red box flash up on the computer screen when the woman typed in his National Insurance number. 'This person has been unemployed for fifteen years.' A waster. A waste of space. A waste of money. A waste of all that was good in him. But he had talent, I thought, a talent that existed outside of convention and needed nurturing.

He was thirty-six now; I was twenty-five. Since getting together, we'd talked a lot about commitment: to each other; to our futures as creatives; to building a good life together; but none of the work he'd said he was going to do had materialised. He had nothing for an exhibition, save that solitary painting he'd finished before we met.

He didn't move now as I clattered about the room, taking clothes off hangers, moving mugs thick with the dregs of ancient coffee, banging my tub of moisturiser hard against the shelf. I looked at him with distaste. He was urban decay: cigarette ash and scattered tobacco on the bedclothes; a smell of dirt and sweat; and on the floor beside him, a bag of weed and three cut-out images of airbrushed, naked women that he wanked over on the nights I wasn't there to do it for him.

I left the room and went downstairs. Maria was in the kitchen, photographing an arrangement of sliced beetroot and coriander. 'It's for the new vegetarian restaurant on Ship Street,' she explained. 'I'm going to take them some samples of my work and see if they want me as their food photographer. I could do their menus.'

'Won't they have already sorted all that?'

She shrugged. 'Worth a shot. Where's Jake?'

'Asleep.'

'Sure. There's a letter for you on the table.'

Oh, God. Another credit reference agency, probably, chasing me for a bill run up by the shit who took my mobile phone two years ago and spent a grand before I'd even got round to calling Virgin and cancelling it. It was the only kind of post I got.

I poured a mug of leftover coffee from Maria's cafetière and reheated it in the microwave.

Maria slung her camera bag over her shoulder and headed for the front door saying, 'Remind Jake he still hasn't paid me for this month's electricity bill. I'm not buying beer until he coughs up.'

I nodded, then turned to the letter on the table. It was from the New Writers' Foundation. I'd given them Jake's address because I was never at my bedsit. I braced myself for a polite note, saying I hadn't been successful this time, but perhaps I'd be interested in one of their other courses, for beginners, at an extra cost of £2,000 because those students suffering my particular level of delusion required a special kind of expensive tutor.

But it didn't say that. It said they were delighted to offer me a place on the course, together with a full grant to cover fees and food, and looked forward to seeing me in May. My tutor would be Bo Luxton, and they strongly recommended I read some of her work before the course started.

I was shocked. I read the letter again, slowly this time, then grabbed my jacket from where it lay on the sofa and set off to City Books, just round the corner. I'd never read Bo Luxton's work before, though her name was vaguely familiar.

The bell above the shop door rang as I entered. The woman behind the counter looked up at me.

'Have you got anything by an author called Bo Luxton?' I asked.

'Her latest has just come out,' she said, and led me to the display table in the centre of the shop.

The Poet's Sister. I turned it over and read the back. '1800. Dorothy Wordsworth has sacrificed all her marrying years to care for her brother. While he writes some of the world's finest poetry, she darns his stockings, cooks his meals and changes his sheets. William cannot live without her, but now he is engaged to be married to their childhood friend, Mary. How will Dorothy survive this loss, and what is the truth of this strange and deep love that the locals of Grasmere call "unnatural and rotten"?'

I took it to the desk, paid for it and left.

Instead of walking back to Jake's, I headed for my bedsit on Brunswick Place. I'd hardly been there for weeks, mainly because I hated it. The size of it, the hard brown carpet, the greasy walls, the depressing kitchen unit in the corner of the room with a rusty Baby Belling that scarcely worked. And the electricity meter that swallowed pound coins until I had none left, and all the lights went out and the food was gone.

But it was a place to be alone. No one would visit me here.

I got into bed and opened the book. The dedication first: 'For Lola and Maggie.' Then the opening:

> 'At last, I was outside again, walking the cottage garden with my brother. The snowdrops had gone now and all over the grass, the daffodils were out, holding the last of the day's sunlight in their petals.'

I read on – fifty pages before I put it down. I envied the writer that lyrical beauty. *Bo Luxton must be lovely*, I thought. Only someone angelic at the core could write those sentences. I wanted to be taught by her, let her pull me away from that brutal voice I'd written in: 'The Japanese always burn their dead.' Bash, bash, bash. Anger on the page.

Bo Luxton wasn't like that, I thought. Bo must write with feathers.

But somehow, I needed to get the money for the fare to Northumberland. The letter said to take the train to Alnmouth and a taxi to the village. I was skint. Since quitting my admin job, I'd worked four mornings a week in a language school run by a man who paid me cash and told me, if ever the Home Office visited, to say I was on work experience. It was hardly enough to cover my rent. Buying that book today had been an extravagance.

I phoned Network Rail and asked for the price of a ticket if I booked it in advance. Round trip: £147. There was no way.

Of course there was a way.

In a box, in a drawer, was a bracelet my mother had given me on my eighteenth birthday, the last day I'd ever seen her, just before...

I rummaged around among knickers and tights and tops and bras until I found it. It was still there, glinting and expensive. I'd never worn it.

I put my jacket back on, slipped the bracelet in my pocket and set off for the computers at the library. I knew I'd be able to sell it quickly on eBay; though I also knew I was heading into danger now. I stored my mother carefully, shrunk her to the size of a trinket, shut her in a box and locked her away in some remote part of me. She only rose up in those moments when some professional was trying to harness my subconscious (it was why I stopped seeing professionals, in the end) or, as I found recently, if I was writing. She became inevitable then, and afterwards I'd have to commit to wasted days – long hours when I could do nothing but rage at the memory of her and the loss of her and the awful, unmendable break of us.

And then I would have to recover.

I walked through town briskly, past the shoppers and the tourists, the beggars and the buskers, keeping my eyes fixed straight ahead. Always, I was aware of my pocketful of silver. But I didn't dwell on it, not until the moment I saw her.

She was right there on the corner of Bond Street, a take-away coffee in her hand and a smile on her face so maternal and serene, it took my breath away.

'Alice,' she said, and held out her hand. 'Alice.'

I stood still, then walked towards her, my hand raised to take the one she held out to me.

She frowned, confused, and I realised it wasn't Alice she was saying, but something else, some other name, for some other child.

As I watched, I saw the little girl she was with take her hand, and then the two of them walked together, away from me, until they were lost in the throng and I could see them no more.

3

Bo

I wrote it all down and stuck it to the fridge – everything Gus would need to remember while I was away in Northumberland. *Monday: Lola ukulele club 6 pm; Tuesday: swimming lessons 4 pm; Wednesday: Maggie drama class, Keswick, 5 pm; Thursday: learn spellings; Friday: maths homework.*

It made me feel like a dictator, but Gus hadn't a clue. He knew the girls went to school and how to get them there, but that was as far as his understanding of their lives went. It was me who knew their hobbies and hatreds, their worries, their friends, the crazes they had to keep up with: loom bands, Shopkins, Moon Balls…

He'd been forty-seven when I met him, with three grown-up children from two previous marriages. He'd thought he was having a meaningless one-night-stand, but I was twenty-five and had my sights set on marriage. I'd been struggling alone for ten years, ever since running away from my parents' old caravan and taking myself to London, where I earned money in any way I could and wrote poetry and stories when the jobs ran dry and I left with time to fill. I took my work to open-mic nights. Then someone told me about an organisation that arranged mentoring. Experienced, well-known authors would take on someone like me – young, enthusiastic, with a lot to say – and work with them, sharing their insight and wisdom and helping new talent reach giddy heights. It was 1994. There were grants available for people like me. I made an application. A bestselling author accepted it, took me under her wing and, after two years, took me with her on a festival tour; she let me read alongside her at Hay.

That was where I met him. He walked in, dressed in a suit, out of place, listened to me read and asked questions afterwards. He said he worked in advertising. We swapped phone numbers.

I played it cool, of course, but I wasn't going to let him go. He was good-looking, solvent, easy to get on with. He was also ancient, with two failed marriages behind him. He wouldn't be looking for deep emotional entanglement or a love that would rock the world. I didn't want that, either. I was suspicious of love and what it did to people – those dark depths of anguish and horror; the thought of it all made me shudder. And anyway, I didn't seem to have it in me. Gus would be stable, reliable, happy enough with a normal, quiet life in a normal, quiet home. He was everything I wanted.

We got married when I was twenty-nine – 'Yes, I suppose we might as well,' he said, when I asked him – and Lola was born three years later. I'd had to push him for children. He was too old, he said, and babies were exhausting. You needed to be young to keep up with them, to chase them round the supermarket when they ran off, to teach them everything they needed to learn: riding a bike, football, tennis … He'd done his time as a father.

But I took care of it, and he was happy when they came along. He wept in the delivery room after Lola's birth, the problem of his age washed away in moments. He spoke of his new lease of life, his unexpected chance to be the father he wished he could have been the first time round.

He was stopping at two, though. There was no way he would consider having another one after Maggie. I still tried, though, now and then. The previous week, the council had placed an advert in the local paper, wanting decent people to act as foster carers for children waiting to be adopted. I'd read it out to Gus. 'What do you think?' I asked.

He said, 'I think we've got enough on our plate without trying to save every abandoned child on the planet.'

'It wouldn't be every child. Just one or two at a time.'

He shook his head. 'We've got our own children,' he said simply.

'We can't risk harming them by disrupting their home for the sake of children who aren't ours. Our concern has to be keeping our own girls safe and well.'

I let it go, for now. He thought I was mad, I knew that, and he was right in a way. This weakness of mine for the unloved … it was probably pathological. If I wanted, I could trace it to its roots, but there was no point looking backwards, picking over old memories. Much better to stay in the present.

I heard his footfall in the hallway and the latch on the kitchen door lifted. 'Morning,' he said.

The kitchen table was covered in manuscripts from the students I'd be teaching the following week. 'Can I move some of these?' he asked.

'Just stick them on the floor. I'm taking them out to the car in a minute.'

'You're not going till Monday.'

'I know, but they're cluttering up the study.'

He flicked through one of the manuscripts, pausing to read the occasional paragraph. 'Anything good this year?' he said.

'The usual,' I told him. 'Murders, drugs raids, dystopian worlds, a few feminist protests. But there's one I love.'

'Oh?'

'Yes. Have a look through. Alice Dark.'

'Is this it? "Last Words".'

'Yes.'

He read it quickly. 'Well, that's all pretty disturbing,' he said.

I stood up beside him. 'Yes, but it's good. Can't you see?'

'It's brutal.'

'But there is so much anguish and pain in here; and longing. Endless longing for repair.'

He said nothing.

Ever since I'd first read it, I'd been thinking about Alice Dark's work; it was rare that students moved me like this. I knew it had stirred up something that usually slumped deep inside me, in the place I didn't like to visit. But I couldn't help being intrigued. I loved the writing and wanted to meet the writer. Alice Dark was, I felt sure, young and vulnerable, and in need of care. I had the urge to reach out to her, to steer her to wellness.

I said, 'I think the author is vulnerable.'

Gus smiled, 'Another one of your waifs and strays,' he said, indulgently, as though my habit of caring for the dispossessed was endearing. 'Be careful this time.'

I sniffed and turned to the fridge. 'Do you want lunch? I was going to use the last of the squash in a soup.'

'I'm fine. I'll grab something later.'

His routine was fixed. A morning spent reading books, then a sandwich in front of the local lunchtime news and an afternoon of brain-training games on the iPad. I mostly shut myself away in the study and worked, and we came together again in the evenings, for a meal and a glass of wine. That was the way we lived, now he was retired and the days were long and threw us together more than we'd ever been used to. It worked. It was what I needed. If he had made demands of me, I'd never have got anything done. Life was quiet and normal, and all I'd ever wanted.

At two-thirty, I set off to pick the girls up from school. Gus hadn't brought the post in today. He usually went out for it straight after breakfast, then handed me the letters I needed and threw away anything he thought I wouldn't cope with. I wasn't sure what else he read, though I had some suspicions that certain things never reached me.

I paused by the tiny red mailbox standing on its post at the end of the drive and stooped to peer inside. In the darkness, I could make out three or four envelopes, though the print was impossible to read. I was still waiting for the contract for my new book. Perhaps he'd have taken it all in by the time I came home, I thought, and walked on.

I followed the waterfall trail. It took me across streams that fell over the rocky edges of the mountains, rushing down to the river that wound through the pastures below.

It wasn't possible to be unhappy here. There was nothing ugly in nature. Human guilt was in the city: in the factories and all their dark fog; in the grey sky that fell into black rivers; in the smog and the damage.

The path took me under a yellow-green canopy of beech trees, where a waterfall raged and ancient boulders, green with moss, soaked up the spray. One of the reasons I'd wanted to move here was because walking like this took me, not just through the landscape around me, but along a path through my own mind. It was when I was walking that I could best think about my work and had all my ideas.

The canopy of beech trees opened out at the foot of the mountain. I stepped into the light and down the stone steps that took me into the village where the school stood. The yard was already full. I talked briefly to some of the other parents, keeping my eye out all the time for the girls' teachers bringing their straggly lines of children out of the building.

Maggie came out first, in her red gingham dress with one sock to her knees and one round her ankles, weighed down by her book bag, her hair in her eyes. She saw me and waved, her face lit with a smile. I smiled back, then the teacher released her and she bounded over and threw herself at me. I returned her hug, took charge of the book bag, straightened her hair and pulled up her socks. 'Good day?' I asked.

Maggie wrinkled her nose. 'Boring,' she said. 'We had to do our six times table and I hate it.'

'They're tricky, the sixes,' I agreed with a smile.

Maggie took my hand, then we spotted Lola and the ritual was repeated.

They were always so pleased to see me, and the happiness it brought me was always tinged with regret, because how much longer would it go on like this? How many years could I hold on to them before I became just a drag: a tedious old woman who nagged about exam revision and wouldn't let them go to Manchester nightclubs every Friday?

Still, I thought, as I nudged the book bags further on to my shoulder and took Lola's hand in mine, they were here now and they were mine, and they were eight and six years old, and I'd brought them this far – happy, healthy, nurtured, secure.

I was not like my own mother. Not at all.

4

Alice

Sunday evening. I was in the bedroom packing. Jake lay on the mattress, headphones in, listening to something meaningful. My train was leaving Brighton at six the following morning, which meant the latest I could get up was 5:15. This was not a time I recognised, or at least not as a time to start the day. I might have passed through 5:15 as part of a late night once or twice, but other than that, the hour did not exist. The thought of it was painful and impossible. It would be easier, I decided, to stay up to greet it rather than go to bed at my usual time and set an alarm for three hours later.

Jake was going to a party. His friend, who owned an attic flat above a health food shop on Bond Street, always threw a party on Sunday nights. The anticapitalist tribal gathering, he called it. Fuck Mondays. Screw the job. Join the hedonist clan. Be happy. I'd been a few times and hated it. The music was too loud, the people too cool, the room filled with the smell of sweat and decaying youth. It was claustrophobic. I wanted to run away.

I'd invited Anna over to keep me company while I waited for morning to roll around. Anna was a police officer and kept unusual hours. She had the next day off, and could go on drinking and talking till at least 2 am. I thought I might do some work in those last hours – carve out a few paragraphs to take with me to Northumberland, something I could finish when I was there.

Jake took his headphones off and sat up, 'Are you nervous about the course?' he asked.

I turned to face him. 'A bit, maybe. No one wants to be the worst one, do they? I'm nervous about that – everyone else being better than me.'

'They won't be,' he said.

'I read somewhere that only old people do these courses. They all retire and then decide to flood the world with crap stories.'

Jake shrugged, 'Then even if they're better than you, you'll still have the advantage – you'll have loads more years to improve than they've got left.'

I sat down beside him on the mattress. 'I know we've talked about this before, but when I get back from this course, I really want to think about moving out of Brighton. There are too many distractions here. Neither of us commits to anything properly. If we really want to be successful, we need to knuckle down and do it.'

'Yeah. I know. Yeah.'

'So you'll move to the country with me?'

'I need to be able to go to parties, though. I can't work if I can't go to parties and hear music. It helps my painting. You know there are links between my art and techno.'

I left it. This particular conversation only ever went in circles: I wanted to move somewhere remote, so I could work without distraction; he wanted to be in a town. I wanted to be successful and knew it involved commitment; he wanted to be successful and thought he could fit his working life into the nooks of crannies of the week. He loved parties and had to ransack the town to find one almost every night; I hated them and didn't go with him, and couldn't bear it when he came home at 6 am, still tripping so hard he thought I was a snake and beat me with a pillow. He thought I was uptight for not wanting to be woken up by someone on drugs at 6 am, beating me with a pillow…

'When's Anna coming over?' he asked.

'About eight.'

'I'll make sure I'm gone by then. I don't want her to arrest me.'

'She won't arrest you.'

'She's a pig. She'll arrest me if she sees what's in my drawers.'

'She'll turn a blind eye.'

'She won't. They're all the same, pigs. Power freaks. They love banging people up.'

'Not all of them. Lots of them are decent. They protect people.'

'They're pigs,' he said.

What he meant was that they were too mainstream for him, too busy imposing rules, and Jake was not someone who liked to live a life with rules. He was suspicious of anyone who cared so much about rules they actually wanted to be the one to bollock him for flouting them.

I said, 'What are you going to do while I'm away?'

He looked at me blankly. 'Just … you know, the usual. I'll try and catch up with Adam while he's in town, and maybe my brother. There's a party on Tuesday night. Might go to the Joint on Wednesday. I don't know.' He shrugged. 'Just see how the week pans out, I suppose.'

Work didn't feature in his plans, I noted. The commitment he'd said he had to becoming a world-class painter was looking more and more delusional.

I sighed, 'Alright.'

He said, 'I'll try and paint something as well. Start something good. For that agent.'

'Great,' I said, without enthusiasm. I'd heard all this before.

The doorbell rang.

Jake looked alarmed. 'It's a pig,' he said. 'I'm going down the fire escape. See you later.' He kissed me quickly on the mouth then climbed out of the window onto the flat roof outside his room and down the steps that led to the pavement.

Bye, Jake, I thought. *See you in a week.*

I ran downstairs and opened the front door. Anna stood there in black skinny jeans, a bright-pink halterneck and leather jacket.

'Wow,' I said, looking at her admiringly. 'If I were criminally inclined, I'd commit robbery just so I could be locked up in an interview room with you.'

'Thanks, love,' Anna said, stepping inside and handing me a bottle of wine. 'What time are you off?'

'Five.'

'Great. Loads of time.'

She sat down on the sofa. I filled a bowl with some Kettle Chips, poured two glasses of red wine and joined her. There was a moment's silence while we both lit cigarettes, then Anna said, 'So what's new? What's this course you're doing?'

'It's a writing course,' I told her. 'It's run by an author. I think we write stuff and she tells us how to make it better. Maybe. I don't know exactly what it will involve, but I've decided it's going to change my life. It'll be the crucial pivot – the thing that transforms me from Alice the waster to Alice the brilliant, committed author. Definitely, it will do this.'

'Great. I hope you become the Beyoncé of the literary world,' Anna said. 'How's Jake?'

I sighed. 'Like he's always been.'

'Which is what, exactly?'

'Sweet, lovely, a dreamer, but utterly useless at life.'

'Are you sure about that?'

'Completely sure.'

'So...'

'Let's drink instead of talk about this. I was mean. He's not completely useless. He has talent and a good heart.'

'Where is he now?'

'At an anticapitalist, fuck-Monday-mornings party.'

'What a revolutionary. He'll change the world with that sort of protest.'

'You never know.'

I sat back and inhaled on my cigarette. I'd known Anna since we were at York together. She'd started as a mature student, twenty-six instead of eighteen. She'd joined the police force straight after school, despite acing her A levels, but then she'd wanted to try out university. She left at the end of the first year. 'Oh, it's alright for some people,' she'd said, 'but really, what's the point in it? What's the point in writing all these essays on fairies in Shakespeare, when I could be protecting women from domestic abuse and getting paedophiles locked up?' So she'd got a new job with Sussex Police. After I graduated and all my friends had returned to live with their parents, I'd lodged in her spare room for a while and paid her in homemade cake.

Now, Anna looked at me and said, 'Maybe you'll meet a rich writer on this course.'

'I don't think writers are rich, in general.'

'Some must be. J.K Rowling. She's loaded.'

'I don't think she has much need to do Advanced Fiction Writing.'

'You could have an affair with the tutor. He'll be rich.'

'It's a woman. Bo Luxton.'

Anna looked blank. 'Oh. Listen, I know you don't want to talk about Jake but if you're worried about money – I mean, if that's what's keeping you here and you need to get out – you can always come and stay with me again. It's no problem. I won't ask for any rent for the first three months. You'll need a job, though.'

'I've got a job.'

'Not a proper one. Not one that pays you enough money to leave your boyfriend. Everyone needs enough money to go it alone if they have to. Seriously. Everyone.'

'Oh, you're so wise, Anna. Please have another drink so it can be knocked out of you.'

We changed the subject and went on talking, drinking and smoking until after midnight, when Anna stood up to leave.

'Enjoy the course,' she said. 'Come back a bestselling author. Buy a house.'

'OK.'

After she'd gone, I busied myself making notes, jotting down images and phrases I liked. This was my trouble. I was full of observations and occasional sentences – but never enough to fill a book, and I had no ideas for plot. I was only twenty-six. I hadn't lived yet. All I'd really experienced was the death of my mother, and I could immediately think of at least ten other books about the death of someone's mother. It wasn't a subject that could be easily made new.

Time ticked on. I was tired and mildly pissed, but excited. I looked over my notes. They were a jumble, nothing that could easily be turned into anything substantial, but they were there – the first stirrings of something. I wasn't sure what was going to happen now, but I had an absolute, deep-soul certainty that my life was about to change. I was on the cusp of something; something important and new.

5

Bo

I'd never been to Northumberland before. When we'd lived in Oxford and I couldn't face the stress of taking young children for holidays in the sun – all that threat of burned skin, diseased mosquitoes, bad plumbing – we'd abandoned the crowds heading to the West Country and come north instead, to the Yorkshire coast, the Dales, or the Lakes, but Northumberland was off my radar. If I thought about it at all, it was in terms of a history that didn't interest me: Roman armies, an old stone wall, digging up the earth and getting excited about ancient pots and toilet seats. And cold. Northumberland was cold.

What struck me most now was the emptiness. I'd left the fast roads behind me at a village called Wall, then driven for miles through a landscape of rolling heath, marked here and there with crags and castle ruins, until I reached the rocky wildness of the coast beyond. This was dramatic and beautiful country, deserted.

The house stood three miles outside Warkworth. I found it easily enough: a sixteenth-century manor, approached by a long, uneven drive, pocked with potholes and interrupted by cattle grids, and with acres of land, a private lake and wide-open views of the sea.

It was run by a young couple. They took bookings, changed the bed linen and smiled at everyone they saw, whether they wanted to or not. As soon as I pulled up in the gravel car port, the man of the pair appeared.

'Bo,' he said, as I stepped out of the car. He came forwards and shook my hand enthusiastically. 'I'm Dan. Great to meet you.'

He had the slightly star-struck look about him that I often saw when I met new people. It was something I'd never quite got used to. I, Bo Luxton, with the travelling parents and no education to speak of, was famous – a fact about my life that mostly made me uncomfortable.

I smiled at him. 'I'm glad to be here, really looking forward to it,' I said. There was nothing else to say, though it wasn't strictly true. It was the first time I'd done any teaching since the drama with Christian. I'd thought afterwards that I'd never teach again, never do any kind of public event again; but later I decided that would make me too much of a victim – cutting off ways of earning money, and increasing book sales, just because of one fan.

Another problem was that, even now, driving so far away from the girls felt as though someone was tugging too hard on the old umbilical cord that I swore still pulsed on between us – the invisible force that made them cry when they saw me again after a bad day, and that stopped me from ever straying too far. It was the old conundrum of motherhood: always, I craved time away. But when it came to it, I couldn't bear the distance between us.

Dan took my bag and showed me to my room. It was at the top of the house, in the en-suite attic conversion, separate from the students, who would sleep a floor below me and would have to share a bathroom. I knew from experience that distance from them was crucial. Students were like parasites. Some of them bore an eagerness so heavy they could barely hold themselves up off the floor. They'd follow wherever I went, trying to get five minutes alone with me, away from the others, so I could say the things they thought it would be tactless to mention in front of the group. They were desperate to be singled out, to have me look them square in the eye and say, 'You are good.' Most writers, I felt sure, had not been loved enough as children.

'A couple of the students are here already,' Dan was saying. 'They're in the lounge, but get yourself settled in. We start officially at five. The usual stuff – a talk about meals and washing up, not flushing anything other than toilet roll into the cesspit, composting the compostable, recycling the recyclable – then dinner together, followed by some horrendous group activity, followed by a piss-up. It's up to you whether you take part in that.'

I shook my head demurely. 'A teetotal week for me.'

'Very wise,' Dan said, and left the room.

I unpacked slowly and checked my phone for messages from Lola or Maggie. Nothing. Nothing from Gus, either. They were fine. The week would fly by for them. Of course, Gus would read all my mail; open all my emails; keep an eye on me, even from a distance. He'd entirely fail to listen to the girls read or take them to their swimming lessons, and they would eat only fish-finger sandwiches and strawberry jelly, but they would have fun together, the three of them, liberated from my boring insistence on homework, health and trust.

I left the room and walked downstairs to meet my students. There they were in the lounge, as Dan had said, five of them aged – it looked to me – between forty-five and seventy. The atmosphere changed as I entered. There was some nudging, a murmured, 'Here she is,' and then silence. Oh, God. This was what I always struggled with – the sense that my presence in a room altered it; that people paid good money to just meet me; that they wanted to hear what I had to say because it was important and relevant. That I was, in some real and vital way, less ordinary than they were.

I had never worked as hard at anything as I worked at being ordinary.

I cleared my throat and smiled in way I hoped was normal and friendly. 'I'm Bo Luxton,' I said.

A couple of them rolled their eyes, as if the introduction was unnecessary. They knew who I was, they'd seen me on book covers, on posters, on television…

'I hope we'll have a great few days, and you'll all go home feeling that this was a purposeful and meaningful week.'

I stopped talking and sat down in an easy chair, feeling the comforting caress of my fleece against my skin.

A bottle of wine was making its way around the room. One of

the more courageous of the two male students approached me with it. 'Bo?'

I shook my head. 'Is there some water?'

Someone else jumped up. 'I'll get it. Still or sparkling?'

'Just tap water. I can get it myself if someone points me in the direction of the sink.'

They wouldn't hear of it, and off they went, competing. Oh, the great privilege of bringing water to Bo Luxton. It was only for a week, I reminded myself. I should try and enjoy it. But I felt – had always felt – that there was something dehumanising about people removing your need to care for yourself. It was why I could never have had an au pair, even though all my friends in Oxford had one. Because really, what was left of you if you couldn't pour yourself a drink, make yourself a meal, change your own child's nappy? And besides all of that, I knew this was how obsession started. It was how Christian started. He raised me to the status of beyond human, then worshipped me.

The students around me went on talking. Their voices were loud and unnatural now because they wanted me to hear what they were saying: all the details of their lives, their commitment to this week, how important it all was, what lengths they'd had to go to, rearranging their careers and homes so they could get here...

Then someone else walked in. She was younger than the others by far, mid-twenties at the most. She was also very pretty, in a sensational, made-up way – a way that knew it would be looked at, and liked it: dark-brown, asymmetric bob; bright-pink boots; black coat with a floppy fabric flower pinned to it; glossy lips, slightly – just very slightly – underweight.

This, I knew straight away, was Alice. The girl – for I could not think of her as a woman – stood in the doorway. She smiled brightly as everyone looked up at her, and said, 'Sorry I'm so late. Bloody trains.'

The men moved over for her, the women bristled. She wouldn't let Ben, the greying man in his fifties, give up his seat for her, and so she sat on the floor, elf-like, her arms wrapped around her knees.

'Alice,' she was saying. 'I left Brighton at six this morning.'

'Early start,' Ben commented.

'A late night, really. I couldn't face a five o'clock alarm, so I just stayed up.'

Suddenly, unexpectedly and from nowhere at all, I felt a lurch of envy. Youth. Vitality. Freedom. Alice was years away from the time when sleep would become a drug she'd risk everything to lay her hands on. She could probably go nights and nights without it. Sleep lurked somewhere at the bottom of her priorities list, beneath dancing, food, sex.

I went up to her and shook her hand. 'I'm Bo, the course tutor,' I said. 'Sounds like you had a bad journey.'

'I missed my train out of King's Cross. It was my own fault. I realised as I stood on the platform that I'd forgotten to bring a pen with me, and I thought how slack it would look – you know, rocking up to a writing course without a pen – so I went off to buy some and the queue was long and the train left without me. I'm not very good with timetables. They always surprise me. The rest of the world moves much faster than I do.'

Ben was eyeing her with amusement. Alice stopped talking and blushed.

'I'm sorry,' she said. 'I'm a bit nervous. I lose all power to edit my speech when I'm in a room full of people I don't know. I suppose the good thing about it is that now you know my life story, I won't have to speak during the getting-to-know-you activity. Thank God. I've always hated those.'

'They have their flaws, I agree,' I said, 'but seeing as no one in the field of group dynamics has come up with something better, shall we begin and get ours over with?'

There was general, murmuring agreement. They went around the room, saying who they were, condensing their identities into three sentences. Most of them were the same: They'd been bogged down in the day job for twenty years, and now, suddenly, they'd looked up and realised half their lives had passed and time was accelerating beyond their control. They needed to do this now, or their lives would be over and all they'd have to leave the world was a two-page CV saying they were good with data.

It was Alice's turn. 'I'm here because … well, because it's all I want to do. I can't do anything else. I know it's hard and brutal and I'm condemning myself to a life of poverty, but I don't care. Normal life is killing me.'

I looked at her. I could see she meant this. In some strange and very real sense, she'd actually been dying of boredom. Alice was a burst of crushed energy. Her skin could scarcely contain her.

She was like no one I'd ever met before. Except perhaps myself, when I was that age.

6

Alice

I was having a great time. I'd been unsure when I first walked in – late, always late – and saw that everyone else in the room was at least twice my age, but I got used to it quickly and decided I liked these people with their steady lives, minds full of books and vintage wisdom. Besides, they all drank just as much as I did. Forget those hateful getting-to-know-you games, I'd always thought (and once tried to tell my boss); the only way to get a team bonding was through the group consumption of too much alcohol.

Bo Luxton was everything I'd expected her to be. She looked the way she wrote: ethereal, gentle, sensual. There was, I thought – probably because I was in an old manor house overlooking the sea, talking a lot about poetry – a touch of the angel about her. It was the way her hair fell in waves around that pale and delicate face and down to her shoulders. It was also to do with the fact that, every time she opened her mouth, gold nuggets of wisdom seemed to drop from it.

I would have loved some time with Bo, away from all the others, but knew I'd have to fight for it. The rest of them hung around her like moths; I'd need sharp elbows to get within a metre of her. I had the sense that Bo was uncomfortable with all this needy worship. Now and then, she had about her the look of a hunted animal, desperate to break away.

Instead, I spent my afternoons writing alone in my room or the garden, or shut away in the lounge. Jake sent me a text message every day at around two, probably when he'd just got up: *Hi baby hows it going missing you started new painting will have it finished before you get back.*

By Wednesday, I'd stopped replying. I had, I realised now, nothing to say to him. I couldn't fit him into this situation, in which people were productive and articulate and managed to lead full, complicated and busy lives without feeling the need to fall down and sleep every hour so they could recover from the cycle of pressure – of walking half a mile for a pint of milk, composing an email, buying a new canvas.

I had to end things with him. I'd do it as soon as I got back to Brighton. If I phoned him and did it now, he'd never stop phoning back, wanting to discuss it all to death in a voice slowed down by his afternoon spliffs. I sighed. Far better not to ruin the week.

The lounge, when I went in that particular afternoon, was empty. I took a seat in an armchair and read over some of the notes I'd made in the workshops in response to Bo's advice about my work. All Bo's wisdom, gathered there on the page. My favourite: *Everyone was a terrible writer once. You just have to keep on until you're terrible no longer.*

As I read on in silence, the latch on the door lifted and Bo herself walked in.

At first, she looked flustered. 'Oh, I'm sorry. I can leave if you're working. I was just looking for somewhere to sit in peace for a while.'

I shook my head. 'It's fine. Come in, please.'

'Thank you,' Bo said, and took a seat in the armchair opposite me.

I went on trying to read Bo's feedback, but her presence in the room was distracting.

'Are you finding the week useful?' she said, after a while.

'Really useful. It's been great so far. Even just being out here in the countryside is so different to what I'm used to. I live in Brighton. We only really get two seasons there – cold and dark, and then a bit less cold and light. It's not like this.'

It was true. In Brighton now, the air would be slowly warming and the sea brightening after the long murk of winter, but there would be nothing else drawing my attention to the shift of the seasons; except for the people – there were more of them now: tourists, foreign students, and that tedious, endless procession of weekend stags and hens. But here, the brilliant green of spring made my eyes ache. Every day I walked the grounds before breakfast, saw the purple flash of bluebells among the birch trees, or the dark spread of the enclosing moors, and thought, *All my life, I have missed all this.*

Bo said, 'I've never regretted our decision to leave the city. It's good for you, good in every way, to live in the natural world. I have a theory – I have lots of theories; you'll get used to it – that it's much harder to be miserable if you live in the country. If you look, you'll see there is nothing ugly in nature. Nothing at all. Ugliness exists only where humans have altered the landscape. Go to the city, and you're surrounded by concrete, industry and damage. It's no good for people to see that all the time. It depresses the life out of us, and we don't even realise it's happening. It's brutal, insidious.'

There it was again. Wisdom. I wondered if Bo ever opened her mouth and talked crap, like me.

I looked at her and asked, 'Where do you live?' The ordinary lives of famous people interested me. I found it hard to imagine them engaged with the everyday: cooking meals, cleaning bathrooms, pouring coffee, being domestic. I imagined their fame lifting them away from all that, placing them so far above the real world, they were godlike.

'I live just outside Grasmere in the Lake District,' Bo was saying, 'in a house halfway up a mountain with my family. I have two girls and a cat. And a husband, of course.'

Straight away, I saw this woman's life and wanted it. The house (it would be big and beautiful), the mountain setting, the family, the talent – God, the talent! – the love. Because I could tell that this woman was loved. It hung around her like an aura.

'Wow. It sounds lovely,' I said.

'It is. We moved there for my last project, which was a novel about the life of Dorothy Wordsworth...'

'Oh, I read it,' I said. 'I really liked it.'

'Thank you.'

Bo seemed to have mastered the art of accepting compliments gracefully. She had no need, I supposed, to dwell on them and dig for more. 'Thank you,' was all she ever said when anyone admired her, and then she moved the conversation on.

Now, she said, 'It was hard to write – much harder than you'd think.'

'Why?'

'Because the facts are all there for you, when you write about a real life – your story is lying on a plate for you before you even begin. That was what I thought, anyway. I thought, *Great. I won't have to think up a plot*. But it didn't turn out like that. Because I didn't want to abandon the facts, they were there all the time, needing to be included, and it meant the book never really took off and had its own momentum. It didn't write itself easily, is what I mean – the way my books usually do.'

I nodded, and imagined what it would be like to be in charge of a book that wrote itself. Bo made it sound like walking a dog.

I said, 'Well, it doesn't show. When I read it, I wasn't thinking, *The great flaw in this book is that it didn't write itself*.'

Bo laughed. 'I'm glad.'

'I'm sure you hear this all the time,' I said, 'but I loved the way you wrote about the natural world...' I hesitated. It was odd, complimenting someone like this. It felt like arse licking. 'I loved the beauty of it. I would love to write like that, instead of like some hard madwoman.'

Bo smiled and leaned forwards slightly. 'Alice,' she said, 'I don't often say this to students – because most of them are hobbyists who will never get anywhere in the publishing industry – but as soon as I read your work I was excited by it. Genuinely. I think you are very talented. Trust me. I wouldn't say it if I didn't believe it.'

I wrinkled my nose. 'I hate that piece I sent in. It's just a load of angst about my mother.'

Bo shook her head. 'Mothers are an underwritten subject. There isn't enough about them, and yet they're so important. Fathers are too, of course; but that's different, because we live in a world where all the expectation is heaped on the mother. For all of us, what we experience with our mothers is the blueprint; it sets the stage for every other relationship we make and if it fails, the consequences can last forever.'

I looked away. I felt understood suddenly, and exposed.

'It's stuffy in here,' Bo said, after a moment. 'Would you like to go for a walk? Then you can tell me your plans for your work. I'd like to hear them.'

I could hardly believe it, but Bo's interest in me seemed real. It was all new, this strange sense that what I had to say meant something to someone. To this particular someone. To Bo Luxton.

I said, 'OK.'

We stepped outside. The sun polished the moorland and struck the lake with spears. The crowds of deep-green sycamores lay reflected in its waters. We walked in silence.

'What do you do, in Brighton?' Bo said at last.

'I live with my boyfriend, pretty much. He's a decent guy – really lovely. He has a great heart and he's so talented, but I'm starting to realise he's a bit of a waster, and it rubs off after a while.'

'What will he be doing this week?'

I shrugged. 'Well, at this moment, he's probably still in bed.'

'Really?'

'Yeah.' I sighed. 'My friend keeps telling me I need to end it, and she's right. I was going to phone him the night we got here and do it then, just so he'd have time to get used to the idea before I saw him again, but then I couldn't be bothered.'

'You certainly don't strike me as a waster, though.'

'Oh, I'm not. I get very frustrated with him. I hadn't realised he was like this at first. I thought he was … you know, alternative but driven. Anyway, I gave up my job after I met him. It was probably a bad move, but I wanted to write a book. And it still seems like a fine idea, until I meet up with everyone I was at university with. They've all got stuff now: careers, cars, houses. And then there's me, skint, trying a different life, and although they never say anything, I can tell they're thinking, *You're a bloody idiot, Alice.* I sometimes feel as if I've been in the school play and got so high on the applause, I gave everything up and moved to Hollywood.'

Bo laughed. 'You've done the right thing.'

'Really? I'm not sure. It was just after my mother died. I probably wasn't thinking things through properly.'

'Oh, Alice. I'm sorry. You're very young to have lost your mother.'

I shook my head. 'It's OK. We weren't close. I hadn't seen her for years.'

Bo said nothing, but looked at me with interest, as though she were waiting for me to say more.

'It's fine,' I said.

Bo said, 'It's no wonder, then, that you find yourself drawn to stories about mothers. It's normal after an event like that.'

'Possibly.'

'Was it … Tell me to go away if you don't want to talk about it … but was it as you described it in your work?'

'More or less. Her last words to me were "put it right".'

'What do you think she meant by that?'

'She meant: find a nice man, get married, have babies, don't beat them, don't get divorced.'

'Really?'

'Really. I only lived with her till I was eleven. I went to foster parents after that.'

'Wow. You've turned out well.'

I smiled. 'You've known me three days.'

'I can still tell.'

'But marriage is a long way off for me, anyway. I haven't been with anyone longer than six months.'

'You will.'

I shrugged. 'Maybe,' I said, and felt a heaviness inside me. This thing with Jake. It hadn't been a disaster, not like the others, but it wasn't what I'd been hoping for. 'We'll see. How old are your children?'

'Lola's eight and Maggie is six.'

'Cool names.'

'Cool girls.'

'Do you miss them when you're here?'

'Yes, sometimes. But motherhood is demanding. It's relentless. It does you good to get a break from it sometimes. To be yourself, as you used to be.'

I nodded.

'Make the most of these child-free years, Alice,' Bo continued. 'Really. You'll never get this time again. Once they arrive, everything is about them. It's great, of course; it's fabulous in so many ways, but *you* will slip down your priorities list. So many women get lost that way. Build up your life as a writer before you have kids; you'll have a much better chance of preserving it if you do.'

'I don't think I will have children, though,' I said.

'Don't you like them?'

'Oh, I like them; I just can't be trusted to bring them up sane.'

'I used to think like that. My own mother is a nightmare – possibly not as big a nightmare as yours, but a nightmare nonetheless – and I used to worry that I'd be like her. But I've learnt you don't have to be: The future isn't written in stone because of your past. You can change it. You will change it. You can be the mother you wanted for yourself.'

I looked at her. I'd been speaking to this woman for less than half and hour, and in that time, it felt as though she'd stripped off my skin and seen right to the very heart of me. It was exhilarating, in a way. And frightening.

7

Bo

I knew the effect I was having on this young woman. I made sure our eyes met as we spoke and could see her, wide-eyed and attentive, and in my thrall: I was the older, wiser writer who was telling her, right here, right now, that she was brilliant.

The two of us were alone, engaged in the one-to-one tutorial that came as part of the course package. Fifteen hours' whole-group tuition, and half an hour alone with the tutor. It was exhausting being the tutor in these circumstances, dealing with all the desperate, breakable egos, the big dreams that would mostly come to nothing. I used to think of it as my duty – some kind of moral obligation – to spell out the difficulties of the publishing world to my students. But I soon found that this attitude did me no favours; they didn't want to hear it. They wanted to knock out their work, send it off and make millions. That was their dream, and nothing I said could talk them down from it. If I tried, they took against me; they thought I was arrogant, showing off: *I might have made it, but don't ever think you will.*

So nowadays, I didn't bother with such warnings. I told students what they wanted to hear and sent them away again, delusions intact. It was only when I found real talent that I bothered spelling it out at all, and that was what I did now, with Alice. 'You must keep on going,' I said, passing her work back to her. 'You must never give up, even if it takes you ten years of hard slog to get noticed.'

'Ten years? Really?'

'Or longer. Maybe fifteen. This is a rocky world, Alice, and you need to find a way to navigate it without getting lost. In my experience, that way is to just keep on going, shrug off failures and take nothing personally. It's hard.'

'OK,' Alice said.

I reached across the desk and touched Alice's hand lightly. 'You have brilliance in you Alice,' I said, truthfully. 'I can see it. But I worry you can't see it in yourself; and I'm afraid you won't succeed in this world without confidence and determination. You need to set your sights on where you want to be and make sure every step you take is a step closer to that goal. Forget about men. Romance will only hold you back. Be on your own, and be strong. Set up home with someone if you want to, get married if you want a cosy life, but make your true love your work, and then you'll find that the whole world loves you. I know you can do it.'

Alice looked away from me but she didn't pull her hand from mine. I had told her only good things about her work. I wanted to reach her. I wanted to be liked by her. And I knew how to do it.

Alice was twenty-five, the same age as the girl I still thought of as Willow. Even now, my heart lurched at the memory of her. I had thought I'd be able to let her go once I'd had Lola and Maggie, but it didn't happen. For weeks after each child's birth, I'd wept and wept for the baby that had once been Willow.

I turned my attention back to Alice. 'Take it from me: You will be a star,' I said.

Alice blushed. 'Thank you.'

I went on holding her hand, knowing she was taking me seriously. She was full of possibility.

Alice was a star in so many ways. Everyone loved her. Even the women who at first had taken a dislike to her – because she was so young, and deliberately sensational, and yet in every way more than their equal – came round to her in the end. She was witty and clever and brought an energy the week would have lacked without her. She made all those people in their fifties feel twenty-five again. They were grateful for it.

But I was worried about her. I had an urge to reach out and take her home with me. It would pass, though, once I was back in Grasmere with the girls and locked into the routine of cooking, school runs, homework, stories … It was just this week off from parenting. The mother in me had clearly become desperate for someone to tend to. I wanted to give the girl a decent bed to sleep in, wanted to feed her properly, wanted to give her everything she needed to make her productive and then push her out into the world. Because the world was where she needed to be – not hidden away in some damp, greasy bedsit that cost more than she earned, or visiting a boyfriend whose only redeeming feature seemed to be that he'd never hit her.

Alice was fragile, I could see that. And she was weighed down by an awful history, which I could sense, but which she couldn't yet bring herself to confide to me. She hadn't learnt yet how to use an abusive past – how to shut herself off and cast herself in mystery. It made her artless, endearing. Easy to reach. I knew I could do it; it wouldn't take much. But what would come pouring out of her? All that grief for her mother. It would be immense. It would be unstoppable. I wouldn't have the strength or the skill to hold her up.

I sighed as I made a pile of everybody's work for recycling, then took myself out to the barn where they were waiting for me. It was the last night: a showcase when the students drank too much and read the best of the work they'd written over the week. Until now, I'd taken myself away early in the evenings, not been part of the wild socialising that Alice had usually been at the heart of. Once, she'd fallen asleep on a sofa in the barn, and someone had to go and get her for the morning's workshop. She'd been miraculously lucid, despite that.

One of the women was dancing when I walked in. She moved like a stripper. Her book was about a stripper, and now here she was, almost being one. No one seemed able to pluck an idea from the air and make fiction from it. Everything was just a constant drone about their own tedious lives.

I sat down beside Alice. She looked at me with raised eyebrows. *What the fuck is this?* she asked, silently.

Exactly, I answered.

The woman stopped dancing. Someone poured wine. The students took it in turns to stand up and read. Alice's piece, of course, was excellent. The girl had no idea how good she was. Because of this, I thought, she was at risk; at risk of wasting it all on the mechanics of just getting through her life – the poverty, the loneliness, the cycle of bad men who drained her energy as if they were babies.

The two of us had talked a lot since Wednesday, when we'd gone for a walk along the cliff path, and it had dawned on me then that I missed all this – the easy company of another female, the sort I'd had so much of when the girls were preschool age. I loved the Lake District, really loved it, but there was no denying its remoteness.

But still, I had Gus and the girls.

I'd spoken to them on Skype earlier. They told me they were making dinner the next day, to welcome me home.

'That's lovely,' I said. 'What are you making?'

'It's a surprise,' Lola said at the same time that Maggie said, 'Pancakes.'

Then Maggie disappeared for a moment; and when she came back, she held up an index card on which she'd written, in glitter glue of all colours, 'Welkoom home, Mummy'.

I couldn't wait to see them. I'd been gone too long.

Alice finished her reading and sat down again. She looked flushed and relieved it was all over.

I patted her thigh. 'You were great,' I whispered.

She smiled; a genuine, deep smile. She refilled her wine glass and offered some to me. Together, we sipped our way through the last two readings and clapped politely at the end. Then I stood up to congratulate everyone and tell them what a great week it had been, and how much I'd enjoyed it, how I wished them well for their futures and looked forward to seeing their books in the shops. Here, deliberately, I fixed my eyes on Alice. *I'm talking to you. Listen to what I am saying. Don't waste this.*

It was half past nine. I collected my bag from beneath my chair and moved as if to leave.

I felt a hand on my arm. 'Don't go to bed yet,' Alice was saying. She was rolling a joint. 'It's the last night. Stay up and get pissed.'

I sat down, let someone refill my glass, listened as Ben came up to Alice and told her he hadn't smoked a joint for twenty years, and would she mind letting him have some? Alice obliged, of course, and I watched as he took the joint from her fingers as lightly as if he were touching velvet or lace. The end was marked with her lip gloss. He held it to his mouth and drew on it. God, he fancied her. That was obvious. But he was fifty-six, married, five kids. I wanted to beat him away. *Take your vagrant cock elsewhere.*

The evening wore on. Everyone's spirits were high. In the end, I pulled Alice away and took her outside. I handed her one of the cards I'd had made up months ago, useful for when I was forced into city networking events with booksellers and journalists. It had my contact details and a thumbnail image of one of my book covers.

'Keep in touch with me,' I said. 'I want you to keep writing. Try a little every day – five hundred words – then email it to me at the end of every week. Then I'll look at it. I want to help you, Alice. There was no one to help me when I was younger…'

Alice took the card from my hand, and looked taken aback. 'Thank you.' she said. 'I—'

And suddenly I found myself held tight in the girl's embrace. It shocked me, this feeling of warm, adult affection, of being clasped against a body strong enough not to demand anything from me. I was unused to it.

I kissed her cheek. 'I'm glad I met you, Alice,' I said, and meant it.

I went to bed that night and found my half-conscious thoughts were full of her. The girl, with all her wit and crystal fragility, was here now, under my skin, where no one had been for years.

8

Alice

I sat on the train back to Brighton, feeling as though I'd been taken under someone's wing but not knowing quite why. Bo Luxton – successful, talented, rich – appeared to have warmed to me, Alice Dark – unemployed, unskilled, impoverished. I looked at the business card in my hand.

Bo Luxton
'The Riddlepit', Nr Grasmere, Cumbria
Bo@BoLuxton.co.uk
07965 324762

She'd said goodbye to me that morning, as I joined Ben and the others in a taxi to Alnmouth station. She'd held me at arm's length, looked at me and then repeated her words from the previous night. 'Keep in touch.' Then she'd leaned forwards kissed me, and I'd been aware of her nearness, the smell of her, the skin of her cheek as it brushed mine. It made me catch my breath.

I'm starstruck, I realised. The thought made me laugh. Twenty-five years old and I felt the way a preteen with a backstage pass to a One Direction gig would feel.

Roll with it, I thought. *It will pass.*

Because it would pass, of course. This train was the hinge between the creative, seductive week I'd just had and the life I was going back to. Already, I could feel my spirits starting to sag. Jake the Waster was waiting for me, half-drunk on Special Brew, his clothes unwashed, tobacco down his trousers. I wasn't sure I could bear it.

The train pulled into the station and I walked down to Churchill Square and then further on, to the sea front. It was a longer route than the High Street way, but I felt as though I was missing something integral, something that mature people like Bo and Ben all had – some sense of being rooted in their environment. They took note of places. Any time they felt like it, they would be able to sit down and write about the sea, and not just some generic version involving ships and azure waves, but the details, the specifics. Hell, I thought, they'd probably get to the heart of it, the very essence of the sea, creating a vision no one had seen before.

I was not part of my environment like they were. I was passing through it, paying it no attention at all. That was what was wrong with my bedsit, I thought now. There was nothing there but a bed, a box that served as a table and a fabric wardrobe from Argos that housed two pairs of jeans, some tops and a few leftovers from the days when I used to pretend I liked clubbing. Everything about it carried a feeling of transience, a sense that it could all be dismantled in an instant and moved somewhere else.

I needed to settle. I needed to get rid of Jake, move out of my bedsit, earn money, acquire the things other people had that marked them out as grown-ups: knickers that matched my bras; my own transport; a living-room rug.

The seafront was crowded. It was half past five. The daytime drinkers were now crossing over with the early-evening drinkers, and the dregs of the Home Counties day-trippers still hung around the craft shops under the arches. Ahead of me, the black skeleton of the West Pier cast its eerie beauty over the water.

I half expected to see Jake as I walked. On sunny days, he often set up on the beach towards Hove. It was more chilled, he said, than standing at the entrance to the Lanes, with all the buses and taxis belching their fumes into his face, polluting the pure colours of his art.

But he wasn't there. I decided to head straight to the house on Brunswick Street East, instead of my bedsit. He probably wouldn't be back yet from wherever he'd spent his afternoon (Jake's life was lived in half-days, rather than days), but I could chat to Maria and wait for him, then go home later, once I'd dumped him. Because I would dump him. Dump him and live, or not dump him and rot. It was a stark choice, like the one between capitalism and the Earth.

As I walked, I planned what I'd say:

– *You're lovely; but I need someone I can rely on not to shit themselves at the end of a night out.*
– *You need a woman who's prepared to be your mother *and* to fuck you. I don't really want to do either.*
– *I know it's shallow, but I would just like the experience of being seduced with champagne and oysters instead of Special Brew and Cheese Footballs.*

He was home when I got there, standing at the worktop, chopping vegetables. I'd never seen anyone chop vegetables like Jake. He did it with the laborious care of a heart surgeon, at a rate of two carrots per half hour. It drove me mad.

He looked up and beamed when he saw me. 'Baby,' he said, and came over and kissed me, his lips tasting only faintly of weed.

'Hi.'

'Was it good?'

I nodded. 'Great,' I said, because how could I explain what the week had been like?

'I'm cooking for you, to celebrate. Do you want a drink?' He opened the fridge. 'I've only got Stella.'

I shrugged and sat down. 'That'll do.'

'Did you do any writing?'

'Some. I met great people.'

'Yeah. Cool. Invite them to stay.'

I took a long slug of my beer and sighed. He looked so earnest, standing there, doing something with aubergines, happy to have me here again; happy with his unconventional life that I no longer wanted to share. I'd never dumped anyone before. I didn't know how to do it, to stand there and watch someone hurt and hurt and know it was because of me.

I began to think I probably wouldn't be able to.

By eleven, I hadn't done it. We'd eaten the aubergine mess, shared two spliffs and drunk some cans of Stella. Now, because I'd been away for a week and so far failed to dump him, I had to go to bed with him and endure reuniting sex.

He set to work on me. I pretended not to notice the extra porn cutouts by the bed, or the balled-up tissues that reeked of spunk, the general seediness of the room. Bo, I felt sure, would not be having reuniting sex in a room like this. She would be having reuniting sex on washed, pure-white linen, with a man who did not grunt like a pig or scratch her tender flesh with the bristles of his beard, and who made her sigh and gasp and part her thighs and buck with pleasure against him and...

Oh God, I thought. Oh, God.

Her Majesty's Prison for Women
Yorkshire

I'm on good terms with the guards here, but even so, they won't let me write to her. They asked the judge, and he said she doesn't want to hear from me, though I don't believe that for a minute. I'm sure she'd want to know what I have to say. I don't suppose he even asked her. It's probably too modern a concept for him. I've read about it. They call it restorative justice, where the criminal writes an apology letter to the victim, showing all their remorse. I still can't really think of myself as a criminal, though; I was just deeply troubled. I hadn't planned to love her like this, and it took my breath away, and my sense. But I can see that the impact of a remorseful criminal is not to be underestimated. It has deeply healing properties for the victim.

But they won't let me write, and there's the end of it.

Perhaps it's just as well. I can hardly hold a pen, my hands are so chapped and reddened from gardening. They gave me gloves, but cheap ones. Prisoners have the worst of everything, although it's true that there are some in here who prefer it to life on the outside. It's the first time many of them have ever had a steady roof over their heads, for a start, or enough to eat. They don't care that the baked beans are grey and the bacon mostly fat. There's enough to fill their withered bellies, and that's all that matters.

I don't complain about the state of my hands, and never will, not even when I get out of here. There's a general belief out there in the world that a decent pair of gloves for a criminal would be a squandering of public money. The guards, I'm sure, think criminal hands are tougher than non-criminal hands and less in need of protection. But this is a misunderstanding, another example of the root of everything that is wrong in the world – that endless failure of nearly everyone to grasp the fact that other people are as real as they are.

But still, there is no space for that sort of thinking here. If I am to survive this I must concentrate only on me. I've done eight months so far. They gave me eighteen, but there's talk of letting me out after a year because I'm quiet and obedient and know how to behave. This is a women's prison and, as such, is not subject to categories of incarceration the way men's prisons are. Men who are really dangerous are sent to Category A prisons; less dangerous ones go to Bs or Cs. The others – though there aren't many of them – are lucky enough to head for an open prison, where they can be trusted not to escape and they'll be allowed out for weekends to visit their families.

We women are not ascribed a sliding scale of dangerousness. We are classed only according to whether we need to be in an open prison or a closed one. I don't know why this is, but I suspect it is a quaint reluctance on the part of the world to accept that women can be dangerous, too. The hand that rocks the cradle is not the hand that holds the knife.

But I am not dangerous. It was passion, that was all. And love like I have never known.

Part Two

LOVING *ALICE*

1

I was useless. I'd been home from Northumberland two weeks and still I was here, in Jake's house, in his bed, still living my life as his girlfriend. Every day, I woke up and resolved to end things with him, and every night, I went to bed having failed to do it. It was hard, knowing the only way to end your own misery was to cause someone else's; but also, I didn't want the drama of it. I'd seen what happened when people finished relationships. They became trapped in the debris for months.

I turned my attention to work, as I'd promised Bo I would. But it was a long slog. I had no real ideas for a story, just a few observations I'd made about how stupid people could be; they were probably more suited to Facebook status updates than a novel. It was a couple of years now since I'd decided I really wanted, more than anything else, to be an author. Someone told me I'd make a good poet – probably because of my ancient tendency toward bleakness and obsession – but no one could make a living through poetry. No, I was going to be a great woman writer of the twenty-first century. I would say subtle yet meaningful things about the world and the people in it, and one day someone would hand me the Nobel Prize for my ground-breaking insights into human nature, insights that would help steer the course of the future.

Jake said, 'Just write a story that people want to read. Put some sex in it, a murder, someone beautiful. Write about that woman you used to be obsessed with.'

'What woman?'

'The lecturer at York. The Shakespeare woman.'

'I wasn't obsessed. I admired her. I enjoyed her company.'

'You used to talk about her all the time. Send her letters and stuff.'

'Probably because you are so profoundly unstimulating, Jake.'

I hadn't meant to say that, but he laughed. 'Yeah, I know. I'm not good enough for a woman of your intellect. But I have a better idea than you and your Shakespeare-loving friends do about what the world wants to read.'

He was probably right. I would settle for knocking out a best-seller, if I could ever think of one. (I thought that was all you had to do to become a bestseller – just knock it out. I had no idea how many other people were doing this, too.)

I sat on the bed and jotted down some ideas in my notebook: 'Child goes missing. Assumed kidnap. Later turns out mother did it. Why?'

None of my characters had motives. It was a problem.

I let my mind drift to Bo. I'd gone to the library and emailed her the morning after I came home.

From: AlicetheEigth@gmail.com
Sent: 15 May 2015, 11:22
To: Bo@BoLuxton.co.uk
Subject: Hello

Hi Bo
Here I am, back in Brighton with my layabout boyfriend and my damp bedsit, missing everyone from the course and wishing we were all still there. It was a privilege to meet you, Bo. I hope you won't think me gushing if I say I think you have changed my life.

Alice

I read back over it and grimaced. I sounded like an idiot. Bo was only doing her job. She wasn't on a mission to change lives. I clicked away from the page and didn't send it. I needed to put Bo in the past. She was a writer. A teacher. She'd returned to her exquisite mountain home and our paths would never cross again. A woman like her had no reason to be friends with a woman like me. That was the end of it.

But then I heard from her that very evening, when we'd barely been out of Northumberland for a day. I opened my inbox, and there it was:

From: Bo@BoLuxton.co.uk
Sent: 15 May 2015, 21:43
To: AlicetheEigth@gmail.com
Subject: Hello

Hello,
How are you? Did you make it back to Brighton in one piece? It must have been a slog on all those trains. I'm glad to be home with my girls again, but it's quiet here. I went out walking after I'd put them both to bed. The evening was bright, the sun still warm in the sky as I made my way towards Langdale, up the fell. I love it there. From up high, you can look back over the valley and see the blue spread of the lake at Grasmere stretched before you, like a slab in the crevice of the mountains. There was a glassy stillness, I thought, hanging over Grasmere, and everything felt subdued. This sort of deep, deep silence was the thing that first attracted me to the Lakes, but suddenly it felt stifling, infinite, something I could get lost in if I wasn't careful. You're a thoughtful sort of a person. Do you ever feel like this?

I'm sure it's just because I've been surrounded by people all week. It takes a while to settle again into everyday life after having such a lively, lovely time.

Anyway, I wanted to say I'm glad I met you. I think you're a very talented writer. I hope you'll keep going.

Stay in touch (or tell me to stop bothering you if you prefer!)

Love,
Bo xx

I read it a couple of times, and for a moment I panicked and wondered whether I'd actually hit send on that message in which I said she'd changed my life. Quickly, I searched my sent items. It wasn't there. She hadn't read it. Thank God.

I returned to her message. Even her emails were lyrical, I thought. It was the most beautiful message anyone had ever sent me. But it was sad, too, undercut by loneliness. There was no mention of her husband, only her daughters, and now, instead of sitting with him – drinking wine or eating cheese or doing whatever it was that the married bourgeoisie did with their evenings – she was going out alone for walks on the fells, and then emailing me.

I began to picture her then as some kind of ethereal heroine from a Victorian romance. I saw her, mysterious and lonely, wandering over the mountains, waiting, waiting…

I was still sitting on the bed, halfheartedly making notes for a novel, when Jake went out.

He said he was going to find a party.

'It's three o'clock on a Sunday afternoon,' I said.

'There'll be one. Someone said last night there was a day party in Hove today. It started at 8 am.'

I found it hard to imagine what went on at a day party in summer. This wouldn't be a barbecue, with people sitting around on the grass, drinking prosecco. It would be held indoors, windows shut, curtains blacking out the sun in protest against the world's tedious habit of living according to the dictates of daylight and time. Music would be blaring, the air thick with heat and sweat and smoke. There was no way of knowing when it might end.

'Are you coming?' he asked.

I shook my head. 'I need to get some work done.'

I watched him go. He was wearing yesterday's trousers, which had been lying in a heap on the floor all night and were still stained with beer and black streaks of ash from his roll-ups. The sight of him now repulsed me. He was never going to become a world-class painter. I don't know why I ever thought he would; he'd told me that's what would happen, and I'd believed him. Being with him was a lesson in disillusion.

I packed up my things and decided not to be here when he came back.

On my way home, I stopped off at the internet café at the top of the road, hoping for an email from Bo. Over the two weeks since I returned from the course we'd fallen into the habit of a daily message. While they were a small thing, they always brightened my day – so much so that I'd already come to rely on them.

There was no email, but she'd updated her status on Facebook:

'The woman on the Clinique counter persuaded me to buy High Impact Curling Mascara by saying it would train my lashes, thereby tapping into this pervading sense of failure I've had for a long time that I've been too busy with my book and not engaged with the important task of training my eyelashes.'

I clicked 'Like' and commented:

'It's a slow process. The desire to train must come from the eyelash itself. You can't just impose curl on it. I recommend *How To Train So Eyebrows Curl and Curl So Eyebrows Train* – a seminal work in the field of facial hair training regimes.'

The frivolity of it lightened my mood a little. I walked slowly back to my bedsit, and wondered if I'd ever see her again.

I'd thought the decision to take my things and head back to my bedsit meant that I'd left Jake, but after he'd been gone for three days, I began to think he'd left me instead. Either way, it was over between us.

I ought to have been upset, and perhaps I would have been if I hadn't unexpectedly received a letter from a probate solicitor, telling me my mother had left me £5,000 in her will. All of a sudden, the world shifted and opened up for me.

It didn't cross my mind not to accept the money. I had no feelings at all for my mother and refused to forgive her, even when she was dying, but I wasn't going to turn down £5,000. I took it as an apology, long overdue.

I signed the form the solicitor had sent me so he could release the money, then went straight to the post office to send it. On my way back, I stopped at the library to tell Bo. An email from her was already waiting for me.

From: Bo@BoLuxton.co.uk
Sent: 13 June 2015, 10:43
To: AlicetheEighth@gmail.com
Subject: Hello
Hi Alice,
I was just thinking about you and wondered how you are. Work is going slowly for me today. I have to do an interview about Dorothy Wordsworth with a proper academic and wish I'd never agreed to it. Learn this from me, Alice: Never say yes to a worthy academic-type project. It will kill you in the end.

Anyway, what's new with you? Send me some of your work. I would love to read it!

Xxx Bo xxxx

From: AlicetheEighth@gmail.com
Sent: 15 June 2015, 13:32
To: Bo@BoLuxton.co.uk
Subject: Re: Hello
I think you need to remember that you're far too important these days to do as you're told. If I were as famous as you are, I wouldn't do a thing I didn't want to do. No, siree. I would tell the academics to go fuck themselves. (Do academics understand that phrase, or would you have to use the actual, dictionary term?)

Anyway, all good here. Jake went out three days ago and hasn't come back yet. I keep wondering if I ought to call the police, but then if they found him I'd be stuck with him again. Sometimes, simply allowing your partner to go missing is easier than dumping them. Have you ever found this?

Also, another good thing: I've just had a letter from a solicitor, saying my mother left me £5,000 in her will. I bought myself a mascara. High Impact Curling Mascara, like the one you mentioned on Facebook, because I thought I would like to train my eyelashes. (My rationale for this is that I can start with my eyes and gradually move to my mind and perhaps one day, my fat arse.) It was £17.50. This is the most I've ever spent on make-up and yet I still got £4,982.50 in change. My mind actually buckles at this wealth. I think I will buy some rainforest and save the world.

Better go. I am living life on the edge, wondering if Jake will come home today. Fingers crossed he got pissed and drifted away to France. Sorry I'm such a bitch. You have my permission to hate me for this level of spite, although in my defence, no normal woman can be expected to sustain a relationship with a man who takes acid and then shits himself. I know a lot of people who have taken acid in the past. It didn't happen to any of them.

Love,
Alice

From: : Bo@BoLuxton.co.uk
Sent: 16 June 2015, 09:43
To: AlicetheEigth@gmail.com
Subject: Re: Hello

Alice, please tell me you haven't spent all that money on a patch of rainforest. The planet is not your responsibility and saving it will cost a lot more than five grand. Keep the money. You'll only be able to buy a couple of yucca plants with that and yucca plants never saved anyone.

I've just come into my study to start work and I can't face it, so am emailing you instead. I like your advice. Perhaps I will say it, though I think it would sound better coming from your mouth than mine. Phrases like that seem to roll off your tongue more naturally.

Has Jake come home yet? What are you going to do about this issue?

Love,

Bo xxxxxxx

From: AlicetheEighth@gmail.com

Sent: 16 June 2015, 11:45

To: Bo@BoLuxton.co.uk

Subject: Re: Hello

I am not going to do anything about this issue. He's still out.

From: Bo@BoLuxton.co.uk

Sent: 17 June 2015, 16:24

To: AlicetheEighth@gmail.com

Subject: Re: Hello

What will you do when he comes home?

Also: let's have this chat on Messenger.

From: AlicetheEighth@gmail.com

Sent: 17 June 2015, 16:26

To: Bo@BoLuxton.co.uk

Subject: Re: Hello

Good idea. I am on a library computer and they will chuck me out soon.

Bo Luxton

Well?

Alice Dark
I won't do anything when he comes home.

Bo Luxton
???

Alice Dark
Seriously. I am a flake. It's my core trait. I will just live with him until he dies. I am confident it won't be many years.

Bo Luxton
NO! Do not do that. You have money now.
You can get out of this.

Alice Dark
OK. I'll write him a note.
'Dear impoverished Jake.
You were OK when I was skint too, but now I have money, I think I am worth more than you and am going to marry rich, old Ben.'

Bo Luxton
Seriously, at this stage I think a letter will do.
You needn't mention Ben (though I feel sure he would have you).

Alice Dark
I'll see. Anyway, he might never come home. Got to go. Librarian giving me evils because someone worthier than me wants to use this computer for something other than frippery. Like getting a job or something. I ought to do that.
PS: Do you really think Ben would have me?

Bo Luxton
Ben would have you.
It might upset his wife, though.

Alice Dark
Going. Bye.

Bo Luxton
Goodnight, sweetheart. xxxx

From: Bo@BoLuxton.co.uk
Sent: 19 June 2015, 13:17
To: AlicetheEighth@gmail.com
Subject: Are you alright, pet? (To be said in a northern, warming voice as I make us a brew.)
You've been very quiet. Are you alright? Has Jake come home? Let me know how you are!

From: AlicetheEighth@gmail.com
Sent: 19 June 2015, 14:53
To: Bo@BoLuxton.co.uk
Subject: Re: Are you alright, pet? (To be said in a northern, warming voice as I make us a brew.)
Jake came home. He'd gone to some weird club thing (I never go clubbing these days. I only ever pretended to like it. The best thing about turning twenty-five was making the decision I'm too old for clubbing now.)

Anyway, he went to a club, took loads of drugs, met some guys who had a van, went back to it with them and stayed there for five days. Apparently, it was like Nirvana in there. His kind of Nirvana, not mine, which is why he didn't invite me to join him.

So that's it. He didn't drift off to France, unfortunately. I'm just going to live in my bedsit from now on. It's a total pit and utterly depressing, but he'll never come over and surely we'll just stop seeing each other … eventually.

From: Bo@BoLuxton.co.uk
Sent: 20 June 2015, 08:16
To: AlicetheEighth@gmail.com
Subject: Take it easy
You sounded flat in your last email. Don't do anything too quickly. Just try and get used to things for a while; but remember you have £5,000 (minus the eyelash-training money) and I think that money would be well used on getting yourself somewhere nice to live, perhaps with people more like you? You are too sociable to live on your own in a bedsit.

Also, if you'd like some space away from Brighton and everything associated with Jake, why don't you come and stay here? I've spoken about it with the girls, and they are very excited about meeting you (I told them you wear pink boots), and Gus asked if you're good looking (I said yes) and he said he'd love to meet you, too. (Don't worry. He's ancient.)

I don't think you drive, but if you want to come you can get a train to Carlisle or Oxenholme (whichever is easiest), and I'll meet you at the station. Stay for a week. I can't promise an exciting time. All I do is look after my girls and attempt to write, but it would be fun if you were here, too. You will love the Lake District.

Bo xxxx

From: AlicetheEighth@gmail.com
Sent: 20 June 2015, 12:37
To: Bo@BoLuxton.co.uk
Subject: Re: Take it easy
Dear Lovely Bo,
Did you mean to invite me to your house in the Lake District, or did you just type that by accident?

From: Bo@BoLuxton.co.uk
Sent: 20 June 2015, 12:38
To: AlicetheEighth@gmail.com
Subject: Re: Take it easy
I invited you.

From: AlicetheEighth@gmail.com
Sent: 20 June 2015, 12:40
To: Bo@BoLuxton.co.uk
Subject: Re: Take it easy
Then I would love to come, if that's OK. When were you thinking?

From: Bo@BoLuxton.co.uk
Sent: 20 June 2015, 12:42
To: AlicetheEighth@gmail.com
Subject: Re: Take it easy
We're here all the time. Come whenever you want. Tomorrow, if you like.

From: AlicetheEighth@gmail.com
Sent: 20 June 2015, 12:44
To: Bo@BoLuxton.co.uk
Subject: Re: Take it easy
Tomorrow is Sunday, which means trains will all be fucked because of a storm in Antarctica fifty years ago. How about Tuesday? (Are you really sure?)

From: Bo@BoLuxton.co.uk
Sent: 20 June 2015, 12:42
To: AlicetheEighth@gmail.com
Subject: Re: Take it easy
Tuesday is perfect. I am really sure. See you then. Hurrah! Can't wait!!!

2

I hadn't eaten properly for days. It used to be Jake who cooked, or Maria, and everyone in our house would eat together. Occasionally, when Maria was pissed off that I'd come to stay the night back in October and still not gone home months later, she'd grumble about the fact that I'd never made a single meal for them. 'Seriously, I can't cook,' I'd say. 'I really can't. I'll buy us all a take-away, but you'll regret asking me to cook.'

'Try,' Maria said.

So I did, and they never asked me again. I earned my keep by sharing my cigarettes and buying a bag of weed now and then. It seemed to be enough.

Now, alone in my bedsit, my meals were usually two cigarettes and a cappuccino. I'd just bought a new espresso maker and a milk frother, because I valued the kick up the arse I got from that combination of coffee and nicotine. Nutrition, I thought, was overrated. I'd once known a girl who could dance till 3 am on nothing but two bananas; but I wasn't like that. I needed the jolting force of chemicals to set me going, push me on.

Bo would expect me to eat, though. Bo was an eater, a believer in nourishment. I sensed that it would do no good to rock up at her beautiful mountain home and chain-smoke my way through five packets of Marlboro Gold (I'd splashed out since inheriting my mother's money; I usually made do with Lambert and Butler). I wondered if I'd be able to go a week without them. I could arrive there, clean-smelling and immaculate, not talk crap, not be chaotic and not smoke. Surely it was possible. Other people made whole lives out of that sort of behaviour. I suspected it could be the key to why they had survived the mainstream and I hadn't.

I checked my watch. 8:30. This was the earliest I'd been up since I quit my job six months ago. It felt good, to have something solid to get out of bed for, instead of arranging the endless space of a day around a single trip to the post office or corner shop.

Forty minutes till my train. I checked my bag. Jeans, tops, underwear, notebook, pen, make-up and a stick of Brighton rock for each of Bo's girls. I hadn't known what else to get them, had no idea what children liked these days; anyway, I suspected that Bo's children would not be like others. They were probably more into naming wildflowers and rare bird species than hauling lumps of neon plastic across the floor. They'd probably already read most of Austen and Dickens. I already felt intimidated by them. Lola and Maggie. They would be the cool girls. I remembered the cool girls – the ones who could get away with being clever because they used it to find out about the dreadful things their parents did in their bedrooms at night and mocked you if you didn't believe them.

I hauled my bag onto my shoulder, looked around the bedsit room one last time, thought how horrible it was going to be to come back here, then walked out, shutting the door behind me. I took the stairs two at a time, hoping to avoid other residents on their way to the showers or toilets. People here were poor – properly poor, not just artistically poor like I was. I would, I knew, find my way out of this. One day, I would have it all together. But these people came from long lines of poverty that went back generations. They'd grown up in bedsits where parents were absent and food was scarce; they'd been to failing schools, been beaten by people who were meant to love them, had any scrap of ambition knocked out of them by the hopeless greyness of their surroundings. Now, they were here, scraping together a living on zero-hour contracts, hardly surviving. Some of them, I knew, received parcels from the food bank: economy soup, economy pasta, treacle sponge in a tin. It depressed the hell out of me, to be here, living amongst it.

I made it to the front door of the building without seeing anyone. Now, I just had to get along Western Road and up the hill to the station without running into Jake. At this time of the morning, I was probably pretty safe, but there was always a chance I'd bump into him, saucer-eyed and cognitively absent, on his way home from wherever he'd been last night. I hadn't heard from him since Friday night, when he finally came back from the van he'd been staying in. On Sunday, he sent me a text message. *Where are you baby.* I didn't reply. He'd been silent since.

Outside was warm and sunny. The streets were already filling with shoppers and buskers, and café owners setting up pavement boards advertising breakfast bagels and wholefoods. I walked quickly. I didn't want to be distracted by shops. That five grand (minus cost of mascara, espresso maker and whisk) kept making itself known to me, like an itch. I can afford it, I thought, passing window displays of things I didn't need but that shone with the promise of happiness. But I couldn't afford it. I needed to do what Bo said and put the money aside.

My train was at the platfrom when I reached the station. Quickly, I collected my tickets from the machine, passed through the barriers and got on board. I'd booked a seat on the quiet coach. I hated the incessant ringing of mobile phones, people's public conversations, the intrusion of their lives into mine. Besides, I'd brought Bo's last two novels with me. I wanted to read them carefully and think of insightful, critically aware things to say so Bo wouldn't regret her offer to mentor me. I had to be worth it. I had to be good.

I settled myself into my seat, my luggage shoved on the shelf overhead, and checked my tickets to make sure I'd got everything right so far. My eyes fell over the date. Dates had become meaningless to me since giving up work, but it was the 23rd of June. Nearly the first anniversary of the death of my mother. I counted the days forward. Friday. I would be at Bo's, distracted, safely orbiting the bright heart of her family.

3

She was just so *normal.* That's what amazed me. This woman – successful, well known, wealthy and clever – lived a completely ordinary life. She squirted her worktops with kitchen spray, applied plasters to her children's wounds, made coffee and packed lunches, cooked evening meals … All of this seemed extraordinary to me. Extraordinary in its ordinariness. There was, I thought, a humility to it – a humanity at her core that wealth and fame could not remove.

One morning, I looked out at the mountains and streams that stretched on and on to the skyline, and said, 'Don't you ever want the excitement of London? The glamour and the parties?' I wasn't above being seduced by a party filled with famous authors.

Vehemently, Bo shook her head. 'There's nothing I hate more,' she said. 'The London writing scene … Some of the people are fine, of course; like people everywhere, but on the whole it's brutal, and so insincere. I can't bear it. Give me my middle-of-nowhere life in the Lake District, looking after my children and doing what I love in peace. It's underrated, this capacity for a life lived privately, competing with no one, having the freedom to be yourself.'

It made it all so easy, being here with her. I'd walked through the front door when I arrived and fit in, just like that. The house was rich with family: the noise, the vivacity, the deep-down wholeness of them all. It wasn't like the home I'd grown up in, where there'd been nothing but anger and hurt, and damaged people who couldn't stop damaging people.

Lola and Maggie were great. Vital, energetic, engaged with their lives at school. And loved. They were so loved, I wanted to be them. I wanted to lay down and feel the tender touch of Bo's hand in my hair; her lips on my face; her endless, patient care.

I said, 'Your girls have perfect lives. It's the childhood we all dreamed of.'

Bo smiled, and looked pleased.

I didn't think much of Gus, though. He was brooding, quiet, and took up more than his fair share of space. The grumpy misery of him filled a room. Even Bo acknowledged it. He went to Manchester on the Friday, leaving Bo and me alone with the girls for the day. When he came home that night, Bo sighed and said, 'And now the atmosphere in the house will change.' And that was exactly what happened. He upset the girls; he shouted at Bo when the geriatric cat shat in the corner of the kitchen; he took himself moodily out of the room and slammed the door.

'Bollocks,' I said, because I didn't know what else to say, and felt too inexperienced to offer words of comfort to a woman seventeen years older than I was. If it had been one of my friends in Brighton, I'd have said, straight away, 'What a cock. You can live without him.' Then we would spend the next month or two discussing whether she really could live without him, until finally, triumphantly, she'd decide that she could.

Mildly, Bo said, 'Don't worry about it, Alice. He's always like this when he sees I have friends and a life away from him.'

I looked at her anxiously.

She said, 'It's fine. I can handle it.'

I knew she was telling the truth. Her shoulders were broad and defended.

Gus had brought a letter in with him and dropped it on the table. Collecting the post seemed to be his job. He usually went off for it straight after breakfast, but he'd left early this morning, and even though we'd walked past the old-fashioned mailbox four times that day on the way to and from school with the girls, Bo hadn't collected it herself.

Perhaps I wouldn't have noticed this if Bo hadn't said, quite pointedly, 'I wonder whether there will be any horrors in there for me today.'

I looked at her curiously, but she said no more.

Now, she picked up the white, typed envelope and eyed it suspiciously for a while before tearing it open. I watched her read the letter inside, which went on for more than two pages. When she put it down again, she stood perfectly still, took some deep breaths and got herself a glass of water.

After a while, I said, 'Are you alright?'

She smiled at me. 'I'm fine. It's just not a very nice letter…'

She didn't finish what she was saying. Then Gus came back into the room, so I didn't have time to ask anything more.

Bo said, 'Could you take that letter and put it in the bin, Gus? It's from our old friend.'

'I didn't realise,' he said, and moved as if to read it.

But she put out a hand to stop him. 'Don't. Just get rid of it, Gus. Thanks.'

He mumbled something under his breath that I didn't catch, then dropped the letter into the recycling bin. He stared hard at Bo and said, 'We need to sort—'

'Later, Gus.'

I looked from one of them to the other. I didn't understand what had just happened, but I could see that Bo was biting her lip, trying hard not to cry.

Later that evening, when she was upstairs putting Maggie to bed and I was at the kitchen table with Lola, I caught a glimpse of Gus rifling through the recycling bin. He took out the letter and spent a long time reading it.

The next morning, Bo was back to her usual self. She made the girls' packed lunches and got them ready for the day, then together she and I walked them to school and afterwards we worked in Bo's study. I was envious of that room, all its peace and blank space, and the view I thought all writers should have: over the rocky fells to the valley below and the slate-grey gleam of the lake.

Bo was shuffling papers around on her desk. She picked up some typewritten pages and said, 'Can I read this to you? It's the first two chapters of my new project. I'm taking a leap into a new area this time.'

'I'd love to hear it.'

'I'm really in two minds about it. I can't tell if it's any good or not, and there's no point asking Gus, because he has no idea of the difference between world-class literature and absolute rubbish. I trust you, though. You know these things.'

I was flattered, though of course there was no way I would ever say anything critical about Bo's work. I'd seen quickly enough that Bo, despite all her success, was insecure. She didn't seem to believe she was as good as everyone said; it was as though she thought she'd tricked the whole world somehow. It was a sad lack of confidence that I blamed Gus for. He was horrible to Bo, I thought. Really unpleasant. A bastard.

Bo started reading. I listened. It was the beginning of something about Britain in fifty years' time, after an environmental disaster had destroyed the country. Everyone had become refugees, but the world was turning its back on them. It was chilling and frightening, even just those first few pages.

When Bo finished, I looked at her and said simply, 'Wow.'

Bo smiled, and I could see the relief on her face. 'Really? It's OK?'

'It's great. Truly. Just great. Oh, God, I'm so jealous of your talent.'

Bo laughed. Then she said, quite seriously, 'I'd like you to write today. Anything at all. Help yourself to whatever you need, whatever you want, but have something done before you go to bed. There's coffee on tap in the kitchen. Have as much as you like. I'll be here, too. I need to get on with this, even though I hate it at the moment. But you've cheered me up about it. We can work together, keep each other going. What do you think?'

'I'd love to,' I said. 'If that's OK.'

'It's compulsory.'

We spent the rest of the day there in the study together. There was no sound between us but the scratch of biros against paper, the gentle tapping of keys, the occasional sigh of thought. I became so exquisitely aware of it all that at times it felt as though Bo were running her pen over my skin.

Towards the afternoon, she said, 'Will you share what you've done with me?'

I hesitated. 'It's junk, Bo. Really, it's shit. No matter what I set out to do, I end up writing about my bloody dead mother.'

Bo said, 'Don't be so hard on yourself, sweetheart. Remember it's only been a year, and you've only just lived through the anniversary. It's bound to dominate. Things like that do. It was the same for me when I started out.'

'Was it?' I heard the eagerness in my voice. *Tell me again that I am like you.*

'Yes, absolutely. Starting out with anything creative is like turning on an old tap. The water comes out brown at first because you're emptying your psyche of rubbish. Once you've got rid of that, it will run clear. I promise you.'

'Thank you,' I said.

Gently, Bo said, 'If you want to, you can tell me about your mother, if you think that will get it out of you sooner.'

I shook my head. 'We just didn't get on,' I said.

Bo nodded. 'I understand,' she said, and I knew that she did. She understood deeply, without me having to say a word more about it.

4

It had been one of the happiest weeks of my life, which seemed odd when I thought about it, because it had hardly been exciting. The nights weren't late, there was no sex, no drugs, no rush of new people. Everything at Bo's was just calm and easy. It was good. That's what it was. Good, in every way. The safety of it, the busyness, the atmosphere of home. I hadn't known how deeply you could long for those things, and hardly even be aware of it.

On my last day, we dropped the girls off at school as usual and walked on, following the river through the woods to Rydal Water for a picnic. Everywhere was in full leaf now, and the beech trees and sycamores hid our view of the mountains.

In the green darkness of the woodland, Bo said, 'I'm glad you came to stay.'

I smiled. 'Me, too.'

'I feel like meeting you has been really special.' She stopped and gazed silently at the lake.

I could hear only the gentle heave of water against stones.

Bo said, 'I wish…' Then stopped.

I glanced at her quizzically.

She shook her head. 'I was just thinking how nice it would be if you could … never mind. Come and stay again soon. Come in September, when the crowds have gone. It's lovely here in autumn.'

I could almost feel my legs buckle beneath me, hearing this woman – this wonderful woman – speak like this. I thought, *It's because it's new to me, such a strange and comforting awareness that someone really cares, really wants me here.*

My mind slipped to my mother – dead one year today, everything unresolved between us and no chance to fix it now – and the old, deep loss of her. I used to feel the absence of my family as a weakness, as though my heart were fuelled only by water, instead of the tender force of blood. But the water had turned stagnant, dried up. I did not want my heart to to crack open again.

Bo didn't mention my mother at all today, but as we walked home she linked her arm through mine and smiled and said lightly, 'I feel like I have another daughter.'

I tightened my grip on my friend's arm but stayed silent. Friend. It was the wrong word. It didn't describe this. I didn't know what to call it.

But then, in the evening, after we'd eaten and Gus had slammed out of the room because of the cat shit on the floor, Maggie said, from nowhere, 'Mum, can Daddy sleep somewhere else?'

Fleetingly – so fleetingly – I saw it: Bo's bed, empty of Gus…

I glanced up at Bo.

Our eyes met.

Bo looked startled. Then she laughed and said, 'Maggie likes to have girls' nights sometimes, where the two of us sit in bed and read together.'

I nodded and could hear myself saying, 'Oh, that sounds fun.'

I knew what this was now. Not friend. Not mother. Lover.

We'd said goodbye at the station the previous morning. Afterwards, I sat on the platform waiting for my train, and Bo took Maggie to the station shop. I looked through the window at them and saw Bo standing at the magazine shelf, wiping tears from her eyes. I thought, *Perhaps she is lonely*. And then I thought, *I am lonely*. And I travelled slowly back to Brighton and my flat, and sighed at the appalling depth of my poverty. No money, no family, a skulk of dreadful memories and a home so basic it scarcely kept out the cold.

I sat on my bed and thought of Bo. I wondered what she was

doing, up there in her beautiful Lakeland home, with her mountain views and her children, and the husband who hadn't a clue what a jewel he was married to. And I wondered whether she missed me.

5

After I'd been home three days, I walked into town and bought myself an iPad Mini so I could email Bo whenever I wanted, instead of always having to use the computers at the library, which ran so slowly I needed an hour each time and always felt guilty when there were other people waiting who needed to apply for jobs or get advice.

The iPad was expensive, but worth it, because Bo's emails were now frequent and urgent.

To: AlicetheEighth@gmail.com

Sent: 3 July 2015, 16:15

Subject: Hello

Dear Lovely Alice,

How are you doing? Things are OK here, though quiet. I have started chapter three now and am slowly picking up pace, but it's a long slog and I'm not convinced I'll make it very far. If I send it when it's finished, will you look at it and let me know your (honest!) opinion? Seriously, if it's shit, just say so. I met a man at a conference recently who has devoted his life to studying the environment and predicted the effects of climate change in the UK; he asked to see it, but I refused in case he is a raging sexist tosser. (I think I am starting to sound like you.)

Actually, I miss you. We ate our meal this evening and then, because I love summer nights on the fells, when dark silences the peaks and I can hear nothing but the vale's rocky falls and the occasional creak of a fir, I went out walking for a couple of hours, and as I walked I thought how lovely it would be, to have you here beside me…

So come and stay with me again soon, dear, sweet Alice.

xxxxx

From: AlicetheEighth@gmail.com
Sent: 3 July 2015, 16:49
To: Bo@BoLuxton.co.uk
Subject: Re: Hello

I'm sure your work is better than you think, but yes, do send it to me and I shall examine it and no doubt find it all so brilliant I won't understand any of the depths of it at all. If you're happy with that kind of critic, then sure. But you know by now that I am only ever going to tell you you're brilliant. Because you are. Maybe that's the sort of criticism you want, but you don't need to send me your work for that. I can just say it. I'll say it as much as you like. I'll say it until your ego grows so large, it can be seen from space.

You're brilliant.

My flat is such a heap of shit. I have decided to take your advice and find somewhere decent to live, but I need to find a job first and … blurgh. My boss has increased my hours to every morning at the language school, but it won't be enough to pay rent anywhere nice. I might sell my ovaries on eBay.

Your walk sounds lovely. I wish I could have been there, too.

Ax

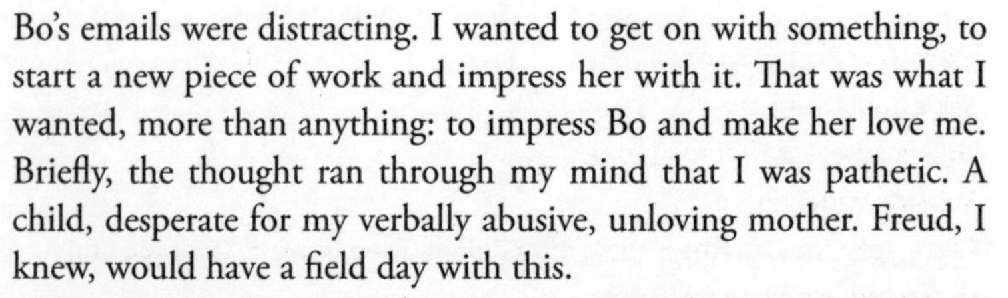

Bo's emails were distracting. I wanted to get on with something, to start a new piece of work and impress her with it. That was what I wanted, more than anything: to impress Bo and make her love me. Briefly, the thought ran through my mind that I was pathetic. A child, desperate for my verbally abusive, unloving mother. Freud, I knew, would have a field day with this.

But Bo wasn't my mother. Bo was a good thing, a positive – someone caring who brought out only the best in me. Last week, in her studio in Grasmere, Bo had started me off, set me going like a watch. 'Write,' she said, and I was going to write.

I turned on the radio. It was tuned to Radio Four. Someone was talking about some new website that had been set up, where anyone who was interested could access transcripts of any case brought before the Old Bailey from 1600 onwards. I listened more intently. A man was telling the story of an impoverished young girl who'd stolen another girl's dress and been sentenced to transportation. A whole life lived in New South Wales instead of here. And that was the last that was known of her. The judge's sentence, her weeping response then nothing.

I thought, *I wonder what happened to her*, and started to make some notes, so I could tell this girl's story.

The day wore on. I read articles online: potted biographies of convicts, facts about life in Botany Bay. At half past six, I made myself some toast, then opened a blank Word document and started writing.

It took me four hours, but I managed to fill a page. Three paragraphs of carefully constructed sentences, not a single one about my mother.

Jubilantly, I attached it to an email. 'I've done it', I wrote, and hit send.

The reply came in ten minutes: 'This is excellent stuff, darling, as I knew it would be. Keep on, keep on…'

I went to bed, exhausted and happy.

I was woken by the ping of the iPad.

From: Bo@BoLuxton.co.uk
Sent: 4 July 2015, 00:32
To: AlicetheEighth@gmail.com
Subject: Wide Awake
Can't sleep, so up in the middle of the night. Tried to work. Too tired and distracted. Wish you were here.

Well done for working today. Goodnight, my sweetheart. I am picturing you lying asleep, hoping your dreams are peaceful.

Love you,

Bxxxxx

From: Bo@BoLuxton.co.uk
Sent: 4 July 2015, 00:34
To: AlicetheEighth@gmail.com
Subject: PS
I forgot to say: Don't sell your ovaries on eBay. You will need them. I want no more of this 'the world doesn't need more of my genes' nonsense. The world would be a better place if it were filled with your genes.
x

I read, and scrutinised every word of the two emails. *Love you.* No one had ever said that to me before. Not that I could remember. *Love you.* I wondered what it meant, what sort of love she was talking about. It kept me awake, trying to work it out.

Everything was sublime and terrible.

6

I needed a project. I woke up on Friday morning and decided today was the day. I was sorting my life out. It would be a major aggravation, but was ultimately for the best. I needed to fill my life. I needed work. I needed a good environment to live in. I needed things to do. That way, I could stop thinking about Bo. No one had ever taken me over like this before. I was like a cliché from a Victorian romance novel. I couldn't eat, or sleep, or concentrate on anything. My head was so full of Bo that I could think of nothing else.

I love her, I thought.

Her.

It came as a shock.

This emotion needed restraining. Bo was married. She was married with two children and lived at the other end of the country. Nothing good could come of this. And, besides, she saw me only as a friend, a close friend, like a daughter or something. That's what she'd said. 'I feel like I have another daughter.'

I didn't want to be her daughter. I wanted to crawl into bed with her and stay there forever.

But I couldn't.

I showered and dressed and went to the language school. When I found my boss, with little preamble, I asked him for more hours.

'How many?' he asked.

'Full time.'

He shrugged. 'OK, but I must pay you cash in hand.'

I gave no thought to the legalities of this. All I saw was cash in my pocket, which was what I needed. I accepted the offer there and then. My next step was to find somewhere else to live.

I'd decided I didn't want to houseshare anymore. If I was going to be working full time, then I needed to be disciplined about how I spent the spare hours around it. I wouldn't get any writing done if I lived with other people. I needed to be on my own, somewhere comfortable and bright.

An agent showed me a place in Kemptown, near the sea. One tiny bedroom and a living space I could write in. £700 a month. It was pushing me to the extremes of my budget, but I could probably manage if I lived on toast and porridge and gave up smoking.

'I'll take it,' I said, and forked out the holding deposit.

I looked at the clock. 2 pm. This new project – sorting my life out – had taken four hours. It was meant to keep me occupied for days. The hassle and administrative hell was meant to have taken my life over.

So, of course, I went home and emailed Bo. Usually, there would have been at least one message from her by now, but today there was nothing.

I allowed myself to picture her, indulging myself in a daydream. But, like every time I thought of her in recent days, I saw her unclothed. The desire was painful. It was no good. I wondered what I was doing,

The message I bashed out was brief. Afterwards, I paced up and down my flat. Could Bo possibly feel the way I felt? Surely not. It would make no sense. But the thing – the connection between us – was so strong, I felt sure Bo had to be aware of it. Of course she was. It was impossible not to be.

Now and then, tentatively, I had dropped hints. At first love was a word we simply tossed between us. We signed off all our emails with it. But then I wrote, 'I love you to Empire State Building proportions. I do not know exactly what sort of love that is, but I do know it's a lot.'

Bo replied, 'I agree. American Architecural Love is huge and hard to define … Love you, adore you. Adore you.'

So love sat there between us, a nettle ungrasped. I didn't want to be the first to take it.

I tried to busy myself for the rest of the afternoon, reading and making notes for my book. Then later, as I was wondering whether to phone someone and go for a drink, the iPad beeped with an email alert.

Bo.

She was telling me to leave her alone.

From: Bo@BoLuxton.co.uk
Sent: 5 July 2015, 19:45
To: AlicetheEighth@gmail.com
Subject: Sorry
Hi Alice. Sorry not to be in touch today. I woke up this morning and decided I needed to give myself a rest from the computer. In fact, I was awake most of the night and I thought, 'I must ask Alice to stop emailing me for a while, as I need my head to myself for a few days.' Would that be OK? I just need to get on with some work. I've been so distracted recently and I hardly know why...

I understood the gist of this message: 'Leave me alone because I can't stop thinking about you,' Oh, God. How long could we keep this up? My heart felt ruptured with it. I could hardly contain it as I knocked out my reply.

From: AlicetheEighth@gmail.com
Sent: 5 July 2015, 19:50
To: Bo@BoLuxton.co.uk
Subject: Re: Sorry
My darling Bo. You don't need to apologise. I understand completely. Loving you in silence, in absence, and always.

I hit send, then regretted it. Too obvious. Far too obvious. I panicked, and sent another one.

From: AlicetheEighth@gmail.com
Sent: 5 July 2015, 19:52
To: Bo@BoLuxton.co.uk
Subject: Re: Sorry
Sorry. Didn't mean to sign off like some kind of bloody Barrett Browning there. Yes, get back to work. Speak in a few days. A.

Originally, I'd typed 'Best wishes, A', but deleted it before sending. That was going too far as well.

Speak in a few days.

A few days.

Ever since I'd come back from Grasmere, we'd been in touch every day. Our talks went on and on. Every couple of hours, she emailed me and I replied. Or I emailed her and she replied. Whatever way round it went, we were in this together.

But now I had to stay away. It was for the best. Of course it was. Perhaps I should take myself out for a drink in that time, meet a man, eat dinner with him, have sex with him, do something sensible instead of … instead of this.

But the thought of days passing in silence between us was unbearable. The clock on the wall ticked on, marking time, but time had become loose and unreliable. Hours were slippery. They shrank or grew, depending on Bo and how far away she was, and the hours without hearing from her would be longer – so much longer – than the hours when she'd been by my side.

This is awful, I thought. It should not be this consuming. The deep shock of love had come with no warning, and ran with the force of water over rocks. It had the power to knock me down.

The next day I wrote. I finished my opening chapter, but I didn't send it to Bo. When I went to bed, I lay awake. It was the first day since we'd met that I hadn't heard from her at all. The silence was a hole I could fall in to.

My sleepless mind drifted. It went to Bo, to my mother, to that night when I was eleven, when they came and took me away from her.

Sometimes, I wondered how Bo had turned out the way she had. She was beautiful, I thought. A truly beautiful person – a miracle, to me at least. She understood everything about the world. It was greater than genius and placed her beyond human.

7

From: Bo@BoLuxton.co.uk
Sent: 7 July 2015, 22:34
To: AlicetheEighth@gmail.com
Subject: Missing you
Nothing to say. Just wanted to say goodnight. And that I miss you. Come and stay soon.

I printed out her emails and took them to the pub to show Anna. I'd caved in to the pressure. I wanted another opinion. I'd asked Anna because she was older than I was and the most forthright of all my friends.

'So what do you think?' I asked

Anna put the sheets of paper down on the table in the bar and swigged her lager. 'I don't know.'

'Really?'

'Quite clearly, this woman loves you, adores you, wants you not to waste your life in a crap bedsit in Brighton. It also seems very possible that she fancies you – there is definitely something sexy about all this. But I don't know. It's difficult to be sure, but if you were asking me to place a bet, I'd put my 50p on you being right. *But* it's easy enough to say all this in emails. Whether she'll be quite as forward in real life, I'm not sure.'

I panicked slightly when Anna used the word 'fancies'. It was feeble in the face of my feelings for Bo. There ought to be a whole new language, I thought, for things that needed to stay pure and not be diluted by words. 'Love' didn't go far enough, either. There wasn't a word in the world that could express this.

Anna passed the pages back to me. I folded them away and put them in my bag.

'So what are you going to do about this?' she asked.

'I'm not sure.'

'From what I can see, it's all looking a bit too late for you to walk away unharmed.'

A rock of dread settled in my stomach at the thought of that. 'No,' I said. 'I think you're right.'

'You need to find out how she really feels and how seriously she's taking it. *If* she feels the way you do, then there's a lot at stake for her. Do you think she'd leave her husband and shack up in a lesbian relationship, and continue bringing up two kids?'

'I don't know,' I said. 'Maybe not.'

Thoughts of Gus worried me. I'd seen his shape before: the moody broodiness of a man who wanted one woman completely to himself. My mother had married a man like him. His jealous intensity had been flattering at first – she saw it as a sign of the depth of his love – but, of course, in the end it turned miserable and violent. And there was something about Bo, I thought – something indefinable and vulnerable, despite all her success and outward calm; it was as though she might be crushed at any moment. I wondered if he'd done that to her, and what he might do if he found out about us. I shuddered at the idea of it.

'I wouldn't, if I were her,' Anna said.

'Why?'

'Honestly? Because it's a bloody stupid thing to do. For a forty-year-old woman to walk away from her tidy, bourgeois life with a husband and two children, and get it on with another woman, practically young enough to be her child, who has no security and no money to speak of, would be insane. Seriously, Alice. If she does it, you need to run a mile, because it means she's not all there. She would be absolutely mad.'

I bristled. 'I suppose it depends.'

'Don't be a romantic idiot about this. She won't do it.'

'Thanks.'

Anna shrugged. 'You wanted to know what I thought and I'm telling you. I think she may well love you, but I also think there's only one direction this can go, and that is straight to hell. You can see that, can't you? If it's not hell for you, it'll be hell for her kids.'

'Not necessarily. If we were careful enough.'

'Kids whose parents separate get fucked up. I see it all the time. The kids I arrest have all come from broken homes. All of them. And that's without their mother moving in with another woman.'

Anna always did this. She could always cite some depressing statistic she'd learnt from twelve years in the police force. Criminals were no-hopers, she said. It started when their parents separated and went on from there. Hers had never been a soft approach, though. She blamed parents for everything. They should just face their responsibilities and stay together.

I said, 'I suppose you're right.'

'Would you wait until her kids are older?'

'Yes,' I replied straight away; I didn't even need to think about it.

'Even if it's fifteen years?'

'Yes.'

'Wow. You've got it bad. You need to be really, really careful, Alice.'

I said no more. I couldn't make anyone understand this. There was no point trying. I didn't need to be careful. This love was huge and magnificent. It would go on and on, and it could never hurt, because it was wise and sublime. It healed and repaired, as if something holy and golden had fallen to earth and struck us down.

I said goodbye to Anna and walked slowly back to my bedsit, her words ringing in my ears: 'there's only one direction this can go, and that is straight to hell.'

But nothing had even been declared between us, not yet. Neither of us had come right out and said, 'More than anything else, I want to lure you away from your conventional, cock-loving ways.' We had, though, once entered into an email discussion about sex (God knows why) and I had reminisced to Bo about the time I'd shagged a bloke in Malawi after we spent the evening together on the lake-shore watching the moon rise out of the water. Bo's reply had been, 'I am still thinking about your last lovely email. Lovely, lovely email, darling. Just lovely. (I am purring here.)' And I got the message.

When I got home, there was a message from her on my iPad.

From: Bo@BoLuxton.co.uk
Sent: 11 July 2015, 12:17
To: AlicetheEighth@gmail.com
Subject: Next week
Gus is going away next Tuesday for three nights.
Come and stay.
Please. Love you, adore you.
Bxxx

8

I boarded the train to Oxenholme at Euston. My backpack was light. I was only going for three days and had just one pair of jeans, two tops, some walking trousers, my iPad and a notebook. I hadn't planned to take pyjamas but at the last minute threw them in, just in case I'd made a terrible mistake and Bo wasn't asking me to stay for the reason I thought she was.

I took the iPad and the notebook out of my rucksack and then shoved it on the rack above my head and took my seat. As soon as I'd set the iPad up on the tiny table that folded down from the seat in front of me a message appeared from Bo. 'So looking forward to seeing you, my darling, darling, Alice. I adore you, Bxxxx'

I replied with nothing but a row of kisses, and felt oddly nervous. Never once had either of us said that this was something other than the ordinary love between friends. But I knew. I knew how I felt about Bo, and Bo had made it plain enough how she felt about me. And now Bo's husband was away, and Bo had invited me to stay, and I was definitely expecting more than a cup of tea, a cheese scone and fresh linen on the spare-room bed.

But I dreaded the awkwardness. I dreaded the strange moments that would take us to *the* moment, where we would somehow seamlessly make the transition from friends to lovers.

I would have to let Bo take the lead, I thought. Bo, after all, was the married one, the one with everything to lose. I had to let her change her mind if she wanted to.

The thought of Bo changing her mind made my stomach sway. Anna was right. This had gone too far for anyone to come out of it unharmed. Bo, me, Gus, Lola, Maggie … I'd tried not to think about it before now, but if I took a moment to stand outside the situation and consider everybody involved, then I had to admit that the odds were stacked against me. My own heart was most at risk in all this.

But no. Not really. Bo was Bo. She might change her mind, but she would never hurt me. That much I was sure of.

I settled myself in my seat and started to write. I wanted to have at least another two thousand words to show her this evening.

This time, Bo kissed me when she met me at the station. The warm smash of her mouth on my lips took me by surprise, so much so that it was over before I could even return it. But it didn't end there. Boldly, as if she didn't care who saw or what they might think, Bo twined her fingers through mine as we walked to the car, and then leaned forwards and kissed me again when we were inside. This time, I felt the warm slip of her tongue in my mouth, the soft smoothness of her face close to mine, the sweet, sweet femaleness of her.

It was all so easy, in the end.

9

After all those years, I felt her as a gift, a dropped jewel.

I lay beside her on the rug, gazed at her in bewilderment and murmured, 'There cannot be anyone on earth like you; no other mind more perfectly sculpted to mine.'

'We are twin souls,' she said. 'Identical.'

'No. Not identical. Opposite. Like life and death, light and dark – one cannot be known without the other.'

We lay together in silence for hours.

I held her against me; the warmth of her breath on my neck; the warmth of her body; her face staring down at me, holding my gaze until her eyes were a mirror and I saw my own in them.

'My beloved,' she whispered. 'My beloved.'

The dark moved slowly over us. We hid inside it, bright stars, our light collapsing.

She rested her head on my shoulder and I read her to sleep, listening to the soft rise and fall of her breath beside me. I kissed her forehead, and did not move after that, or even stir as she slept on. I simply lay beside her and felt it a sacred and hallowed hour.

She woke in silence and drew me into her gaze. No words passed between us. We had learnt not to speak of love, just let it be.

10

Of course, I'd heard the expression 'walking on air' before, but only now did I truly realise what it meant. I felt weightless, my whole body elevated, raised off the ground through joy. Bo loved me, wanted to be with me, was risking everything for me. It was breathtaking, wonderful and hard to believe.

In the morning, we dropped the girls off at school then walked on through the woods to Loughrigg Tarn. The day was warm, the sunlight gold against the dark water. I took Bo's hand in mine and thought, *Do not mention the future.*

We walked in silence. It was blissful at first and I sighed, deeply happy. I looked at Bo. But she wouldn't meet my eye, and the bliss was suddenly shot through with a bolt of tension.

I said, 'Are you alright?'

She said nothing.

Clouds gathered in front of the sun and I shivered. Still she wouldn't look at me. I kept hold of her hand and felt myself clinging. I didn't dare speak, for fear it would all be ruined.

In the evening, Bo cooked dinner and, as we were eating, she said, 'I can't keep pretending Gus isn't coming back.'

I said, 'Where do we go from here?'

She shook her head and said, 'I can't make any promises.'

I said, 'Do you regret this?'

She shrugged.

I spent the night in the spare room, waiting for her to come to me.

She didn't, and I wept.

She was better in the morning. She talked happily as we made the girls' breakfast. I warmed porridge in the microwave, Bo put bread in the toaster and poured juice and coffee. The atmosphere was busy, and whenever she caught my eye, Bo smiled at me and I knew there was flirtation in that smile, and when she brushed against me as I passed, we were both jolted by a force of desire much stronger than we were.

At night, our last night, everything was fine.

Two am. We lay in bed, still not sleeping.

Bo said, 'I've written a poem.'

I said, 'Read it to me.'

She did, and I listened. A sad poem, of course – about being trapped in paradise, and afraid.

When she finished, I took her hand in mine and said, 'It feels so sad to me – full of loneliness and fear and a longing to escape.'

I wished I hadn't spoken, because it was as though Bo's body became hard and sharp. And then she laughed and said, 'I am longing to escape. I am longing to escape from that ancient bloody cat downstairs. I spend my life sitting around, waiting for him to die so I can go on holiday again.'

I said, 'Is that all?'

She retreated from the question, said nothing more.

After a while, I said, 'I feel as though you know everything there is to know about me, but whenever I try and find out about you, you ignore it.'

This was true. I had tried a few times to talk to Bo about Gus and the way he treated her, or why she was always so dismissive of her mother, or thought the only way to live was shut off from everyone else. Always, she stepped around my questions, wouldn't talk, moved the conversation onto something new.

She said, 'What do you do when you feel angry or upset like this?'

'What?'

'You're angry and upset. How are you going to deal with these feelings?'

'I'm trying to talk to you about it. And I wouldn't say I was angry and upset. Just … frustrated.'

'But what do you usually do when you're angry and upset like this?'

'I'm not—'

'Sweetheart, you are. You have a lot to be angry about. You're angry with your mother…'

'I—'

'You need to find ways to get rid of that anger; to heal; get yourself to a place of wellness. You won't find it through alcohol or smoking or…'

I remained silent, confused.

Bo went on, 'When you feel like this, the best thing you can do is walk. Get outside. Walk for miles through beautiful scenery. Feel your feet on the earth and yourself as part of the earth, and let the beauty of your surroundings enter your senses and heal you. Now, come on. Let's sleep.'

But I lay awake, a strange, cold sensation in my gut, as though I were a child who'd just been told off. I tried to brush the feeling away. Bo hadn't told me off. She was being kind and wise and wonderful. I closed my eyes and felt Bo's arms around me. Everything was fine.

Morning rolled around. I woke up bereft. This was our last day. My train was leaving at three. I thought of the journey home, my empty flat, my empty life. All I wanted was to stay here with Bo and her girls. A family.

The girls didn't know, of course. Officially, I stayed in the spare room. It was where I stored my things, and I crept back there every morning before they woke up, like a teenager disobeying my parents' wishes. Or, perhaps, a filthy homewrecker. I turned away from that image of myself.

I could hear Bo and the girls in the kitchen, eating breakfast. I hung back – showered, dressed, packed my rucksack, busied myself with small tasks, quietly weeping at the thought of leaving and not knowing when I'd be back again.

After a while, Lola and Maggie ran upstairs to get ready for school. They were shouting at each other about something – I couldn't make out what and wasn't especially interested. It seemed they were always arguing, always shouting about something. My own mother would have banged their heads together, but Bo muscled on, always guiding, always negotiating, always patient.

I wiped my eyes and went downstairs. Bo was there, clearing the breakfast things. She looked up at me and smiled.

'Morning, darling,' she said, and there was a breeziness to her voice that offended me, because I wanted her to be sad. I wanted to know I wasn't the only one upset about this day.

But before I was able to say anything, Bo went on, 'I need to work today, and I think you should get out for a walk. It will clear your head and help you keep strong and calm.' She reached for a green book on the dresser and handed it to me: *Walks around Grasmere*.

I stared at it, speechless, and felt the stinging threat of tears. We barely had six hours left to spend together, and Bo had decided to work them away. I had an odd feeling inside me – something like shame; as though I'd become an uninvited guest, was being cast out.

I flicked through the pages of the book. 'Which would you recommend?' I asked, without enthusiasm.

She said, 'There's a lovely one starting at Dove Cottage and following the coffin route to Rydal, then you just cross the road to the lake and walk the lakeshore back to the village. It's only about six miles. You'll be done by lunchtime.'

I managed a laugh, 'The coffin route. That sounds right up my street.'

'It's just the path they used to use, linking two villages if one didn't have a church. They had to carry the dead between the parishes. It's pretty steep.' She smiled and added, 'They knew how to suffer in those days.'

I nodded.

'I've made you a lunch to take with you.' She paused. 'Please don't look as though the world's ending, darling. I just need the morning to work. Get yourself out. It will help you think and you'll come up with new ideas. I promise.'

'OK,' I said. I took the lunchbox and a bottle of water from Bo. 'Thanks.' And because there was nothing else to do, I walked out of the door.

What Bo had said was true. The walk was beautiful. The steep climb took me into the hills and gave a view over the lake, still and clear in the sunlight. But it didn't free my mind to give me ideas. All I could do was worry. I didn't want to be walking alone. I wanted Bo at my side.

I trudged on. Perhaps I was too needy. That was probably it. Bo was a famous, successful author with all sorts of demands on her time and she'd sent me away because she wanted some space. I wished I'd sensed it earlier. I wished I'd had the idea to go away and leave her to work, instead of reaching the stage where she'd had to tactfully push me out the door with a lunch she'd made me. My cheeks flamed.

At the end of the coffin route, the path rounded a bend that took me downhill to the road. I crossed it and went over a wooden bridge to the lakeshore. There were families there now, lying at the water's edge, children paddling or swinging daringly on a rope that hung from the branch of a tree.

I kept walking, on and on round the lake. No ideas came to me. I just felt chastised.

I dragged out the time in Grasmere, feeling I ought to leave it as long as possible before going back. I wandered around the shops, looking at bags and books and other things I had no need of. Eventually, the clock rolled round to one-thirty and I began the trek back up the fell to Bo's. There would only be time now to collect my things, say goodbye and head to the train station.

It was with hesitancy that I approached the front door. I wasn't sure whether I ought to just let myself in, or knock and wait, a visitor.

But she was there at the kitchen window, looking out for me. Her face, when me saw me, looked flushed with relief.

'You were gone for ages,' she said, opening the front door and kissing me warmly, urgently, sexily on the lips.

'I had a look round the shops,' I said, lightly.

'You were cutting it fine,' she said. 'We have so little time now before you go … Sweetheart, what's the matter?'

I looked away. Tears had sprung into my eyes, but I would not make a scene. 'Nothing.'

She reached out and put her arms around me. 'Oh, Alice,' she said. 'I didn't mean to hurt you.'

She held me for a long time.

When she finally pulled away she said, 'I only wanted to get on with this because I listened to what you said last night – about me not sharing things with you. You're right. I know you're right. And you'll have to forgive me, sweetheart, because I'm just not good at this sort of thing. I'm no good at talking. I prefer to just get on with life, without drama or conflict or anything like that. So what I've done this morning is written a couple of short stories; they're for you to take with you, to read on the train. You can consider them the story of my life, if you like.'

The relief came all at once. The cold heaviness that had weighed me down all morning lifted.

I smiled, 'Thank you. I thought … I thought…' I shook my head.

'No,' Bo said, and clasped my hand in her own. 'Don't think that.'

11

For Alice, From Bo

We were a family of wanderers. Not gypsies – though we went everywhere in our red gypsy caravan and met a lot of travelling people on our way – but roamers. My parents never liked to stay in one place too long. They said the work dried up if you did, and, besides that, my father had a way of making enemies everywhere he went. You'd know leaving was on the cards a week or so before it happened. Word would reach our ears that men were after my father, and then there'd be nights when we'd be woken up by the sounds of shouting and bodies being hurled against the sides of the wagon, and in the morning, my father would have loaded up the horse and we'd be off somewhere new, all our debts and worries behind us, he would say.

But the trouble with debts and worries was there was no getting away from them, not for long. If they didn't follow us, they just greeted us at the new place. We never had money, or if we did, it wasn't the sort of money that bought food or new clothes. It only ever paid for old things we'd never seen. Money was loose and slippery. It got away before it even reached us.

Most of the time, my parents weren't there. I never really knew what my father did, but my mother dealt in rags and bones. She scoured skips and front yards for other people's discarded belongings, polished them up or took them apart, then piled them into her pack and sold them, door to door. She foraged during the day, sold in the evenings. My brother and I were free to wander.

We hunted food. We learnt which plants were edible and which would poison us. In summer and autumn we got by, picking wild fruit from the hedgerows and eating it fresh and unwashed. 'Make sure you stay away from mushrooms,' our mother said, and she and my father laughed. We knew from the laughter that there was something exciting and forbidden about mushrooms. Like so many other things, they lurked in the dark world children weren't allowed to enter.

Winter was harder. In winter, my brother and I squeezed into our caravan and the cold would come blasting down the hills and freeze us – skin, flesh and bone – till we were stiff as the dead and not much happier, either.

Our mother stayed out later on winter nights. She had to. Hardly anyone opened their doors on winter nights, she said, and she paced twice as many streets to sell half what she sold in summer. But late at night, when she stumbled back to the caravan, there was always the sour smell of beer on her breath and anger in her fists.

'It's a bloody shithole in here,' she'd slur, and I would pretend to sleep on, hoping the beer would knock her down before she could work herself into a frenzy. Sometimes it did, and she'd just lie there on the floor till morning. Other times, she would stand above my bed and shout: 'I don't know what I was thinking, having children. Having a child like you. You do nothing and you cost me a fortune. A bloody fortune. Look at you! Fourteen years old. You're old enough to start bringing some money in to this place, or you'll have to find someone else to take you in.'

Soon after that, it started. When our parents were out and we were both in bed, the first man came in. I recognised him from around the site. A builder. A drinker. A shouter. For a while, he sat on the edge of my bed, then pulled back the sheets.

My brother sat up. 'What are you doing?' he asked.

'Never you mind; and there's no point telling yer mam about it, neither,' the man said, and he went to my brother's bed, grabbed his sheet and wrapped it over his head.

My brother didn't try to take it off.

The man came back to me.

I laid still and silent, and bore it, feeling myself turning to wood.

After he'd gone, another one came, and then another.

And they kept on visiting, night after night, and the more they visited, the richer we grew.

I was the little money tree.

12

For Darling Alice, From Bo

When I was fifteen, I spent three months being sick as a dog. Every morning I woke in panic, threw the covers off me and ran out the door of our old gypsy wagon into the scrubland behind, where I hid myself on my hands and knees and threw up until there was nothing left. Even then it kept on coming. My stomach went on buckling, and I gagged until I thought the life might leave me, but my mouth stayed dry and empty.

After a week of it, my mother looked at me, suspicious. 'What's wrong with you?' she asked.

I didn't meet her gaze. 'It's something I ate. Maybe we killed a bad duck.'

She nodded and said nothing more. I spent my days lying in bed, sometimes too weak to even go outside when the sickness came. My brother brought me a bucket. I cleaned it out when I could.

The caravan stank, and I knew I was in a sorry way.

Eventually, the sickness stopped, but it had left me wrung-out and thin. I thought, *Let the baby in me have been killed by this.*

But it wasn't, and even my mother realised it in the end. 'There's only one thing wrong with you,' she said.

I thought she was going to get it out for me, because I knew you could do that. I knew there were ways. You could go to a doctor and he'd give you a pill and the baby would disappear from the world, like smoke.

But my mother hated doctors. She called them 'the authorities'. The authorities were snoopers, prying eyes who wanted nothing but to lock us up. The authorities were schools, social workers, police, doctors and the government. They were to be hated and avoided at all costs. The authorities were why we never stayed long in one place. As soon as they got a whiff of children not in school, they were on us like rats.

So she didn't take me to the doctor. Instead, every night for a month, she dragged me with her to the Black Horse and asked the owner to give me two double gins. 'She's got herself in a bad way,' she explained. 'It wants getting out, quick. I can't afford more babies.'

The owner, a man everyone called Huggs, but which can't have been his real name, shook his head, as if he didn't have any words for the shame of it all; and then he passed me a glass and my mother handed over the money, paid her by the men who visited me at night.

I drank the gin quickly, four measures of it, neat. It made me feel sick to my stomach and sometimes my head would spin and my words would come out slurred. Walking back to the caravan wasn't easy. When I got there, I'd kneel on the floor and pray like a Christian girl for that gin to work its violent magic and get the baby out of me. But it never did, and I couldn't understand how a potion that could leave a girl seeing double and without her mouth or legs working properly, could still manage to keep the bones of a baby inside her, growing and healthy. There wasn't any sense in it.

There was one good thing about all this, though, and it was that the men stopped coming. Word got out that one of them had planted a child in me, and now they were all saying it wasn't them, and they'd never done it, and to prove how the child wasn't theirs, they stayed away.

Once the sickness had stopped and I could eat what little we had again, I had to start making room in my clothes by cutting the sides of my tops and undoing the button of my jeans.

'How long's it been?' my mother asked, looking pointedly at the round swelling of my belly.

I shrugged. 'I don't know. Five months. Maybe six.'

'Well, there's no getting rid of it with gin now. We'll have to find some other family of mugs to take it in.'

I said nothing.

Time went on. The baby in me grew and I felt so tired and heavy from it, and so afraid of what might happen, I wanted to lie down in the dirt and let the earth claim me and turn me to dust.

But it didn't.

My mother set me to work, fixing and painting tiles. She'd come across a whole sack of them in a builder's skip, bashed to pieces, and she wanted me to sit outside and glue them together again, like some impossible jigsaw. When I'd done that, they needed painting with a thin paintbrush, in beautiful patterns, so they could be sold to rich people, each one ten pounds.

And so that was how my days went by – sitting alone on a plastic sheet in the scrubland, matching up pieces of broken tiles, gluing them together and then painting them. All the while, the baby got bigger and fought me for the space to move.

Once, I said, 'What's going to happen when the baby comes?'

My mother said, 'There's a woman over the other side of the site whose daughter wants it.'

But I hadn't meant that. What I'd meant was what would happen to me, and how would I get it out? Mostly, I tried hard not to think about it, but there were nights I dreamed bad dreams of giving birth here, in the wagon, on my own, with no one to help me at all.

The baby came. It came earlier than I was expecting. I didn't have any idea what day of the week it was, or what time, except that it was light outside and not the grey sort of light of the early morning, but quite bright.

The wagon was empty and it took me a while to work out what was happening. At first I thought I must have wet myself, but my dress and the floor were soaked, and there was water everywhere. I was worried about how I could clear it up before my mother came home.

But soon I realised this was my baby on its way, so I went outside to the toilet block and sat there for a while.

When I grew uncomfortable sitting on the toilet, I took myself back to the wagon. There were only four wagons now on the site. All the ones with the visiting men in them had moved on. Everyone looked to be out.

I stood on the grass and called out: 'Help.' Then I waited a while, but nothing happened, so I decided to set up my work again, as a way of taking my mind off things.

The pain came after a couple of hours or more. And it wasn't that bad at first, but even so, I called 'Help' a few more times to try and get someone's attention. But no one heard. I thought perhaps it was Sunday, because on Sundays most people on the site spent the day in the Black Horse. I wondered if it might be a good thing for a baby to be born on a Sunday, because maybe there'd be a bit more hope for that sort of baby than there'd be for just the ordinary Monday or Tuesday sort.

Then I decided I couldn't sit down anymore, and I went walking instead. I walked and walked, pacing the scrubland, and the pain started to get bad, I did some more shouting. But still no one came, and I started to think maybe I was going to have to do this thing by myself. I didn't know what I was meant to do, or if I might die.

And I thought maybe it'd be a good thing if I did.

And then more pain came, so I didn't think anything for a while.

In the end I had to stop walking, because the pain was coming too often, and it wasn't an easy thing to walk through. I took off my nightdress and sat down in the grass. And when the pain came, I cried out, but it wasn't screaming – it was a strange noise, like I'd never heard before. I wasn't sure it could even be coming from me.

I kept hoping someone would hear me crying and come running, but no one did and so I just carried on sitting there, cross-legged in the grass, with my back leaning against a tree. I cried and grunted and shouted, and when my body said I had to, I started to push.

The grass got a lot of blood and mess on it, but in the end the baby came. I caught it myself in my hands – a wrinkled-up, grey, crying thing, covered in white wax that disappeared into its skin. Then the baby itself turned from grey to red and screamed, and I wasn't sure what to with it, or if it was getting cold, or how I was meant to keep it alive. All I knew was that the cord needed cutting and I didn't have any scissors, and everything was a mess and not at all clean.

So I put the baby down in the grass and picked my nightdress up off the ground. It was the only thing I had, and I thought I'd better cover the baby in it so it could keep warm, and when I did that, I saw that the baby was a girl.

It went to sleep. I carried it back to the wagon and sat with it in my bed.

My mother came home eventually. I heard her coming up the steps and got a horrible feeling inside, like I'd done something shameful and was about to be punished for it. And so I quickly moved the baby under the covers and hid it, and I sat there looking normal, as if nothing had happened.

But she'd seen the blood and the mess outside. She looked around and said, 'Have you had the baby?'

'Yes,' I said.

'Where is it? Why didn't you tell us?'

I pulled back the cover on my bed and showed her the baby, lying there on the mattress. 'I tried calling, but no one heard me.'

She didn't say anything, but she picked up the baby and held it close to her, and said hello to it, which was more than I'd done myself. But it was a difficult thing, to know what you ought to say to a body that'd just come out of you, and which you hadn't ever wanted in the first place.

I'd thought someone would come and take it straight away, but they didn't. I kept it with me for days. It lay in the bed next to me and I looked at it, but it didn't look like me and I wasn't sure it was really mine.

My mother told me to feed it, but I didn't know what I was meant to do, so I did nothing. The baby shuffled a bit, and waved its arms like it didn't know who they belonged to, and then it started crying so I covered it up with the sheet.

Mostly after that, I just wrapped the baby in a sheet, took it outside with me and got on with my painting. There wasn't anything else to do. The baby didn't cry much in those first few days. It mostly slept, and when it woke up, I covered its face with a blanket and put my fingers in my ears and then, eventually, the crying would stop and sleep would come again, which was good.

Sometimes at night, I got a sight of the baby when I'd thought it was asleep, and I'd see it wasn't asleep at all, but just wide awake and silent, watching me in the dark. Its eyes made me afraid, as if they were the eyes of a terrible fish.

My mother made sure there was food around now, but she still went out all day and most of the night. She never said much to me, except to ask how the baby and I were. I'd say we were both fine, thank you, and she'd go away again. But one time she said, 'Remember to feed the child.'

So I opened up a bag she'd left on the floor, took out a bread roll, and went over to where the baby was lying on my bed and held the crust to its mouth. It sucked and sucked on it, and its eyes got wild, as if it was half mad, and I was afraid.

So I left it there with the bread, and went to sit in the corner away from it.

I supposed other people would have given the baby powdered milk, but I didn't have any of that. I'd seen other women suckle their babies themselves, but I didn't really want to go picking it up and holding it to me like they did because I was afraid of doing it wrong. So I just gave it bread and some water now and then, and it didn't die, so I thought I must have been doing alright, though it was sick a lot.

Then one day, my mother came home early and with her was another woman – a young one I'd never seen before. My mother said, 'Where's the baby?'

I nodded towards the bed, where the baby was sleeping. It was always sleeping. She went over to it and picked it up, then took it to the other woman and handed it to her.

The woman looked at the baby in her arms and started to cry. 'Thank you,' she said. 'Thank you.'

And then she took it away.

13

On the train back to Euston, I read each story over and over. So this was it. This was Bo and what had made her who she was: a beautiful soul locked away from the world, strong and pure, not shrivelled with anger and bitterness.

But things were changing now. Slowly, I knew, the hot shock of our love was warming that heart. 'I've never…' Bo had said that first night, then shook her head and couldn't continue. But I knew. Bo had never done this before, never put her heart on the line for anyone. Her steps toward intimacy were small and cautious.

I looked down at the crisp, white pages in my lap. It astonished me that Bo had written this work just because I'd said I wanted to know about her life. It was something we'd argued about; only once, though – when I grew fed up with asking Bo questions she never answered. Now, I read and understood. Bo couldn't speak. She turned her face away, and handed me the words on paper instead. 'This is me.'

All I wanted now was to get off the train, turn around and go back to her. We needed to be together. That much was clear. This had been a collision, a wild combination of souls; a big bang, destiny…

14

I'd been back in Brighton a week, and had only heard from her once – just one brief email saying she hoped I'd made it home safely and that the move to the new place went well. 'Get in touch when you're settled,' she'd said, as though she were expecting some sort of halt in our daily contact, the contact I would move heaven and earth to keep going, the contact I relied on to know that Bo was still OK with all this, that she hadn't changed her mind, wasn't retreating to the husk of her family.

Amidst the wide hole created by Bo's silence, I tried to get on with life. I didn't contact her. I got up in the morning and went to work, taught my classes of Italian and Spanish beginners, then came home and forced myself to write five hundred words of my book. Afterwards, in the evenings, I would focus on sorting the flat out, making it as pleasant as I could: I hung pictures, bought flowers for the sitting room and a crimson throw for the old, worn sofa. I ought to have been happy. This was a step up, so much better than the damp bedsit with greasy walls over on Brunswick Place. But Bo's absence hurt, and the pain outweighed all the excitement of moving my life forwards. *Why aren't you here?* I thought, as I lay in bed at night. But I knew the answer to that. Marriage. Children. Wealth. Of course she wasn't bloody here.

It shocked me, how awful this was. Like a sickness. We'd said goodbye at the station the previous week. I'd walked away from her, settled into my seat on the train, stared out of the window and wept. It wasn't an ordinary goodbye. It felt like grief; the deep, deep pull of it dragging me beneath the surface of sense. I was flailing, drowning, lost in this love that was too big for me.

I tried to plan my future. Bo was always telling me to commit to my writing, to make it my priority, give it greater importance than money or love. But finding the discipline was hard and I needed forcing. I went online and looked up postgraduate degrees in creative writing. They were everywhere. Nearly every university in the country had cashed in on the ambitions of people who'd been led to believe that they, too, could be just like J.K. Rowling if they only dreamed hard enough and forked out the tuition fees.

On Friday evening, I sent out six applications: Manchester, Lancaster, Brunel, UEA, Sussex, Goldsmith's … That should do. Someone would take me, and if Bo ever did come back into my life, I could go to Manchester or Lancaster and live near her.

Where the hell was she? Where was Bo?

I couldn't carry on like this, with the whole length of the country between us. I needed to be near her.

A text message came from Anna: *Drink? Now?*

Sure. Where? I replied.

Ancient Mariner. See you in ten minutes.

I pulled on my denim jacket, brushed my hair and headed down to the beach. It was only seven, but the bars were filling up, as they always did on sunny evenings. I found Anna sitting at a glass table, smoking. 'I ordered you a beer,' she said as I approached.

'Thanks.' I sat down opposite her.

She said, 'So. What's new?'

'Nothing.'

'You went to the Lake District…' she said, as if trying to jog my memory.

'I did.'

'And?'

'It was great. Oh, God, Anna. This is so awful.'

'It was always going to be messy. She's in her forties and she's married with two kids. It can only go one way. I told you that…'

'I thought … I haven't heard from her since I came back.'

'You need to sack this off.'

'I can't.'

'You can. Stop wallowing; stop thinking about her. Get pissed with me, find a man, move on.'

I nearly choked on my beer. The very thought of finding a man and moving on was impossible. Impossible. *You have no idea about love,* I wanted to say. Instead, I slugged my drink and said, 'OK.'

The night passed in a blur. Money was spent, drink was drunk, nightclubs were hit, music was loud. I remembered, at some point, sitting on a purple-velvet sofa in the dark of an underground bar, thinking, *It's too loud, I hate this, I've always hated it*, and wishing I could be with Bo instead, reading poetry.

In the morning, I woke up in a strange bed, next to a bloke I didn't know, in a house I'd never been to before. My mouth felt like Gandhi's flip-flop, my head ached. All the signs were there that I'd shagged him. I needed the morning-after pill, an STD test. I was twenty-five. I was too old for this.

A hangover with self-loathing. The old familiar.

I got dressed and left before he opened his eyes.

When I got home, there it was. An email from Bo. Just two words.

'Call me.'

15

I needed a shower before phoning her. I needed to wash last night away. How would Bo feel if she knew what I'd done? She would probably be fine about it, I thought. She'd accept that she was hardly in a position to demand fidelity. The thought of her not being bothered by it hurt.

I washed the bloke off my skin and the stale smoke out of my hair. My head still ached. I stepped out of the shower and slipped into my pyjamas. I was going nowhere today. As soon as I'd spoken to Bo, I was going to crawl into bed and spend from now until night reading. A book not written by Bo.

I dialled her number. She picked it up immediately.

'It's me.'

'Alice,' she said. 'Gus is out. He's in Manchester again this weekend. The girls are at their music classes. I wanted to talk to you.'

Gus away, and she hadn't asked me to stay.

I got straight to the point, 'Have you got cold feet?'

'No,' she said immediately.

'That's good,' I said, and could hear the relief in my voice. 'It sounds serious, though.'

'It is. I think we need to stop the emails.'

'What?'

'Listen, you've met Gus. You know he's not an easy man. He's always been jealous, but it's been worse over the last few years, ever since my career took off and he hasn't … Anyway, he uses my computer and it's normal for him to read my emails. Can we agree to just talk on the phone instead? Every morning. I'm free then, and he won't know.'

'But I work.'

'Evenings, then. Please, darling. I can't risk this yet. I need to do it in my own time. If I handle this badly, Gus could…' She let her voice trail off, made me read the implications.

Gus could …What could he do? Hit her? It didn't seem impossible to me.

I said, 'OK.'

'And if you have any of my old emails, could you delete them? I know that sounds paranoid, but you just never know…'

I paused again. Then I said, 'OK.'

'Do you understand why I'm asking you to do this?'

'Yes. I do understand. Of course.'

'We'll be together again soon. I'll make sure of it,' she said. 'Look, I have to go now.'

I waited for her to explain why. She didn't. She just said a quick goodbye and ended the call.

I put the phone down beside me on the sofa.

So Bo was all about protecting her life, pretending I didn't exist, hiding me away like some dirty little secret. I knew, of course, that Bo wasn't like my own parents. She wouldn't recklessly pursue her own passions through the wreckage of other lives. She was a careful mother; the well-being of her daughters lay at the heart of every decision. She might go wild for a time, but sense would take over in the end.

I knew this. It was what I loved about her.

She was building a fortress around her life.

It was the distance that was the problem, we both knew that. If she lived here or I lived there, then we could see each other every day, and Gus would think we were friends – two writers working together. But like this, everything had to be clandestine, every moment stolen from the edges of her life.

I had an offer from Lancaster University. I accepted because it was close to Bo. I went to work, stuck with it, pocketed the money, dreamed of something better.

I taught a group of Mexicans how to say 'knickers'. It was a word that appeared in their reading comprehension task and I thought they probably wouldn't know it, so had to teach it first. The task involved standing in front of the class, holding up a picture of knickers, modelling the word for them and getting them to say it back to me. Knickers.

This was not, ever, what I'd planned for my life. When I was twenty-one, I'd been for an interview for the graduate training scheme at the accounting firm, Arthur Andersen. They'd asked, 'Where do you see yourself in five years' time?' I hadn't answered, 'Standing in a run-down language school in Brighton, teaching a room full of Mexicans how to say "knickers".'

Now, I told myself it was part of the joy of life – the endless surprise of it all. Like falling for a married woman fifteen years older than me. That had been a surprise, too.

Another beep. A text message. Another surprise.

Bo: *I have a suggestion. I know you've only just moved, and I know it's a lot to ask, but … why don't you let your flat go and come and live in Grasmere? There is plenty of accommodation in the village, and I'm sure you could find work to keep you going. I can help you financially if you need help. I know it's not perfect, but it would at least mean we didn't have almost the entire length of England between us. We could see each other every day while I work out what to do. I need to come up with a plan that causes the least damage to everyone.*

I typed back: *Are you serious?*

– *Yes.*

– *Erm … move to Grasmere. There is one reason to do this (you), and a million reasons not to, such as having no job, your husband being there, and the possibility of him killing me. Also, I am due to start my MA in five weeks.*

– *He won't kill you (as long as you delete these messages).*

– *But I might kill him in a fit of bunny-boiling jealousy and rage.*

– I trust you not to.
– I don't know anyone in Grasmere.
– You know me.
– I suppose that's true. It is a major selling point.
– So? Will you?
– Yes.

From: AlicetheEighth@gmail.com
Sent: 22 August 2015, 11:04
To: rentals@lakelandproperties.com
Subject: Property to rent
Dear Lakeland Properties,
I am looking for a small property to rent in Grasmere as soon as possible. I am single and have no pets and a budget of up to £600 a month.
Yours,
Alice Dark

From: rentals@lakelandproperties.com
Sent: 22 August 2015, 11:04
To: AlicetheEighth@gmail.com
Dear Miss Dark,
At the moment, we have one property matching your requirements. It is a studio flat in the village centre, about two minutes' walk from the lake. It is available immediately. Let us know if you would like to view it.
Lakeland Properties

– B, There's a flat in Grasmere. I phoned the agent at Lakeland Properties to say I want it, but I have to view it first, or have someone else view it on my behalf. Will you? A xx

– Yes, of course. I'll go asap and get back to you.

Dear Miss Dark,
Thank you for your letter confirming that you intend to end your tenancy at Flat 3, 26 Burlington Street. The remaining rent payable for the early end is £2,800.
Regards,
Halls Lettings

– A. It's lovely and I've held it for you with a deposit of £200 (don't worry about paying me back). It can be yours in two weeks. Bx

Dear Miss Dark,
Please find enclosed the details of the tenancy at The Studio, Grasmere, Cumbria. The outstanding deposit of £700 together with the first month's rent of £600 is payable when you take over the tenancy on Wednesday, 9th September.
Yours,
Lakeland Properties

That was it. All my money. Spent on going to be near Bo.
I told her I'd done it.
She didn't reply.

16

From: AlicetheEighth@gmail.com
Sent: 29 August 2015, 13:04
To: Bo@BoLuxton.co.uk
Subject: Hello

Oh, darling Bo. How do you want me to prove my love for you? Is it through fleeing my home, my town, my job and everything I have always held dear in order that I might be near you? Is it through squandering the only money I have on a wasted six-month tenancy and risking poverty just so I can be closer to you as you struggle to squeeze the dreadful secret of me into your otherwise tidy life? Is it through knowing that you and I will never truly be together and yet doing these things anyway? Tell me, my love, is this enough?

Sorry. I was just seeing if I could mimic the voice of a Victorian poet for a while. How did I do? I've often thought I would be better as a Victorian. Feminine hysteria was expected in those days, and I am feeling slightly hysterical at the moment, as I am behaving in a manner underpinned by no sense whatsover. What we are doing – well, what I am doing – is folly. Absolute folly. I fear I have been manipulated by Hollywood. Only in Hollywood does someone behave like this and it all turn out OK. I am assuming you plan to rescue me when I can't get a job or pay my rent, cos seriously, I have nothing now. Except you, which makes everything worthwhile.

Dammit, I think I have lost my senses with love.

Ax

From: AlicetheEighth@gmail.com
Sent: 30 August 2015, 13:04
To: Bo@BoLuxton.co.uk
Subject: Hello?
You've been silent for a whole twenty-four hours. I tell myself that this is normal and means nothing except that you are busy, but when I have just parted with my every penny and have started packing up my life in order to be near you, I could really do with you tellling me (a few times) that I am not making a crazy mistake.
Love you,
Axx

From: AlicetheEighth@gmail.com
Sent: 31 August 2015, 09:17
To: Bo@BoLuxton.co.uk
Subject: Hello?
Still silent. Are you OK? Please speak to me.

From: AlicetheEighth@gmail.com
Sent: 1 September 2015, 02:28
To: Bo@BoLuxton.co.uk
Subject: Hello?
Bo, what is going on? Please get in touch.

From: AlicetheEighth@gmail.com
Sent: 2 September, 2015 04:43
To: Bo@BoLuxton.co.uk
Subject: Hello?
Day five. No word. I really need to hear from you.

I won't contact you now. I'll leave it to you to get in touch.

From: AlicetheEighth@gmail.com
Sent: 2 September 2015, 04:43
To: Bo@BoLuxton.co.uk
Subject: Hello?
I have tried to leave this, but you really need to let me know if I am still moving to Grasmere. I'm meant to be going in four days. You are being very unfair. Or you're dead. Which is it?

From: AlicetheEighth@gmail.com
Sent: 3 September 2015, 15:35
To: Bo@BoLuxton.co.uk
Subject: Hello?
WHERE THE FUCK ARE YOU?

17

The 8th of September. The day before I was meant to be moving three hundred miles to Grasmere, and I still hadn't heard a word from Bo. This silence had gone on for more than a week. My mind was wrecked with the confusion of it. Why? I told myself that if I hadn't heard after five days, then I would cancel the move and stay here. But I'd paid all that money and bought a train ticket, and besides, Bo – beautiful, lovely Bo – would never do this. Never. She would never ask me to live near her and then suddenly discard me. There had to be a reason for it.

I wondered if the reason was Gus. I didn't know him well, but I'd seen enough of him to understand: he read her letters, her emails; he was always bad-tempered and angry; he spoke to her without ever showing love or respect. And I knew she was scared of him. She'd pretty well told me that.

I tried hard not to worry, but dramatic images kept placing themselves in my mind: Bo, bruised and battered and afraid, unable to contact me…

I pushed the thought away as I packed the last of my things. I didn't have much, just clothes and books. The flat was furnished, and the only things I owned were a television and a wooden stand for it. I'd already packed the books into four boxes and arranged for them to be couriered to Grasmere the following week. It didn't take long to get everything else into the battered old backpack, which had once gone overland across Africa with me, back in the days when I was able to delude myself that sleeping in a shack on the beach and getting sick on rancid meat meant I'd had a profound cultural experience.

I propped the backpack against a kitchen cupboard and sent a message to Jake. *Are you awake?* It was 11:30. Probably not.

The reply came quickly. *Yes.*

– *Do you want my telly?*

– *Don't you want it*

– *I'm moving tomorrow. Going on train. No space.*

– *Sure*

– *Can I come over?*

– *Yep*

– *Now?*

– *Yep*

– *See you in 10 mins.*

– *K*

I hauled the television to the bus stop. I couldn't walk from Kemptown to Brunswick Street East with it, not without attracting attention from someone who would offer to carry it for me and then ask me for a drink and expect sex afterwards. I'd done that before – accepted help from a bloke and then shagged him out of politeness. It was no way to conduct a romantic life.

I loved Kemptown, would have liked to stay a bit longer. All the crazy shops and quirky bars: Doggy Fashion, where people took their dogs to be groomed and dressed in diamante collars; the bookshop with the art press out the back, where they printed unknown works by artists on the fringe; the Honey Pot, a girls-only bar that sold three hundred different types of gin because the owners thought that was what girls liked…

But still, I'd met Bo and I was moving to the Lake District. It was astonishing, the turns that life took.

The bus pulled up beside me. I clambered on, refusing help from everyone who offered, then paid and sat down. It rocked down St George's Road slowly, a vessel made especially for the conveyance of the elderly and frail. I pulled my iPhone out of my pocket. I'd signed up for it when I left my bedsit and started working full time. £25.99 a month. God, I needed to find work in Grasmere. Was there work in Grasmere? Bo had said yes, but Bo had said lots of things…

I checked my emails. Nothing from Bo. I looked at my sent items. I'd last emailed her yesterday afternoon:

From: AlicetheEighth@gmail.com
Sent: 7 September 2015, 16:22
To: Bo@BoLuxton.co.uk
Subject: Wednesday
Bo, I have no idea what is going on in your head. I've tried to cancel the termination of my contract in Brighton, but the agents have someone else lined up to move in soon after I leave, so I would have to find somewhere else. (I am sick about the money this has cost me.) I arrive at Oxenholme on Wednesday at 2 pm. I thought this would be a good time as I will need a lift from the station to Grasmere and had assumed you'd be happy to meet me before the school pick-up and drive me to the flat. I am really hoping that the reasons for your silence will become clear when I see you.

I put the phone back in my pocket. All I really knew was that Bo wouldn't do this to me on purpose. She was forty years old and, instinctively, she took care with people. She didn't carry them, like some dirty angel with prey in its claws, soaring to a great height, and then drop them. That wasn't who she was.

So where was she? My mind turned again to Gus.

I thought, *If she is dead, and only the smallest part of her remains, I could still identify her. I would recognise a finger, a knuckle, a nail. I could run my hand over one small patch of skin, and I'd know if it were hers. They could send me her hair. I'd find her in the smell of it.*

Gus, I knew, couldn't do any of that. I wished he would get Alzheimer's, forget who he was married to and leave. I'd said that to Bo once: 'Tell your overbearing pillock to fuck off, so we can be together.' I fretted about that now. It was spoken in jest, of course, but maybe Bo had been offended. He was her husband, after all. And although Bo said she'd never loved him – never truly loved anyone apart from me – and married him because they got on well, and she knew they could make a good life together, and in exchange for a house all she had to do was fuck him once a week or so … despite all that, maybe I ought to have restrained the urge to insult him. It clearly wasn't going to make Bo leave him any faster.

But perhaps something had happened with Gus that meant she couldn't answer her emails. Perhaps he had deleted her account.

I had a notepad in my bag and a biro. As the bus faltered along through the traffic, I scribbled a quick note.

B, I don't know if you're getting my emails. I will be arriving at Oxenholme on Wednesday, 9th September at 2 pm. Please meet me on the platform. Can't wait to see you. Ax.

There was a newsagent's near Jake's. I could buy a stamp and an envelope there and catch the last post. Bo would get my letter the next day. It wasn't too late to fix this.

The bus came to a stop at the bottom of Jake's road. I swung my way to the front, stepped onto the pavement and felt knocked about the face with wistfulness, as though I were walking back into my past life; it was a simpler one, less fulfilling in every way, but reckless and easy.

I suddenly felt my youth was gone.

I banged on Jake's door. He let me in and took the television from me.

'Thanks for this,' he said. 'Are you sure?'

'Yeah. I never watch it. No room for it where I'm going.'

We sat down on opposite sofas. The usual mess of empty mugs, cigarette papers, rolling tobacco, overflowing ashtrays and take-away foils lay on the coffee table between us.

Jake didn't meet my gaze as he said, 'Where are you going, anyway?'

'Grasmere.'

'What's that?'

'A village in the Lake District.'

'Is it where that woman lives?'

I nodded.

Jake said, 'I thought this would happen.'

'Really?'

He nodded. 'Yeah. You're gay as you like, Alice. You love women. Especially literary women. That Shakespeare professor…'

I ignored him and changed the subject. 'I wanted to apologise for—'

'Not telling me you'd left?'

'Yeah.'

'Don't worry. I think I'm meant to be single. I mean, it wasn't very nice of me to just go off like that.'

I brushed it away. 'Never mind.'

He rolled a cigarette and offered me the packet. I took it.

He said, 'So are you really a lesbian now?'

I laughed. 'I don't know. I suppose so.'

'Isn't she married?'

'Yeah. With kids.'

He let out a low whistle. 'That's heavy.'

'Yeah.'

'So are you moving in with her?'

'And her husband? No. I've got a studio flat in the village. It's just so we can be near each other while she works out what to do.'

He took a long drag on his roll-up. 'Wow. Alice the homewrecking lesbian. I never expected that.'

'Fuck off.'

'It's true, though.'

'It's not that simple.'

'It's love, yeah?'

'Yeah.'

'She must be taking it seriously, if it's come to this.'

'She is. Well, I thought so. I mean, she's the one who suggested it, but she's suddenly gone silent on me. I haven't heard from her for a week.'

'Blimey.'

'It's driving me a bit mad.'

He glanced down for a moment. 'And you're definitely sure it hasn't been a misunderstanding?'

'What do you mean?'

'Just … Are you definitely sure she feels the same way?'

I felt myself begin to flounder. Was I sure? Yes, I was sure – deep in my gut, I was absolutely sure. But my head was a mess.

I said, 'I know she does.'

'Then there'll be a reason for it. Don't worry.'

'Do you think so?'

'Don't you?'

I shrugged. 'I don't know why she'd be quiet for this long, right when I most need her not to be. It's a huge step I'm taking – moving to some far-flung part of the country where there's no work and no one I know, to be with someone who is married … I really need her to tell me it isn't lunacy on my part.'

Jake appeared to think about it. Then he said, 'No one would do all that, or get you to do all that, unless they were serious about it. Really, don't worry.'

'Thanks,' I said. I didn't mention my fears about Gus. It would have felt like a betrayal.

'But anyway, if it doesn't work out, you can just come back.'

'I've got no money, Jake. Everything I owned has gone on this.'

He shrugged. 'You can stay here. Really, if it turns out she's got cold feet or something, you can come back here for a while. There's only a floor to sleep on, but you wouldn't need to pay anything.'

I smiled. 'Thank you,' I said. 'It's been driving me a bit mad over the last few days. I keep wondering if I imagined it.'

'Well you've always seemed very sane to me. Sensible and stuff. Do you want some coffee?'

'Please,' I said.

Cold feet. While he made the coffee, I played these words over in my head. I tried not to dwell too long on them, but it did feel now as though Bo was in retreat, backing off, unable to face me. And I was here, hours away from moving to Grasmere, with no money and nowhere to live if I didn't do it.

I would go. I had to. Bo would be there, and we could talk and mend things, and if Bo had cold feet, then I could take on my most irresistibly gentle, understanding way and win her back.

I would love the fear away from her.

18

Once again, I boarded the Oxenholme train at Euston. Once again, I shoved my backpack on the shelf above me and settled down in my seat with my iPad. But this time I also had a package I'd received in the post the previous afternoon.

It was from Bo's publicist. The previous week, I'd emailed her and asked for the details of all Bo's work – stories, novels, poetry – since the start of her career, so I could look them up and make sure I'd read everything she'd ever written. I wanted to trace the emergence of Bo Luxton from unknown but talented scribbler into a world-class, world-famous novelist. Flushed with pride and amazement, I'd thought, *This author loves me.*

Back when she still seemed to be talking to me, I'd asked Bo if she'd give me copies of all her work, but she didn't have it. She said she'd been through so many computers, so many documents, and her earliest stuff – the stories that had been published in obscure magazines – weren't even written in Word. They were gone, lost to history. She didn't even have copies of the magazines. She'd been twenty-three when she was first published and had moved house so many times since then … But her publicist would have an index, she said, and told me to contact her. 'She'll be able to point you in the right direction. If you say you're a critic, or an English postgrad with an interest in my work, she'll probably send you some free stuff – books, story collections and probably things I've forgotten about, too. Try it and see.'

She'd been right. In the post the previous afternoon, waiting for me when I came home from Jake's, was the parcel:

Dear Ms Dark.
Thank you for your interest in Bo Luxton. Please find enclosed photocopies of some of her early work and a copy of her first novel.

Triumph. Three stories, each about twenty pages long. I couldn't wait to tell Bo. I'd been too irate and anxious to read them properly, before, but now I had a three-hour journey with no interruptions and I was going to savour every word, and then I would do something with them. I wasn't sure what yet. Stick them on the walls of my new home, perhaps, or turn them into postcards and send them to everyone I knew to let them know my change of address. *Alice Dark has moved to The Studio, High St, Grasmere. She is now a lesbian, hoping to form a civil partnership with the author who wrote the story on the front of this card. Please come and stay.*

The train began its slow movement out of the station and I sat back in my seat and started to read. 'When I was fifteen,' the first one began, 'I spent three months being sick as a dog…'

I stared at the words in front of me. This wasn't right, I thought. This wasn't Bo's early work. This was something Bo had written recently, only for me.

The story went on. It was the same, exactly the same. I turned the pages over in my hands, looking for the publication information at the front: 'Published in Newcastle-upon-Tyne, June 1993.'

So Bo had lied. She hadn't written her life story only for me, and she did have copies of her early work, and there had been no need at all for me to contact her publicist. I shook my head in confusion.

My iPad beeped with the ping of an incoming email alert. Bo, I thought. Please let it be Bo.

It was.

My heart began to leap, but then almost immediately, I caught the first few words of her message:

'Alice, I'm sorry. I can't…'

I knew what this was. I knew without even opening the email properly, but I did it anyway.

'Alice, I'm sorry. I can't do this. It's better for both of us to take some time away and start again at a different place. I have thought of nothing but this for weeks. I know how you're going to feel when you read this, but in time you'll see that I'm right. Stay safe. Bx.'

I felt something bright collapse inside me. A falling star.

I wrote back. 'Has Gus found out?'

She replied, 'Please leave this.'

Then I wrote another one. 'You cannot seriously do this now. I am on the train to Oxenholme. I've let my flat in Brighton go. I can't just turn round and go back. I have nowhere to stay. I think I at least deserve an explanation. Meet me at the station.'

'Alice, please don't. This isn't safe for either of us.'

'What do you mean? Has he hurt you?'

'Alice, this is over. I'm sorry, darling. I'm so sorry.'

'Can you at least meet me and talk about it face to face?'

'I don't think I can. I have so much to do today. The girls have swimming after school and I need to keep things normal for them. Please will you delete all my emails, if you haven't already?'

'Please don't do this, Bo,' I typed.

But there was no reply. She was gone.

19

Eight pm. Daylight lasted longer up here. I poured myself a glass of wine, stood at the studio window and lit a cigarette. Still barely dusk. The studio was in the centre of the village, the village enclosed by the darkening mountains, and the evening burning with stars. The beauty and the deep peace of it surprised me, and went on surprising me. It was hard to get used to, after so many years in Brighton.

I pulled hard on my cigarette. I'd given up smoking, but this was a celebratory one. It marked the fact that I was here, I liked the flat and after all the doubt and despair on the journey up here, everything was alright. Everything would be fine.

But God, the chaos. The wild rocking of my mind. Bo's silence, then the messages and all my angry confusion. I had the urge to walk straight to Bo's house and confront her. It was fervent and intense, this longing to punch her lights out. I'd never felt driven to violence before. Not ever. It was frightening.

My mind cannot be trusted, I thought. It swings wildly around, as if dangling on a rope, instead of being held firm in a hard case of bone. Bo wasn't like this. Bo was steady. Her mind would never wander or fail. And her heart was huge and reliable. It didn't ache and buckle the way mine always seemed to these days. I wanted my old heart back, the rocky one I'd spent a lifetime building up, a heart that was able to tick away time until the day when it would just beat the life out of itself.

I stubbed my cigarette out on the wall beneath the window ledge and looked again at Bo's note. It had been on the doormat when I let myself in.

So sorry, darling. So, so sorry. I can explain it all (though you can probably guess – it begins with G). Settle in and then we'll find a way of meeting up to discuss this. I'm always at the café round the corner on Saturday lunchtimes with the girls. It's called The Grasmere Cake Shop, although it sells lots of things other than cakes. We'll meet there soon.

The relief was huge. I felt as if I'd been pulled from a crumbling building that was about to collapse and take me with it. I was grateful now to my rescuer. To Bo. Grateful for not having been abandoned. I needed to watch that, I thought, that desire to fall into bed with her and let everything be fine again. And anyway, why Saturday? Why not tomorrow? Why not now? This minute?

Because she's married, I reminded herself. *Because she's married and has two children and can't just drop everything to have sex with you. You knew this. You knew it from the start.*

But no one had ever left me feeling as humiliated as I'd felt on the train that morning, and then later at the station, where I'd waited and waited until I could hope no more. Bo wasn't coming.

I had got into a taxi then, and gave the address of the lettings agent to the driver, then I huddled in the back seat and wept. The driver politely ignored me. He drove down lakeside roads and through market towns and hamlets until finally we came to the place I recognised: Grasmere village and Rydal Fell, halfway up which lurked Bo's house.

I wanted to get out of the taxi right there, find Bo and take her away from the horrible, aggressive man she was married to. The only things stopping me were Lola and Maggie. They were children. They didn't deserve this.

The driver pulled up in front of the agent's office. I paid him then went inside, signed the papers and handed over more cash. I'd stopped counting how much all this had cost me now. A lot, I knew that much. More than I could afford.

A bored-looking woman handed me the key to the flat and told me which way to go. I slung my backpack over my shoulders again and followed her directions, stopping on the way for a bottle of cheap wine and ten cigarettes. A temporary lapse. Just for tonight, while I worked out what to do.

The flat was above a bakery. Even now, late in the afternoon, the smell of cakes and fresh bread drifted onto the pavement and up the flight of stone stairs that led me to the front door.

Inside the flat was cold and dark. I turned the light on, dropped my backpack on the floor and looked around. A small studio room with uneven stone walls and beams, and a kitchen off it with just a sink, a mini fridge and a couple of units. It would have been charming and beautiful if only Bo had shown up; if only Bo was here.

I was crying again. I was angry with myself now for not staying in Brighton when Bo's emails had stopped. I should have known she was in trouble, should have done things differently, more carefully.

That was when I caught sight of the note on the doormat. It was just a piece of scrap paper, lying inconspicuously among flyers for National Trust properties and places to visit.

'So sorry, darling…'

Happiness overwhelmed me. Instead of using wine to blank out my life, now I was going to use it to celebrate. I was going to smoke at my open window, gaze out over exquisite Grasmere, drink and imagine my life here with Bo. My beautiful woman, my love, my drop of gold.

The time until Saturday passed slowly. I busied myself getting to know Grasmere. I walked round the village, down to the lake, popped into the tourist information office for a bus timetable so I could get out to the far-flung fells around Buttermere and Ennerdale. I visited Dove Cottage, just so I could see the place where Bo had set her novel, so I could wander the rooms around which Bo had moved and sense her there. I reached out and ran my fingers over the display cupboard housing Wordsworth's ice skates and imagined that Bo had touched this wood, left her fingerprints in the space that I now caressed.

Then I wondered if this was how people behaved when they were bereaved, if this was what it was like to lose someone: to be constantly looking for them in familiar spaces, wishing the force of your love was enough to bring them back, and going slowly mad when you realised it wasn't, would never be. I recoiled from the thought of it.

On Friday, I woke with no idea how to get through till tomorrow. The clock on the kitchen wall ticked on, marking time. And time was slow.

This is awful, I thought. A love so consuming it had the power to flatten me. But it would be better now I was here, now we could be together at some point of every day instead of snatching moments in the nooks and crannies of the year.

Nine am. At the moment, Bo would be dropping the girls off at school, then beginning that long trek home up the fellside. If I hurried, I could probably catch her on the way, say hello, kiss her, walk with her for a while, listen to her news.

But Bo had said Saturday. She must be working, making up for all those months that had gone by when she'd felt blocked and couldn't do it. I would just have to wait. But God, I didn't want to. I wanted Bo to drop everything and run to me, the way I would have run to her, if she would just let me…

I spent the day in bed, reading her books.

I woke up early on Saturday. What I needed, more than anything, was a job that could distract me. For now, I'd do any old thing, then, once the money was ticking over again, I'd find something better. I picked up my iPad, typed 'Lake District jobs' into Google and scrolled through the pages. Lots of the jobs were seasonal, and the season was ending, but there were hotspots that stayed open all year round. I fired off emails to the National Trust, a bookshop, and a few organisations offering walking tours. I was sure I could take people for walks.

I showered and dressed, then spent the morning wandering the village again. I visited the church and Wordsworth's grave and the tiny old schoolhouse that was now a shop selling world-famous gingerbread (though I had never heard of it).

In my head, I played out all the possible ways I could greet Bo when I saw her. Should I just walk over and kiss her delicately, on the cheek? Should I be cool and distant, make it clear I was still pissed off about her long silence, the vicious dumping, and the two-day wait to see her? Or should I just do what I most wanted to do: abandon all decorum and snog her, right there, in quaint, heteronormative Grasmere?

I decided to just see what happened. I'd give it a moment, and respond to whichever way Bo greeted me.

At one-fifteen, I went for one last walk around the churchyard before heading down to the café. I didn't want to look as though I'd been killing time all morning, wandering aimlessly, unable to concentrate on anything but Bo…

When I got there, the café was noisy and crowded. I scanned the tables and couldn't see her. I went outside to the terrace.

There she was, right there, sipping tea from a bone-china mug, her glossy lips smiling, smiling.

And there was Gus. And Lola and Maggie.

Bo saw me and gasped.

'Alice!' she cried. 'What are you doing here?'

I was speechless. I looked at Bo and then at Gus and the girls. 'I…'

Bo turned away from me and murmured something to her husband.

She turned back to me. 'I have told you to leave me alone,' she said.

I shook my head. 'I…'

She looked exasperated, like someone at the end of her tether. 'I have tried to be kind to you, Alice. I have tried to be patient and sympathetic. But there is nothing going on here. I do not return these feelings you have, and I have never given you any reason to suggest that I did. Now, you need to pack your bags and go back to your house in Brighton; back to your friends and your job. You are young, Alice. You have the world at your feet. Go and get on with living, and leave me to get on with living, too.'

People at the tables around us were watching.

Shock rendered me speechless.

'Please leave,' Bo said again.

I glanced at Gus, to see what he made of this, but he was busying himself with the children, telling them not to worry.

I left. The shock of it overwhelmed any pain I might have felt. It drowned the anger. Fury. Rage. The desire to go back to that café and split Bo's pretty little face and her tidy little life in two.

I found a pub with free Wi-Fi, ordered a pint of ale, sat at the window with my iPad and bashed out an email. 'What the fuck is going on? You've just made look like a complete lunatic in front of your entire family. You asked me to move here, and now you're saying you want nothing to do with me. Is this because of Gus, or is it because you're a bitch? I have tried very hard not to think you're a bitch, but at moments like this, I don't see that there's any other option.'

I pressed send. Almost immediately, the message bounced back. I went onto Facebook and typed Bo's name into the search bar. Bo had removed herself from my friends list, but she hadn't blocked me. I retyped the message and sent it from there. Then I wrote another one. 'I suggest you give me some money. It has cost me around £3,000 to come up here from Brighton. £3,000 that you know I haven't got. Please pay it into my account by the end of today, or I will make sure your husband knows what a lying, cheating cow he's married to. The bank is HSBC. My account number is 51478934 and the sort code is 40-87-43. Three grand, or Gus will find out. I mean it.'

I drank the rest of my ale quickly and went back to my studio. My hands were shaking. Cold hung in my chest. I ransacked the flat, looking for Bo's note, but couldn't find it. I checked my pockets. Not there. Where was it? Where had I put it? I wasn't stupid, or crazy. I knew that note had existed. I hadn't dreamed it up, any more than I had dreamed up Bo asking me to move here, any more than I'd dreamed up three glorious nights with her when Gus was away.

I sat down on my bed. There was so much to sort out. I couldn't stay here, not now. But I was poor. I had nothing, not even a train fare. Jake's words came back to me: 'There's only a floor to sleep on, but you wouldn't need to pay anything.'

But Jake was Jake. So lovely, so useless, and so distant from me now. I felt I'd aged years since that night I left him.

I wasn't going to cry. No, I wasn't. I wasn't going to think about Bo, and this horrifying love that had gone deep enough to unhinge me. I wouldn't think about the beautiful woman who'd lain beside me in bed and run her fingers over my skin and said, 'There can be no one else on earth like you, no other mind more perfectly sculpted to mine.' Nor would I remember my response. 'We are twin souls. Identical.' Or Bo saying, 'No. Not identical. Opposite. Like life and death, light and dark – one cannot be known without the other.'

I would remember none of it at all, I thought, as I felt something inside me crack open and break. It wasn't my heart, I knew that. It was everything I was. It was all of me, derelict.

Her Majesty's Prison for Women
Yorkshire

As long as I'm outside, I can make it through the days. The troubles start when evening falls and I have to come in and they send us to our cells. Summer is easier than winter. Then, I can just slip beneath the sheets, take a sleeping pill and lie in the black until the bell rings for breakfast. Winter is different, though, when the hours from dusk till night stretch out ahead of me and I have nothing to fill them with but my own thoughts. I try to be strict about directing them. My mind is my escape. I am solitary. I stay far away from the others, and they don't come near me. I write notes, write diaries, write poetry. Anything to keep me creative and away from that old black cat, despair.

It's easy to get Prozac here. They prescribe it with no questions, without telling us to seek therapy or counselling, or a deeper cure than chemical sunshine. It is generally accepted that the prison population has every reason to miserable.

No one seems to have any clear idea of what this place is for – whether it's a holding pen or a place of rehab, a place where we can learn how not to be criminal, so we can live good lives on the outside again. But I'd lived a good life on the outside. And that's the fact I reflect on the most – how quickly a well-lived, ordinary life can be reduced to this, just by letting the wrong person into it.

That was the trouble. We were a potent mix, she and I. The passion was deep, and shot straight to our cores, where other people couldn't reach. It was divine love, but when it turned, it dragged us both through hell.

There was a time when I wanted revenge. I hated her for what she'd done to me. Now, all I want is peace. Forgiveness. Another chance. Her.

I would do it differently, if I could do it again.

I've already written her a letter. They won't let me send it from here, but I can send it when I get out. They'll probably make it a condition of my early release that I don't contact her, but she'll want to hear from me, that much I'm certain of. I googled her recently, when they let me have internet access. She's just had a book out, and although she's made herself difficult to contact directly – she has no Facebook page, no Twitter account, no public email – I'll be able to get hold of her through her publisher.

I want her to know that I'm sorry.

Part Three

DENYING
BO

1

The moment of change was easy to pinpoint. It was the day I came home from Northumberland. Before then, I'd been the happy owner of everything I'd ever wanted – a beautiful home, two lovely children, a successful career and a man I could live with well enough. If someone had asked me to sum up my life in one word, I'd have said this: peaceful.

A peaceful life. Unexciting, but vital. You can't measure the value of a peaceful life until it's gone.

Alice came at me unexpectedly. After saying goodbye to her, everything felt dreary and flat, like an endless Sunday afternoon with no one to break the boredom. At home the next day, I was meant to be reading a new biography about Dorothy Worsdsworth, ready for a joint radio interview with the author, to see if it shed any more light on the eternal question of whether she'd slept with her brother. But getting down to work was like walking through an intellectual marshland. I couldn't be bothered with it.

I abandoned work and went to the kitchen. Gus was there, in his usual spot. 'What are your plans today?' he asked.

I shrugged and tipped biscuits into the cat's bowl. 'The usual,' I said. 'A bit of work.'

I stepped towards the sink to fill the kettle and tripped over the cat as she came stumbling out from her bed by the stove. She was ancient, this cat. I'd had her since I was nineteen. It hadn't occurred to me when I'd picked up a tiny, playful kitten that one day I'd be stuck looking after a geriatric with feline dementia, who'd lost one eye and used the fruit bowl as a toilet.

I went on. 'I might walk up to Grisedale Tarn later. Do you want to come?'

He shook his head. Of course not. Recently, he'd become less interested in my company. I didn't know why. All I could think was that a quiet resentment was eroding him. My work brought in most of our money, and so it was me who made the decisions about our life together. What was more, I'd brought him here, to the middle of rural Cumbria, where he knew no one and where his only chance of meeting people would be if he joined some local society that didn't interest him a jot. He'd had friends in Oxford – people he'd worked with most of his life, people who understood him. Now, he was drifting away into invisible old age.

There was still tension lingering between us, left over from the conversation we'd had the evening before, when I'd suggested he look for work to keep him occupied.

'Yeah, like what?' he'd sneered. 'A farmhand, or a Sherpa carrying people's backpacks up and down mountains so they don't have to do it themselves? Those are the only jobs in Cumbria.'

'I didn't mean that,' I said. 'I meant freelance work. Get in touch with your old organisation and say you're available for projects if they need you.'

'Maybe,' he said, and fell silent.

But I heard his unspoken words, his anger with my success, my fame and what he saw as my ability to let bestselling novels fly from my fingertips while all his achievements lay buried in the past. He wasn't going to fight, I could see that. It was a conversation we needed to stop having.

It hadn't bothered me, until now. Until Alice.

I went to my study and fired up the computer, with the aim of finding some reviews of this new biography. Perhaps they'd give me enough information that I wouldn't have to read it. Instead, though, I clicked on to Facebook, scrolled through the endless political posts in my newsfeed from friends campaigning for climate justice, or for an end to the bedroom tax or, curiously from one, for an end to what he saw as the hard-left ban on fox-hunting. I hovered over it, left a comment: 'Poor countryside-dwelling Tories. Always having their fun ended by the emotional left. They are like helpless foxes, pursued by commie hounds for their blood and taxes.'

I didn't know why I'd done that, only that the words had slipped from my fingers more easily than the ones I was being paid to write.

Alice never posted politics. Today, her status read:

'*The Girl on the Train* ought be renamed *The Girl on the Rail Replacement Bus.*'

I clicked 'like', then went to my emails. There was one there from her, telling me she'd split up from her boyfriend. She joked about it, but the tone was flat. I invited her to stay. It would be good, I thought, to have her here. She'd breathe life into me again.

As soon as I told them a friend was coming to stay, the girls were beside themselves with excitement. On Monday afternoon, they came in from the garden laden with hollyhocks and rhododendrons, then spent half an hour arranging them in jars of water, which they carried to the spare room and set down on the bedside table and the chest of drawers.

Lola said, 'I'm going to make her some rose perfume,' and so I gave her four miniature honey pots I'd picked up in London hotels, then Lola took Maggie's arm and dragged her back outside.

I could see them from the kitchen window as they busied themselves with plucking rose petals and filling the jars with water from the garden tap. I was looking forward to seeing Alice, although I had the odd moment of anxiety about it. Gus thought I was reckless.

'Are you sure this is wise?' he asked.

'I know what you're thinking…' I said.

'I'm just worried. The last thing you need is to take a starstruck young author under your wing – especially one you've already said is vulnerable and needy – and for things to go wrong.'

I sighed. 'I know. But Alice isn't like Christian. She's sweet. She's…'

'I remember a time when you thought Christian was sweet. You thought he was lonely. Young, sweet, lonely and talented.'

'I—'

'How do you know this girl is OK? You've spent five days with her.'

'I just know.'

'She's young.'

'So what?'

'She wants to be an author. She'll expect you to help her make it in the world.'

I said, 'Well, I might be able to help her. She's very talented. If I can, then I will.'

Gus shook his head. 'Another one of your causes,' he said. 'Another orphan. I sometimes think you look for trouble.'

He spoke with weariness and suspicion. Gus wasn't a man who found selflessness easy to believe in. The motives, for him, were always dubious. It was against human nature, he said, to care this much about strangers when there was nothing in it for you. I brushed him aside. It was against *his* human nature, perhaps, but not everyone's. Not mine.

2

At last, Alice arrived, and there was life in the house again – interesting, adult life; not simply the clatter and chaos of children. I could feel myself coming out of the slump, my mind lit again by someone else who was excited about the things I loved. I took her off, walking the fells. We hiked from Grasmere to Ullswater one morning after heavy rain, listening to the cold rush of the waterfalls and the gentle crash of the lake on the shore.

Alice stood still beside me, held in Cumbria's rocky edges, and said, 'It's beautiful here. I've never seen anything like it.'

I said, 'There's a link between walking in natural beauty and an increase in mental well-being. Have you ever been aware of it?'

Alice shook her head. 'I've never really walked futher than the kebab shop before.'

'You should walk. It will make you feel better.'

'I don't feel bad.'

I said nothing to that. This girl, I knew, felt bad. Badness shimmered like moonshine beneath her skin. *I was like you once*, I wanted to say. *I can make you well, if you would let me.*

She wouldn't let me. Not yet.

We spent our evenings at the kitchen table, drinking wine, while Gus watched television dramas in the living room and then took himself to bed. I didn't care. He wasn't interested in my writing life, other than the money it brought in. But Alice was interested, and she was animated and clever, and I realised while she was here how deprived I'd been of clever company since we'd left Oxford. There were my friends on Facebook, of course, talking politics, hoping to enlighten the unenlightened and change the world, but it wasn't the same as having someone here beside me – real flesh and blood that spoke words I could hear, and had hands I could take in my own as she talked on and on and then said, casually, 'It's the anniversary of my mother's death tomorrow.'

The mother. That old, recurring theme.

I said, 'Will you be OK?'

'Yes. It's fine. A year. I hadn't seen her for six years. It's hard to miss someone you haven't seen for that long, and I hadn't even lived with her since I was eleven.'

'I'm sure you do miss her, though.'

Alice shrugged and shook her head. 'I think it's … complicated. It will do me good not to examine it too much.'

I smiled. 'Probably wise. But you're so young to have lost a mother. And grief is such a funny, unpredictable thing. It can attack without warning, especially when it's someone you've grown used to living without. Suddenly, for whatever reason, their absence makes itself felt, and it can knock the breath from you for a while.'

'Maybe.'

'All I mean is that we can do whatever you like tomorrow. We don't need to make any plans. Don't feel you have to come downstairs if all you want is to lie in bed all day. Be gentle with yourself; and if you do feel bad about it – and I'm not saying you will – just know that it's normal and will pass.'

I spoke tenderly. Alice looked away from me. Oh, the vicious knife of tenderness. I knew it could cut the most hardened heart in two.

Alice turned back to me. 'You said your mother was a nightmare…' she ventured.

'Oh, my mother is alright now. I spent many years being angry with her, but after I got married and settled down and was able to look after myself better, I found I could let go of the mother I wanted to have and build a relationship with her on different terms. I have an eye for people like me, though. I can pick the unmothered ones out in a crowd.'

'What was wrong with her?'

'She wasn't maternal,' I said. 'She didn't know how to look after people.'

An old image flooded my mind: my family's gypsy caravan, bright red on the outside, dark within; my parents always absent, and the men who knew it, who came in one by one. My mother knew what happened. She knew and turned away, and I understood now, aged forty, that it was OK. It was OK not to forgive the unforgiveable, but live with it quietly, healing myself, loving myself as my mother never could.

We sat in silence for a while, and then she spoke. 'My mother was violent,' she said. 'That was why they took me away from her. I didn't realise it wasn't normal for mothers to beat their children like that. I thought it happened to everyone. It took a long time for people to see what was happening. We had money, and that makes a difference. People don't suspect you when you're successful and own a big house; and she was clever enough to know not to send me to school when the bruises were bad. But eventually, one night, a neighbour heard me screaming and called the police. She'd broken my arm. Not long after that, they took me away.'

Gently, I said, 'And did you see her again?'

She nodded. 'Yes, but not often. She was always involved in emotional dramas with men. Always falling in love or having her heart broken. It was exhausting. I don't think she had much energy left to repair things with me, although she did try when I was older. I was lucky. I had good foster parents and they kept me with them. They let me stay on after I turned sixteen – till I went to university.'

'You did well.'

She shrugged. 'It was my escape. I knew it was my only way out.'

'And how did you feel when she died?'

'I didn't feel anything. She wanted me to forgive her, but there wasn't really anything to forgive by then.'

'That's very generous of you.'

'No. I mean there was no relationship left. It was gone. The time for forgiveness had passed. She was just someone who used to hurt me. I didn't want her back. What would be the point in forming some emotional bond just as she died?'

'You were afraid of the grief?'

'Yes,' she said. 'Yes, I think so.' Then she looked at me and added, 'You're very understanding.'

I smiled and said, 'I'm just very old.'

She laughed.

I went on, 'Mothers are important, Alice. Everyone needs one. It's important to acknowledge that, to acknowledge the gravity of what you never had. You know you can be your own mother. You can be for yourself everything you wanted the first time.'

For a moment, she seemed lost for words. Then she said, 'How?'

'Start by learning to cook,' I said. I was beckoning her forwards, watching her take slow but certain steps further into my world. 'Just simple things at first. Learn to make yourself vegetable soup. Take time to care for your body, and the rest of you will start to heal as well.'

Alice nodded.

We went on talking – about her boyfriend, the bleakness of her life in foster care, her hopes for the future. Children.

At midnight, the wine ran out. At the top of the stairs, we said goodnight. For a long time, I held her tight in my embrace, and told myself that this unexpected, constant desire to be close to her was maternal. As instinctive as holding a newborn baby to your chest.

3

And then she was gone. After a week, Maggie and I dropped her off at Oxenholme and the house was empty again. I was left with a feeling in my chest I hadn't experienced since I was a child, as though someone had reached beneath my skin and taken a scoop out of my insides. It shocked me.

I thought I'd moved beyond all this. Self-preservation was my art. It always had been. Back in that caravan, when the men came and went, when Willow arrived and then was gone, I'd felt my body turning to wood. I'd thought my mother would find me there one day, old and stiff as a dying tree. Maybe she'd make something of me – a table, perhaps, or a blanket box.

If they cut me open now, they'd find the rings of my life: the hidden pain of the early years; the healing growth; and deep in the middle, a core. Ancient trees had dead wood at their core. Heartwood. The heart died, and the tree went on growing.

I was as magnificent and hard as old oak. And no one knew it but me.

Alice was not Willow. But she'd reminded me of Willow because she was twenty-five and beautiful and lovely and clever, and all the things I knew Willow would be by now, too.

I took myself into the study, fired up my computer and went straight to Facebook. It was stupid, futile, but in the search bar I typed 'Willow Luxton'. Six profiles appeared on the screen in front of me. I clicked on each one, searching for a face the age of Alice's, with features that carried genetic hints of my own. There was one:

blonde, young, green eyes. It could be her, I thought. It could be. I looked at it a while longer.

My hands were shaking when I finally pulled myself away. You're being ridiculous, I told myself. No one knew I'd ever even named her Willow. The girl probably had some other name now, something like Lucy or Kate or Nicola. And she wouldn't be Luxton. Every part of me would have been erased from her long ago. I didn't exist.

Anyway, Alice's sheets needed changing. I often let things like that slide – the boring, non-urgent stuff – but my work was slumping again and I couldn't face it. It was a bad sign, when I'd rather change sheets than write, and I wondered if this new project was ever going to get off the ground.

Upstairs, the spare room stood empty and bare, nothing left of Alice save the wrinkle of an untidy bedspread. I took the duvet cover off and started a wash pile in the middle of the room. I could smell her in the bed linen – the warm, broken and beautiful heart of her, ingrained in the fibres. And I couldn't help myself: I stood and stared at the empty space on the mattress, knowing her imprint would be fixed in the memory foam below; and then I climbed into the bed, curled up and wept.

4

From: AlicetheEighth@gmail.com

Sent: 11 July 2015, 11:07

To: Bo@BoLuxton.co.uk

Subject: Hello

Dear Lovely Bo

This week, I made the decision to take your advice and sort my life out. It takes a lot of commitment to sort out a life as disordered as this one, which is why you haven't heard from me for a few days. But I can now report:

1. I am employed full-time.
2. I have found a one-bedroom flat in Kemptown to rent. I move next month.
3. I am fit to reproduce.

Ha ha. That last one is unexpected, I know, but while I was walking along the beach the other day, I came across a van that said 'Free Chlamydia Test' on the side, painted in friendly, non-threatening pink writing. I thought, *Well, why not? This is the week for getting my life together, after all.*

So I went inside and had a free chlamydia test, and, lo and behold, it turned out positive. Cue: visions of a lifetime spent alone, with seven cats and a house that smells of piss. After a number of calculations, I worked out that I'd probably had it five years.

The woman who did the test was breezy about my crisis. 'Make an appointment to see your GP,' she said. But when I phoned the surgery, I was told my GP couldn't see me before the end of this century.

So that night, I stayed up till about 4 am, googling like a fuckwit, and came away knowing everything there is to know about the clap, most importantly:

– It does not always cause infertility.

– It only causes infertility if it becomes pelvic inflammatory disease, which is more likely the longer you've had it. But many people have it for hundreds of years and still have babies.

That was OK, then. On Monday, that was OK.

On Tuesday, I found an alternative doctor and went to see her, weeping silently.

She gave me some degree of hope that I would not have PID. So that was also OK.

On Wednesday, I decided, after a lot of research and adding up and such, that my chances of having PID were about 40%.

On Thursday morning, after some more sums, this had risen to 60%. By Thursday afternoon, it had gone up again to 80%.

On Friday morning, I rang the Centre for International Adoption and asked them to send me three baby girls from China. They said they would send me a form. On Friday afternoon, the test results came back from the doctor, who said I didn't have the clap after all, but advised me to visit my local GUM clinic, a place for irresponsible people to go to learn about safe sex and the horrors that might befall you if you don't have safe sex – such as a family. Cruel and vicious irony.

So on Saturday, I went to the GUM clinic, where I sat for half an hour, the oldest person there by approximately eleven years. Then I was called to see a counsellor, who gave me about three hundred condoms and some sheets of rubber whose function I have not yet worked out, and also made me get tested for all other STDs, including HIV, something I have always avoided doing on the grounds that I would rather not know.

So on Saturday afternoon, the blood was drawn and I was fairly confident I would not have HIV, having never slept with men from the tropics, or homosexuals.

On Saturday evening, I had a few doubts.

In the early hours of Sunday morning, I began to grow a little fearful, so got out of bed and returned to Google.

By 6 am, I had worked out that my chances of having HIV were about 0.2%.

By 7 am, this had risen to about 98%.

At 8 am, I made a will. (You were in it. You got nearly everything.)

The rest of Sunday was a bit of a write-off.

On Monday morning, the form arrived from the International Adoption Agency re: the three baby girls I'd ordered from China. I thought I should fill it in, because if I had HIV, I would not be able to conceive a child myself, for reasons of ethics. One of the questions was, 'Have you ever been tested for HIV?' There was a choice of two boxes to tick – yes or no. Even in my state of slightly controlled hysteria, I could see that there was a definite right answer here. So I threw the paper aside, murmuring something about bureaucracy and a load of small-minded bastards because really, who hasn't had a bit of a wild time in their youth? And all my dreams of motherhood were shattered.

I then waited for lunchtime to roll round, because after lunch, I was allowed to phone the GUM clinic for my results. Which I did. I then punched in my unique identification number, which made me feel special and warm inside, and listened to a recorded message saying this:

'Your test results are as follows:

Chlamydia: negative. (That disembodied voice had a slight change in tone as it declared 'negative', like the one at train stations that says, 'The next train will be calling at ….')

Gonorrhea: negative.

Herpes: negative.

Syphilis: negative.

HIV: negative.

Thus I continued my day in a happy state, with all my dreams of motherhood restored.

And that is the end of the story of my week. But what I have been left wondering is whether this is how they break it to people that they are, in fact, HIV positive? Because if so, I don't think it's very caring.

I hope your week was as productive and happy as mine.

A xxxx

I was still laughing as I typed my reply: 'Alice, you are a comedy genius. Please come and stay again soon. I think about you a lot. I miss you. xxxxxxxxxxxxxxxxxxxxxxxxxxxxxx.'

From: AlicetheEighth@gmail.com
Sent: 11 July 2015 12:04
To: Bo@BoLuxton.co.uk
Subject: Re: Hello
I think about you a lot, too. And I miss you, too.
A xxxxxxxxxxxxxxxxxx

From: Bo@BoLuxton.co.uk
Sent: 11 July 2015, 12:14
To: AlicetheEighth@gmail.com
Subject: Re: Hello
Dear Sweet Alice,
I suppose now that you're employed full-time, you won't be able to come and stay again for a while. How much time off do you get? I was thinking that next time you come, we ought to climb a fell. Do you like climbing? I don't mean real climbing, obviously, with ropes and equipment. I just mean a steep path up to a peak, from where you'll see magnificent views of lakes and valleys. Really, there is nothing like it. I want you to experience it because I know you'll love it.

Also, I used to love walking alone, but now it is just not the same without you. These days, I walk out alone and feel the space of you beside me and wish you could be here to fill it.
Love you,
Bxxx

From: AlicetheEighth@gmail.com
Sent: 11 July 2015, 12:43
To: Bo@BoLuxton.co.uk
Subject: Re: Hello
Dear Lovely Bo,
I have no idea whether I like climbing fells. I've never done it before. It sounds fucking energetic to me, and you know I am at heart just a slobbish,

workshy youth who rarely walks beyond the front door if I can help it. But I am happy to give it a go. I'm sure if you are next to me, talking away about your books, then I will be happy whatever we're doing. I would probably be happy lying beside you on a rubbish dump.

Love you,

A xxxxx

From: Bo@BoLuxton.co.uk
Sent: 11 July 2015, 12:52
To: AlicetheEighth@gmail.com
Subject: Re: Hello

A rubbish dump? Really?

From: AlicetheEigHth@gmail.com
Sent: 11 July 2015, 12:56
To: Bo@BoLuxton.co.uk
Subject: Re: Hello

A rubbish dump. Really.

That's how much you mean to me, Mrs Luxton.

From: Bo@BoLuxton.co.uk
Sent: 11 July 2015, 13:06
To: AlicetheEighth@gmail.com
Subject: Re: Hello

Darling Alice, you make me smile and laugh more than anyone I've ever met.

I adore you. I wish you were here.

From: AlicetheEighth@gmail.com
Sent: 11 July 2015, 13:08
To: Bo@BoLuxton.co.uk
Subject: Re: Hello
I wish I was there, too.

Also: I adore you as well. Really. I love you to Empire State Building proportions. I do not know exactly what sort of love that is, but I do know it's a lot.

From: Bo@BoLuxton.co.uk
Sent: 11 July 2015, 13:12
To: AlicetheEighth@gmail.com
Subject: Re: Hello
I agree. American Architecural Love is huge and hard to define, but it definitely exists, whatever it is.

Love you, adore you,
B xx

5

Sunday. Gus and the girls were still asleep. I kicked off the morning with a pint of coffee. All night, I'd lain awake, my mind flitting between work and Alice. There was nothing, really, for me to worry about as far as work was concerned. My seventh novel, *The Poet's Sister,* had come out in April, and the older ones were selling steadily enough. But that last book hadn't been published to a fanfare like my others had, and I had a niggling sense of myself now as a fading light in the book world. No one said as much, and my agent was as encouraging as always, but I knew. Younger, more exciting writers were emerging, and unless I could shed my skin and adapt, I'd be just another dead voice from the past.

Ideas floated into my mind and drifted away again. I couldn't concentrate on one thought long enough for it to take shape. Alice was in my head perpetually – a beautiful boulder that nothing could pass.

I needed to get her out.

But I didn't want to. I liked having her there.

Alice was good for me, I thought. Her youth meant she could help with my work. There was a freshness and a freedom to her that had gone from me. I was bogged down in the everyday, the domestic, the drudge; Alice could show me the world through young eyes again, and I thought, if I could somehow combine the vitality of youth and the wisdom of experience into my work, then I might be on to something.

Alice also reminded me of what it was like to be young. Her emails could take me soaring to a peak of giddy, reckless laughter that made me feel, just briefly, twenty-five again. It was gold. It was addictive. I wanted more of it.

This, I felt sure, was the reason she was taking up all the space in my head. Nostalgia for youth, a yearning for the freedom to eat takeaway chips every night and not worry that they'd have killed me by morning. The freedom to stay up late and then lie in bed for half the day without other lives crashing around you.

That was all. The longing for youth was powerful. Like pining. Pining for the person you used to be. But that didn't change the fact that I'd spent most of yesterday sitting at my computer, unable to stop emailing her, unable to stop talking about love...

I swallowed a large gulp of coffee, then sat at the kitchen table to apply my make-up, which I kept in a bag on top of the fridge. I didn't wear much, just mascara and lipstick most days, enough to keep me from becoming washed-out and invisible to the world. I remembered something Alice had said last week, about people's personalities being reflected in their faces. I peered at my own face in the mirror and wondered what the world could see there.

Christian once had said I had an 'aura'. He said I carried the air of a beautiful, creative woman being crushed by an oppressive man. I'd liked that idea, and besides, it was hardly untrue.

I put the mirror and the make-up away and set to work. Today, I was not going to be seduced by the computer and all the chat it contained. I would not let my desire to hear from Alice drag me away from work. I was just going to write. Write and write and write. Anything at all. I would do what I told beginners to do: 'Don't worry about what you're trying to create. Just learn to love the act of writing. See what happens.'

So I set to work, the ideas barely formed, but the paragraphs emerging anyway. I scarcely looked up. Time opened its mouth and took the morning, the way it used to do.

I locked the door so I wouldn't be disturbed.

I described a woman, lying on her side in bed – the white curve of her breasts, the arc of her stomach, the strip of hair between her legs alluring beneath the translucence of the thin, white slip that covered her.

The image of her – beautiful, remote, untouchable – made me catch my breath. I knew that this was Alice. I went on writing – another woman appeared in the scene, her lips touching Alice's, her hands against her skin…

I had to stop there. This was something I'd never known before, but I wanted Alice here. I wanted her near me, beside me, beneath me. I wanted her unclothed. Beautiful Alice. Beautiful, beautiful Alice.

The house was empty and the study locked. I lay down on the floor and let thoughts of Alice flood me. This was passion, I thought. Ecstasy. I pictured Alice, lying in bed, naked as she was in the image I had created, and it made my breath come faster, until I slipped my hand beneath my clothes, caressing my own skin lightly, then harder, until my fingers slipped slowly under and into me, and I imagined I had Alice beside me, touching me, moving with me, kissing me, and I sighed and whimpered and wished it could be real.

So now I couldn't ignore it. Alice was in my head because I fancied her. Loved her. Was in love with her. Wanted to make love to her.

But it was ridiculous. I was married. Alice was fifteen years younger than I was. It made no sense. I laughed at that. I'd read enough of love to know it couldn't be held to reason. But this? Really?

In the evening, after I'd put the girls to bed and made myself a quick pasta supper – Gus and I hardly ate together these days – I checked my emails. There were two from Alice, one sent that morning and another an hour or so ago. The first was light-hearted and chatty. She said she'd been writing and had plans to move out of her flat and find somewhere better. The second was brief. 'I haven't heard from you today. Are you alright? Drop me a line, as it seems I cannot make it through the day without hearing from you. xxx'

How should I reply? 'I haven't been in touch because I've been lying on my studio floor, running my hands over my own wet flesh, imagining you naked and sweating beside me, and the image of it was so glorious I now want you to come here and make it real.'

Instead I wrote: 'Hi Alice. Sorry not to be in touch today. I woke up this morning and decided I needed to give myself a rest from the computer. In fact, I was awake most of the night and I thought, "I must ask Alice to stop emailing me for a while, as I need my head to myself for a few days." Would that be OK? I just need to get on with some work. I've been so distracted recently and I hardly know why…'

I hit send. The reply came back almost immediately: 'My darling Bo. You don't need to apologise. I understand completely. Loving you in silence, in absence, and always.'

I thought, *I am not the only one.*

Another email. 'Sorry. Didn't mean to sign off like some kind of bloody Barrett Browning there. Yes, get back to work. Speak in a few days. A.'

Oh, God, I thought. I was in love with Alice and as far as I could see, Alice was in love with me.

It was like being given permission to fly.

But it was impossible. Eternally impossible. Eternal, impossible love. But there was romance in that, I thought, and my heart ached and ached.

This was it. This was it. Not waving, but loving.

6

I muscled on with my work. There would be nothing in my inbox from Alice so there was no point checking. My story was taking shape. At the heart of it now was a couple, separated after environmental disaster made refugees of them; long years in Europe passed by, the husband presumed dead, the wife slowly liberated…

I wrote on and sighed. Everything hurt with hopeless promise. Impossible love. Alice herself was impossible. She was so uncontainable, so open and so fragile, I knew she would never last. Not in this form. She would mature, learn cunning, shroud herself in smoke and mirrors. She couldn't stay this artless for long.

I'd never met anyone like her. Alice's range of emotions was astonishing. Even in her emails, she could drag me with her through the hot, loveless hell of her early years. Then the next day, she could make me cry with laughter.

'You are gorgeous,' I would say. 'Just absolutely gorgeous.' And I meant it.

I had no idea how her mother could have let this young woman go; not realise the treasure she'd possessed, right there in front of her nose. It made me angry. But there was no point being angry. Her mother was dead and all I could do now was pick up what she'd left behind.

I came away from the computer and took myself to the kitchen for a drink.

Gus looked up from his usual place in the rocking chair. 'How's your young friend today?' he asked, lightly scornful, as he always was these days, of my friends – the ones I had that were separate from him, that were tied up in my work.

'Fine,' I said.

'How many emails has she sent this morning? Fifty?'

Clearly, he'd been at my computer. Jealous snooping, as always.

'Three,' I said.

'Remember this was how it started with Christian.'

'Christian was a one-off,' I said. 'He was troubled. He was dangerous. And now he's dead.'

It was the first time I'd said it out loud since it happened, and it surprised me how matter-of-fact I sounded. But the letters from his mother were still coming, still hurting.

Gus returned to his paper in silence.

I looked at him with contempt. I'd have liked to reach out my hand and strike him across the face, just to see if he'd respond; just to see if he had it in him to get out of that bloody chair and move.

I didn't mean to, but I imagined Alice there in his place. But then, Alice would never spend her days in a rocking chair, not even when she was old (and Gus wasn't even old yet; he was barely into his sixties). When she was old, Alice would still wear full make-up and sensational clothes, still go out on the lash, still be sexy and outrageous. She would fill her life with things more exciting than reading news about Cumbrian sheep.

It was nearly noon. Five hours before I could click on my emails and hear from Alice. Five hours. It was the agreement we'd come to. One message a day, in the evening. Otherwise, neither of us would get anything done. It was meant to be a sensible move, meant to bring us both back down to earth. This thing between us – whatever it was – had never been spoken of directly, but we both agreed that we were each other's terrible distraction and it was too easy to let hours slip by, just talking on messenger.

It was like being starved of her, I thought now. Hours and hours each day had to roll on without her, but she was still here, still in my head, and my body still ached to have her here, in my home, in my bed.

I'd given up trying to fight it. It had taken me over.

Sod it, I thought, and went back to the study and turned on the laptop. Just in case Alice had written this morning. Just in case.

Nothing.

I went back to the kicthen, where Gus was making his lunch. I wished he'd just bugger off sometimes instead of being here, cluttering up my space.

'What are you doing with the afternoon?' I asked.

He dug his knife in the butter. 'I need to book some train tickets. Dave phoned from Manchester. He's got some work he wants overseeing. He's asked me to help. I said I would. He'll pay me.'

'You're going there?'

Gus nodded, 'It's easier to do it in person. It's three days' work.'

'When?'

'Next Tuesday.'

Immediately, I went back to the study.

From: Bo@BoLuxton.co.uk

Sent: 11 July 2015, 12:17

To: AlicetheEighth@gmail.com

Subject: Next week

Gus is going away next Tuesday for three nights.

Come and stay.

Please. Love you, adore you.

Bxxx

7

After all those years, I felt her as a gift, a dropped jewel.

She lay beside me on the rug and gazed at me in bewilderment and murmured, 'There cannot be anyone on earth like you, no other mind more perfectly sculpted to mine.'

'We are twin souls,' I said. 'Identical.'

'No. Not identical. Opposite. Like life and death, light and dark – one cannot be known without the other.'

We lay together in silence for hours.

I held her against me; the warmth of her breath on my neck; the warmth of her body; her face staring down at me, holding my gaze until her eyes were a mirror and I saw my own in them.

'My beloved,' she whispered. 'My beloved.'

The dark moved slowly over us. We hid inside it, bright stars, our light collapsing.

I rested my head on her shoulder and she read me to sleep. Later, I woke in silence and drew her into my gaze. No words passed between us. We had learnt not to speak of love, just let it be.

8

Through the night, I woke repeatedly and wondered what I was doing. Here I was, in bed with Alice, in love with Alice, everything happening so quickly I hardly knew how I'd got here.

But then I looked at the woman lying beside me and felt happy. Deeply, deliriously happy, in a way I'd not known before. Somewhere, in some distant part of my mind, was a warning, reminding me that I was married, I had two girls who needed their father, and none of this was ordinary after all I'd ever fought for. All my life, all I'd wanted was to be ordinary and I was putting everything at risk.

But it didn't matter. For now, tonight, it didn't matter. This was irresistible.

In the morning, the sun woke us early. Alice opened her eyes and smiled at me: a rich, beautiful smile, tender with love.

I looked at her, and felt appalled.

9

In the morning, she took herself to the guest bedroom to get dressed while I went downstairs to see to the girls. They sat together at the kitchen table, their hair unbrushed, spooning Cheerios into their mouths while I busied myself putting bread into the toaster and finding the jar of peanut butter that could have been in any cupboard. There was no system in this house, just the whims of the tidiers.

Maggie paused for a moment between mouthfuls, looked up and said, 'When will Daddy be home?'

'In a couple of days,' I said breezily, and all of a sudden, I felt sick.

She returned to her cereal. I began to spread their toast with butter and saw my hands were shaking. Not once, in all the time I'd been planning for Alice to come here and share my bed, had it crossed my mind how I'd feel in the morning when I faced my children. All that trust they'd put in me their whole short lives to keep them safe within our family, and I'd betrayed them.

Alice stepped into the kitchen, dressed in blue jeans and a strappy pink top. My heart lurched at the sight of her. Beautiful. She was beautiful and I wanted only to keep her here.

I could barely look at her.

Together, we dropped the girls off at school, then walked on through the woods to Loughrigg Tarn. She took my hand in hers. Happiness radiated from her, like sunlight. I felt like I could walk through it. *I've done this to you,* I thought, *I've made you this happy*. The responsibility was huge.

We walked in silence. I could see her from the corner of my eye, casting anxious glances my way.

She said, 'Are you alright?'

I couldn't speak.

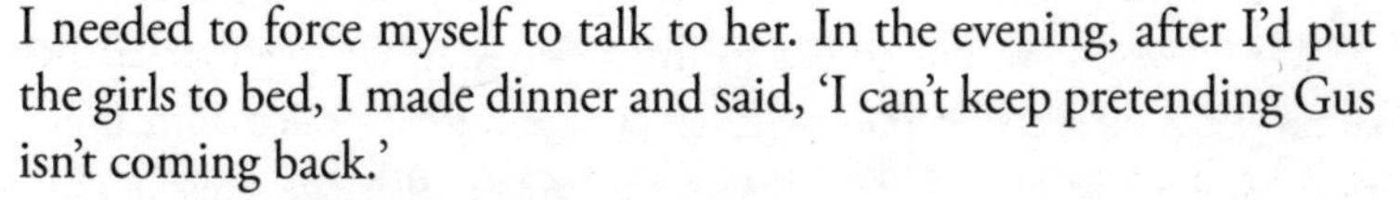

I needed to force myself to talk to her. In the evening, after I'd put the girls to bed, I made dinner and said, 'I can't keep pretending Gus isn't coming back.'

She said, 'Where do we go from here?'

I spoke the truth. 'I can't make any promises.'

'Do you regret this?'

I said nothing.

She said she would sleep in the guest room. I could see she wanted me to say no, that it wasn't necessary, she must stay with me. But I didn't. I thought we could both do with the space.

All night I missed her. I missed her and missed her and missed her.

It was dreadful, to love like this. I'd thought a love like this was beyond me.

The next day, I gave in. The night was long and perfect, and I was wrecked.

10

What I needed was to cool everything down. This was intense – emotion so strong it took my breath away. Love had weakened me. If I kept it up, unchecked, then I would die from it.

On the last day, I told her to go for a walk while I worked. If we'd spent it together, we'd have fallen into that whirlpool of emotion and drowned in it. The imminent parting, the love, desire, the tears, the anguish. We couldn't do it. We had to stay calm.

She was hurt. But someone needed to take control.

While she was gone, I dug around old files on my computer and found those earliest stories – the ones I'd written at the beginning of my career, when nothing but the past would come out. I wanted to give them to her. I wanted her to know who I was. I wanted her to know the heartwood at my core, and to understand.

It was our only hope.

Later, we said goodbye, and for days afterwards I felt wretched, as though my heart were a gaping wound. I couldn't heal it.

It was more than I could bear.

11

From: AlicetheEighth@gmail.com
Sent: 18 July 2015, 10:32
To: Bo@BoLuxton.co.uk
Subject: Hello, Beautiful

Dear Beautiful, Darling Bo,

I won't open this email by telling you how much I miss you because you already know that. Instead, I will simply say that I have moved into my new flat and it is bright and lovely and I ought to be happy, but instead, everything is crap because you are not here.

That's enough of that.

Let me tell you about my new flat. I am sitting in the sitting room, which is mostly wood. I fret now and then about the glorious trees that had to be slain for this luxury, but until someone comes up with an alternative, I must pillage the earth for my comfort, just like everyone else.

Anyway, that is the sitting room. Wooden floors, an ancient sofa and a bookcase filled with books, of which your own are on most prominent display. I look at them sometimes and remember … Well, never mind about that.

There is a small kitchen off the sitting room. It's tiny. Two units on one side and a fridge on the other. You couldn't really call it a kitchen. 'Kitchen' is not the right word, or even 'kitchenette'. There needs to be a whole new language, I've decided, for these days of tiny-property-related bullshit. In reality, this kitchen was probably once a cupboard. A more accurate term for it, instead of kitchen, would be 'cupboard space with fridge', though admittedly, that's not terribly catchy.

I might write to the Oxford English Dictionary and ask them to give me a job, inventing this new language of estate-agent crap.

After you've walked through the kitchen (it can be done in two steps, one if you have long legs), you pretty much land on the double bed. That's it. That's the next room. I am practically camping here. You, my darling Bo, live a life of unimaginable bourgeois luxury compared to me. I live in boho hell.

So, let's move on. I read your stories. They broke my heart and made everything clear. But do not worry. I will never mention any of it again, unless you want to. Thank you for telling me that stuff. xxx

I suppose I had better go. My boss has given me more work, so I have lessons on the finer points of the the first and second conditional to prepare. Actually, it's interesting, in a way. Here's a lesson for you. I will give you two sentences. Think about the difference in meaning between them:

1) If Bo Luxton marries me, I will live happily ever after.
2) If Bo Luxton married me, I would live happily ever after.

Have you got it? You probably have because you are a woman of deep genius, who can work these things out without the assistance of your protegée. However, just in case, here is the explanation:

You use the first to talk about something which is quite likely to happen.

You use the second to talk about something you don't believe will happen. It's wishful thinking.

Many people think I am incredibly boring to find the rules of grammar so exciting, but there are times like this when you can read a person's mind, simply by the language they choose. You can also work out whether they are delusional. 'If Bo Luxton marries me, I will live happily ever after.' There it is. Me. Totally delusional but I can't let the idea go…

Love you,
Alice xxx

I read the email on my phone and sighed. I didn't reply. Not straight away. Dear, sweet Alice. So desperate to be with me.

I looked around – at my kitchen, at the magnificent view of the fells from the window, and thought of Alice, alone and lonely in her tiny flat. 'Totally delusional, but I can't let the idea go…' There it was, the quiet request for commitment. I could read between the lines. I was adept at it, and what I read here was, 'Please tell me we have a future.'

Oh, God. This was where it had got to with Christian. I still remembered his beautiful young face, so trusting, wanting me to follow him into that wide trench of intimacy. And I tried. God, I tried, but I couldn't. I stood on the edge and peered in and all I could see was love and squalor: suffocation; disaster; death.

I put my head in my hands and wept.

12

I told myself, *The only cure for desire is distance*, and didn't contact her for a week. I hoped she might sense it, understand my worries and then take some steps back. Get this love to a place of sanity and start again.

But she didn't.

The emails came thick and fast. Every morning, every afternoon, every evening. 'Please let me know how you are. If you want to end this, that's OK. I'll understand. Just talk to me about it.'

How could I? This young woman had her wellness wrapped up in me. If I walked away from her, she would break. Besides, I didn't want to walk away. What I needed – what we both needed – was just to back off, slowly and carefully.

After six days without contacting her, I sent her a text message: *Call me,* I said.

She phoned at 11 am on Saturday. She sounded flat, slightly hoarse, and I wondered if she was hungover, turning to drink after my silence.

I said, 'Gus is out. He's in Manchester again this weekend. The girls are at their music classes. I wanted to talk to you.'

I could hear the unsaid words: 'If he's away, why haven't you asked me back there?'

Out loud, Alice got straight to the point, 'Have you got cold feet?'

'No.' I spoke immediately. I didn't have cold feet. I wanted this. I did. I loved this young, clever and troubled woman, but there was too much at stake. Lola and Maggie, just six and eight years old, and so happy they didn't even have to think about happiness. It was just who they were: stable, happy girls. I couldn't destroy that.

Alice said, 'That's good,' and I could hear the relief in her voice. Then she said, 'It sounds serious, though.'

'It is. I think we need to stop the emails.'

'What?'

'Listen, you've met Gus. You know he's not an easy man, and he's always been jealous, but it's been worse over the last few years, ever since my career took off and he hasn't … Anyway, he uses my computer and it's normal for him to read my emails. Can we agree to just talk on the phone instead? Every morning. I'm free then, and he won't know.'

'But I work.'

'Evenings, then. Please, darling. I can't risk this.'

Alice paused. After a long moment, she said, 'OK.'

'And if you have any of my old emails, could you delete them? I know that sounds paranoid, but you just never know…'

Alice paused again. Then again, she said, 'OK.'

'Do you understand why I'm asking you to do this?'

'Yes. I do understand. Of course.'

'We'll be together again soon. I'll make sure of it,' I said.

Alice said nothing. I said I had to go and ended the call.

13

At nights, now, I lay awake and tried to return to my family.

It would be a lovely summer. Summers were always lovely here, even without the warm sun of the south. Almost every morning, we'd be out on the fells, or down at the lake to swim, then we'd come home for a late lunch and the girls would spend the afternoon in the garden while I sat on the terrace and read a novel or wrote ideas in my notebook. Now and then, Gus would come and join us. Last year, the evening before the girls had gone back to school, he'd brought a tray of sandwiches and cakes, and a jug of lemonade, and the four of us had stayed out there for hours, eating and drinking until the sun collapsed and night fell, and the moon rose out of the lake and silvered the mountains. I had felt deeply happy.

I thought now, *What is wrong with me?*

Next week, the girls would be finishing school. There'd be no time to write and no space in my head for anything but them. I wasn't sure where I'd be able to fit Alice in. There was no possibility of us stealing time together before Christmas.

Alice.

She made the whole world brighter and more meaningful than it had ever been before. It reminded me of those days in my awful twenties when I'd eaten magic mushrooms and been flooded with a sense of calm and wellness that later turned to ecstasy. All around me, everything would grow brighter: the sky bluer, the grass greener, the turning autumn leaves a deeper shade of russet, as though someone had turned up the colours of the earth and then bathed it all in light.

It was like that now. Just ecstasy. I tried to rationalise it, even tried to control it, but it couldn't be restrained, and went beyond the reach of language. I hadn't the words to describe it, except that it was overwhelming and exquisite and right. But sometimes the joy would turn and the sharp ache of despair take its place. There was always grief in love. It was bound in with it – the quiet threat of loss. It was why I'd never loved before, I knew that.

Apart from my babies. Of course. But those first few weeks and months after Lola was born … they were awful. Wild, hormonal emotion, like falling into an abyss, fragile and about to be broken by it. I was so naïve and the baby so helpless, and always, I was terrified I wouldn't be able to feed her, or keep her alive, or that someone would take her, and then I would die from the pain of it. Motherhood was a place for me. A terrible, vulnerable place. For weeks I wept, knowing it was all grief for the first baby. Grief and fear and shame. God, so much shame, even then. But I pushed on, took control, and it wore off after a while, and I was able to look after the baby steadily and carefully, without panic.

Never have your well-being wrapped up in someone else – that had always been my mantra. Never. And if you do, retreat or get rid of them.

I wasn't stupid. I knew Alice's age. The baby's age now. The baby I called Willow. That was what I put it down to. This lovely young woman, like me in so many ways, could have been that baby. I'd thought my feelings were maternal, but they raged on, until I grew exhausted from trying to push them back and I just collapsed and let love erode me.

Because it had eroded me. It had ground down my energy and my sense. And now I was here, debilitated, and really thinking of risking all this, all that I had: this home, this family, this normality. God, the normality – the precious ordinariness that I'd waited so long for.

When I'd been reading all those biographies for the Wordsworth project, trying to decide my answer to the age-old question of whether the great man had been shagging his sister, I'd read that family members who were separated and reunited years later often fell in love. That mix of strangeness (someone unknown, mysterious) and familiarity (so like you, in so many ways) was a potent one. It went straight to their heads and wrecked their lives.

Something like this had happened between Alice and me. We weren't family, but we were wounded; and the wound in each of us was gaping and was shaped exactly like the other. Alice was my missing piece, the beautiful girl that made me whole again.

And I knew what I was to Alice: the shape of the mother.

14

When I was young – in those years before Gus – I'd loved men. I'd loved them with obsessive, unrequited emptiness. Unrequited love had been all I was capable of. It gave me all the emotional jolts of real love, without ever having to drown myself in intimacy. Now, I realised, that drama had been reversed. Now, I drew people in and then retreated. Their hearts broke and I watched from the sidelines, guilty and ashamed, but with all the satisfaction of knowing I was deeply loved, while never having to make any of it real.

For all my success, at base I was deeply dysfunctional.

I sighed. I'd just had another letter from Lucy Winter. The typewritten envelope fooled Gus into giving it to me, and me into opening it, instead of leaving it for him to deal with, as I usually did. It contained her usual hate-filled diatribe. But her letters were becoming less frequent now. More time passed between each one, and I assumed that one day, eventually, they would just stop altogether.

'Some power greater than me will make sure you pay for my son's death', she wrote.

I wanted to write back to her, but had no idea what to say. The story was settled in my mind. Christian had been a lovely young man. I had been very fond of him – in a maternal way. I'd tried to help him, not realising he would fall in love with me. When I had to set him straight, he wouldn't accept it and became obsessed, a stalker. It went on and on. He made my life a misery, and in the end, I had to come down hard on him. And he killed himself. That was what happened. It was tragic, awful, but Christian was troubled and it wasn't my fault. I was not guilty. No judge would have ever found me guilty. I was a good woman, a kind woman, a woman that people loved. I was not guilty.

That was how I remembered it, and that was how it was.

I watched the girls in the garden. I'd set the sprinkler up for them and they were running through it, shrieking and getting wet and cold. We could only do this when Gus wasn't around. He disapproved of such a frivolous use of water. By 2050, he said, half the planet would be suffering from famine and water shortages. We had no right to fritter it away like this.

I said, 'Then don't we owe it to ourselves to just make the most of the time we have? If all we have is now, I'm going to let my children jump through as much water as they can.'

Gus ignored me. He probably didn't want to dignify my remark with a response. I was too selfish for him, not galvanised enough to take my part in the massive collective effort to preserve a healthy, living Earth. It was true. I wasn't. The thought of it exhausted me. Besides, what was the aim of all this? Was it to protect the planet, or to protect humans from dying out? Humans had had their day. We were peaking, right now, anyone could see that. Why not just wipe ourselves out; give plankton a chance?

'There will be no plankton before long,' Gus murmured darkly, citing figures about plastic in the oceans – more plastic than fish by mid-century. The Great Barrier Reef was falling apart as we spoke. In the last hour, six thousand acres of rainforest had been felled and another section of the Arctic had plunged into the sea. Everything was dying. The girls were going to inherit an environmental catastrophe.

Gus suffered from a permanent depression that had been brought about when he decided to read about the state of the planet. I wished he'd never done it. It filled our house with gloom.

Lola abandoned the sprinkler first. 'I'm cold,' she announced, standing in front of me and shivering.

I reached for a towel from the pile on the table beside me, wrapped her in it then hauled her onto my lap to warm her up. We sat together like that, quietly, for ages, and again I thought, *What is wrong with me?*

If Gus were to go on my computer now, catch sight of my emails (which Alice went on sending, despite what I'd said), then life here would be over. He would leave me, and the girls would become just two more children from a broken home, so common these days people could easily fool themselves into thinking it was OK, that the children would be fine. But I'd read the articles, the data, the research that covered half a century. The evidence was there, irrefutable: If you want happy children, stay together. Always. Even if it's killing you. Better that you die from a lack of emotional fulfilment than you inflict a separation on them. And they will surely punish you for pursuing your own happiness. They will grow into depressed adults and you'll watch them fail and fail and fail, and it will all be because you left their father, thinking the children would be fine, that they'd be glad to see you away from the bastard and happy at last. The truth was the children didn't give a shit about your happiness. They gave a shit about their family being together.

I couldn't do it.

I couldn't.

But the thought of not doing it made me sob.

Instead of myself, I tried to focus on Alice. To be with me, she would have to give up everything. All that longing for children of her own, that need she had to put her own damaged childhood right, to heal with the next generation. I couldn't let her abandon that, just for me. It mattered. It mattered to her. It mattered to me that she could do it.

Someone here needed to take control. And I was the elder of the two of us. It needed to be me.

15

I washed my hands and washed my hands. I felt sick. My guilt was everywhere. Gus, the children, Alice, I'd betrayed them all, every one, and now I had to stop. I needed to take control of this and head away from it, down the path that would destroy the fewest lives.

There was only one choice, only one sacrifice. Alice had to go.

I dried my hands and sobbed.

Alice. Dear, sweet, beautiful Alice, whom I adored with every cell in my body. Alice, who had been so deeply hurt, who loved me like I had never been loved before … and now I was going to take that girl's heart in my hand and crush it.

Alice wasn't going to recover from this easily, I knew that much. It would set her back years. It would be too much pain for her to bear.

I buried my face in my hands. What was I doing? Dear God, what had I done?

I can't face her, I thought. *I cannot do it.*

The emails kept coming. Needy, angry, desperate. God, there was something abhorrent in distress like this. It was vile, like shit or guts. I had some primal need not to see it.

One night, I lay awake, thinking of the best words I could use to break my decision to her. But no matter what I said, the result would be the same: Alice, knocked to the floor, shocked, devastated. I shook my head, and for a moment allowed myself to think how she must be feeling right now. My heart snagged on it.

I got out of bed at 4 am and went down to my study, where I googled 'mid-life crisis.' I needed to find a reason for this love I had for Alice. That was the first step, the first stage of rationalising it all away.

Yes. A mid-life crisis was probably all this was. I'd seen it happen to friends. Marriages that had seemed happy and stable for years and years suddenly fell apart as someone started craving excitement, passion, a new direction. Secretly, smugly perhaps, I'd watched other lives crumble and felt absolute certainty that it wouldn't happen to me. Never in my life had I desired love or passion or excitement. All I wanted was to be ordinary. I wanted marriage, a home and a family so I could blend in with everyone else, but I did not need to love or be loved. It was much easier to be ordinary when you banished yourself from the roaring world of emotions.

But here, where I was now, was not ordinary. It was not normal, or sensible. It was foolish, risky, dangerous. For the first time in my life, I understood what it meant to be madly in love. That was what I was; what we both were: we'd been rendered insane with emotion.

On the screen in front of me, it appeared: 'Top ten signs of a mid-life crisis.' I clicked the link:

1. Going to Glastonbury
2. Taking up a new hobby
3. Wanting to make the world a better place
4. Buying a motorbike
5. Looking up ex-lovers on Facebook
6. Switching from Radio 2 to indie stations like 6 Music
7. Dyeing your hair
8. Quitting your job in the city and moving somewhere rural
9. Questioning your sexuality
10. Having an affair

So there it was in black and white. I was having a mid-life crisis. Of those ten things, I had done eight in the last two years, and the final three on the list were deemed by its author (a psychotherapist) to be the most dangerous. They could tear homes apart, and lead to lifetimes of regret.

I needed to stop it. I couldn't abandon the father of my girls and bring up my children with another woman. That sort of thing was fine in forward-thinking, youthful Brighton, but here in Grasmere, it was not. The girls would stand out, they'd be talked about. They would not be like everyone else. They would not be normal.

But Alice. Beautiful, hurting Alice. She wouldn't sit back and accept it. She'd come here, demand conversations, arguments, make scenes that I couldn't have because I had children, a husband, a life that could not accommodate another's heartbreak…

I clicked onto my email account. Sure enough, there they were: four emails from her sent since midnight, each one asking where I was.

I felt a surge of anger rise inside me. I had asked her, more than two weeks ago, to stop emailing. I'd made it clear that I needed space, some distance from this, a chance to protect all that I was risking. She'd agreed to it for a day or so, but now she was back, emailing frequently, too frequently for me to keep up with, to keep track of, to protect myself from. They came at me like the wail of a newborn child at night.

How dare she do this? How dare she put so much pressure on me? She was twenty-five. She was old enough to know what she was letting herself in for when she fell in love with a married woman; old enough to have a life to get on with, old enough, for God's sake, to look after herself.

This wasn't all my fault. It was Alice, too. Of course it was Alice.

I opened my sent folder and deleted every message I'd ever written her.

16

I went back to bed at five and slept. Maggie jumped into our bed at seven. I was heavy with tiredness, could barely open my eyes, and instead left Gus to the drudge of the morning – the breakfast shift that continued through yet another half-showing of *Annie* or *Mary Poppins*; the arguments about getting dressed, cleaning teeth, washing faces; and finally, the long walk down the fell to school.

Even now, at nine, I wasn't ready to face the day. I wanted to crawl back under the covers and hide.

I forced myself out of bed, wrapped my dressing gown around me and went downstairs, straight to my study.

Three emails from Alice, sent between 4 and 6 am. The girl was losing her mind. She had been up in the middle of the night, just as I had been.

Oh, God.

I heard the front door open and Gus go into the kitchen.

I didn't open the emails. I left my inbox on the screen and went out to make coffee.

'Morning,' I said to Gus. 'The computer's free, if you need to use it.'

He mumbled thanks, then took himself off.

I sat at the table, picked up the morning's *Guardian* and read the front cover while I waited for him to return.

When he did, the first thing he said was, 'How many messages has Alice sent you today?'

I made a dismissive gesture with my wrist. 'Oh, God knows. I've stopped reading them. She has nothing else to do.'

He nodded and left it.

But I picked it up again. 'I've been a bit worried, to be honest.

She seemed lovely when we first met, but there's something troubled about her. Needy. She won't leave me alone.'

Gus raised his eyebrows. 'Another stalker?'

'I hope not.'

'Do you reply to them?'

I shook my head. 'I used to, but I haven't for ages. She's too demanding. She wants a lot of attention.'

'Well, she can't keep it up forever. Ignore her and she'll move on.'

'I hope you're right,' I said. And something in me shifted. I shuddered at the thought of her, this troubled and troubling young woman.

17

I passed night after night in tumult. I was exhausted and angry; furious. How could I possibly set my own head straight, when Alice insisted on dumping all the wild content of hers on my computer screen, every hour, every minute? For my own health, I had to stop reading her messages.

One morning – I don't know which; time by then was indistinct – I got out of bed before six and went downstairs. I pulled back the curtains in the kitchen and looked out. Mornings were a little darker now, but as I watched, dawn smashed the night and burned over the rocky edges of the fells. I stood there for a long time, seeing the darkness fade and the mountains emerge, and wondering how on earth I got into this mess.

Alice wasn't going to just disappear, that much was certain. She wasn't the disappearing sort. And even if I went to her and explained, and even if, in some miracle of reason over emotion, Alice accepted it and stayed away from me, she would still be here, because this was where she was: here, in my head, messing up the tight, neat order of it. And she was in my heart, too, filling it up when I had worked so hard to keep it empty, keep it functioning.

What I really wanted now was to be able to brush her off, as if she were nothing more than the drone of a fly. I wanted to prove that the moment was over, the madness of love was finished and I could walk away, magnificent, unbreakable, heartwood at my core.

But it was impossible, and I knew that. Alice would cry. She would cry and cry and make a scene. She'd declare a love that was forever, eternal, undying. She didn't care about children, she'd say. She would give everything up for me, for me and my girls. I was her real love, her soulmate, all she wanted.

But love would never erode me. I was locked in and alone, and God have mercy on the person who tried to get near, because I knew I had a weapon that surfaced at moments like this. It was a beast that lurked at the very heart of me, usually quietly sleeping, but other times ready to pounce and shred someone's wellness to pieces.

18

Alice was working herself into a frenzy, and I couldn't stop it. Every day, the emails and texts rolled in. They felt like an assault. I had no energy to read them.

I thought about blocking her email address and her Facebook account so the messages would be sent back to her, but I wasn't convinced it would work. Alice wouldn't stop at that. She'd find some other way to contact me. She'd probably end up here at the house, banging on the door or the windows like something out of *Wuthering Heights.*

Madness. She was a troubled young woman who'd lost her mind.

My inbox was full. I didn't know where to start.

Eleven am. The 8th September. I sat at my computer, watching the messages drop in. It had become frightening now.

I clicked on one and opened it. She was talking about moving to Grasmere. She was coming to live near me so we could be together, and she spoke as though we'd arranged all this between us. We hadn't. I didn't know what she was talking about.

'Bo.'

It was Gus.

He walked in and handed me a letter. 'This just came,' he said.

The postmark was from Brighton, the writing large and feminine. Alice, of course.

I put it to one side. 'Look at this,' I said to him. 'Just look.'

A whole page of emails, all from Alice Dark, all with aggressive subject lines. One was, 'Where the fuck are you?' Another: 'Speak to me'; followed by the most recent: 'I am on my way'.

'Good grief,' Gus said. 'What is going on?'

I shook my head. 'I've no idea,' I said. 'I don't know what's happening. She emailed too often, and I started ignoring her, but she went on, so I blocked her address. I thought the messages would be sent back to her, but they're just here in my junk folder instead. I hardly ever check it.'

Gus looked at me doubtfully. I knew he was remembering Christian. 'Really?'

'Yes.'

'Good God, Bo. What is this?'

I said nothing. If I were to have any hope of protecting all this – my life with Gus, my children, myself – then I had to lie. I'd had a mid-life crisis, a trauma, an affair, and now I regretted it. I could be forgiven. But he must never know.

'Open them,' Gus said.

I clicked the one called 'I'm on my way'. She'd sent it at five o'clock that morning. 'I will be at Oxenholme at 2 pm. Please meet me at the station platform. I would really like to just talk to you. If you're having doubts, that's fine. I understand. I understand completely. We can just be friends if you prefer. I want you to know that I will never, ever ask you to make sacrifices for me, but please don't leave me in the lurch like this. Let's just talk. A.'

Gus frowned and looked at me seriously. 'What have you been doing?'

'Nothing.'

'This woman clearly thinks there's something going on between you. Where has she got that from?'

'I don't know. I really don't know.'

'She speaks as though you two are having an affair.'

I laughed incredulously. 'Yes, of course. Bo Luxton, married mother of two, gets together with woman young enough to be her child.'

He went on looking at me. 'We've been here before, Bo. Don't you remember?'

'Stop it, Gus.'

He sighed. 'I've learnt better than to try and talk to you.'

I scrolled down all the emails. They went back four days. I opened the oldest one, aware of Gus reading over my shoulder: 'I haven't heard from you for too long' it said. 'I don't know how many days it has been, but this silence is torture and feels like a lifetime. Please get in touch, darling Bo. I miss you.'

Then: 'For fuck's sake. You are being so unfair. I have made a massive commitment to you and all you can do is fucking ignore me.'

And another: 'Are you alright? I love you and I'm worried about you. Has he found out about us, and hurt you?'

Gus and I sat together in silence. Eventually, he said, 'Either she's insane, or you're not being honest.'

I sighed. 'She is troubled, Gus. I always knew that. I thought I could help her, but I was wrong. She's become … something else. Not what I thought she was.'

'But she's coming here today? Is that what she's saying?'

'She seems to be.'

I opened the letter.

B, I don't know if you're getting my emails. I will be arriving at Oxenholme on Wednesday, 9th September at 2 pm. Please meet me on the platform. Can't wait to see you. Ax.

Gus stood up and said, 'I don't want to be a part of this. Do whatever you want. Go and spell it out to her. Meet her at the station like she says. If something has gone on between you, or she's got the wrong end of the stick, tell her it's over. If she's stalking you like you say she is, then tell her she needs to go away and leave you alone, or you'll call the police.'

'I cannot believe you're doubting me, Gus.'

'This is your second stalker in five years. I could sympathise with the first, but I can't help losing faith with the second. Also, let's be honest here. I like you less than I did five years ago.'

I said nothing to that. I didn't like him, either.

19

I was afraid. There was such rage in her emails now, I couldn't face her. This woman, hurling abuse and foul language at me, telling me I was evil and behaving as though we were on the brink of living together … She was unrecognisable from the beautiful, funny Alice I'd met and loved. The thought of meeting her as Gus had told me to do filled me with dread. I'd seen anger like this before, as a child. It was violent.

I took the car and drove aimlessly for a while. But then I thought, perhaps I should meet her. Perhaps I should go and talk to her, say I no longer wanted this and that she'd made a mistake – I had never, ever asked her to move to Grasmere to be with me. Perhaps if she heard it from my lips, that would put an end to it.

I made it to Oxenholme in time for her train. I parked by a verge a few minutes' walk away, then hung around among the silver birch trees on the footpath that linked the station to the village. I wouldn't be seen from here, though it gave me a good view of the platform and the taxi rank outside. I thought I'd just watch her at first. I thought I might be able to tell, somehow, how crazy she was and whether going to her was a good idea.

The train from London pulled in on time. I stood and waited. The passengers stepped onto the platform and then moved quickly on with their lives. They knew where they were heading. Then a lone woman with a shabby backpack slung over her shoulders simply stood and gazed about. She scanned the whole area around her, and looked ready to cry.

I watched her take a seat on the platform bench and wait. Five minutes passed. Ten minutes passed. Eventually, she stood up and walked to the front of the station. She looked around again, then went towards the last waiting taxi.

I could see the wild anger on her face, even from here.

I didn't go to her. I couldn't.

I picked the girls up from school, then drove home slowly up the fell to The Riddlepit. Gus was waiting in the kitchen. He would be angry, I thought, if he knew. I'd had enough of anger and hatred.

'Lola,' I said, 'will you take Maggie up to your room and get your swimming things together so you're ready for your lesson?'

They went off. Gus turned to me. 'Well?'

I sighed. 'I told her,' I said. 'I told her there seemed to have been some confusion – a mistake – in all this, and that I don't feel about her the way she thinks I do.'

'And how did she take it?'

'Not that well. She didn't seem to accept it, kept saying she knows I love her.'

'Did you tell her to leave you alone?'

'Yes.'

'Do you think she will?'

My voice wavered as I spoke, 'I hope so, Gus. I really hope so. I can't take much more of this.'

He said nothing.

20

After that, things quietened down for a while. The rest of the week passed peacefully enough. I'd been afraid Alice would turn up at the front door, demanding answers to questions I couldn't understand, but she stayed away and I began to hope that perhaps she realised now that things were over between us and she'd made a mistake – I had never asked her to move to Grasmere. Never. I never would.

I thought she must have gone back to Brighton.

With relief, I slipped back into my normal life. On Saturday, Gus and I took the girls to the Grasmere Cake Shop for lunch. We sat on the terrace by the river, and were happy, the four of us – a family surrounded by the best of the Lake District: wild swimming, hikes to remote waterfalls, stickleback catching in Little Langdale tarn.

Maggie said, 'You said seven was old enough to climb Helvellyn. Can we do that before we go back to school?'

I wiped soup from her chin with my napkin, 'I did not say Helvellyn,' I told her.

Then suddenly, excitedly, Lola said, 'Look! It's Alice!'

I looked where she was pointing. Alice stood in the doorway to the terrace, shielding her eyes with her hand, searching for us. Then she saw me, smiled and walked over.

I gasped. 'Alice! What are you doing here?'

She looked from one to the other of us. 'I…' she began, and her voice trailed off.

I turned to Gus and said quietly, 'She must have followed us here.'

I went back to Alice. 'I have told you to leave me alone,' I said.

She shook her head. 'I…'

'I have tried to be kind to you, Alice,' I said. 'I have tried to be patient and sympathetic. But there is nothing going on here. I do not return these feelings you have, and I have never given you any reason to suggest that I did. Now, you need to pack your bags and go back to your house in Brighton, back to your friends and your job. You are young. You have the world at your feet. Go and get on with living, and leave me to get on with living, too.'

People at the tables around us were watching.

'Please leave,' I said again.

I watched her go. Oh, God. It was awful. I knew I was partly to blame, of course. I had lied to Gus. I'd lied to protect our life and the girls' lives, and when I'd first done that, I hadn't realised how messy it would all become, how many more lies I would have to tell to keep that first one believable.

Inside, I felt shabby. Cheap. Horrible. But I'd made a mistake. That was all. A big mistake, a bad mistake; one I badly regretted and now I was getting lost in runaway consequences.

We came home and I went straight to bed to lie down. It was the shock of it all, I said, after telling Alice so clearly that she'd made a mistake, that I didn't return her peculiar feelings and wanted to be left alone.

I was still uncertain whether Gus believed me, but the scene in the café seemed to have been a step forwards. He said he'd check my emails, to see if there was anything more from Alice. 'There won't be,' I told him. 'I blocked her ages ago, and deleted her as my friend on Facebook.'

'She definitely can't contact you there?'

I shook my head. 'I don't think so. Check and see – I'm logged in – but I don't think she can, not if we aren't friends.'

I gazed up at the ceiling and focussed on Alice. Damaged Alice, who could barely move without me, she was so obsessed. She was needy and desperate, like a child crying for its mother. And that's exactly what she was. An abandoned baby. Unstable.

Gus came back into the bedroom, looking grave. 'There are no emails,' he told me, 'but she's sent you two messages on Facebook.'

'Oh, God. What?'

'In the first one, she says you're vile. In the second, she says you need to put three grand in her bank account or she'll tell me about your affair.'

'That's ludicrous.'

'It's definitely blackmail.'

I was silent.

Gus said, 'Listen, Bo. You can't blame me for having doubted this at first. I just … I find it very difficult to accept that someone can have two stalkers in five years. I know Christian Winter was a strange case. I know he was ill. But I've met Alice before and she struck me as very normal, very rational. The girls liked her. And from what I read of those messages, she seemed absolutely convinced that something had happened between the two of you. Where did she get that from?'

'I have no idea,' I said. 'I think she's very troubled, and very imaginative, and also desperate to be loved. And she looks up to me. She's an aspiring writer. I am everything she wants to be. It's classic stalking material.'

He nodded. 'If what you're saying is true, then I think you need to consider taking this to the police.'

'Maybe.'

'Bo, come on. What you're saying is that she's bombarded you with emails, she's cooked up some fantasy lesbian relationship between the two of you, she has *moved* to Grasmere, and then failed to take any notice of the fact that you told her she'd made some strange mistake. She followed you and your family into a café when you were having lunch, and now she's demanding three thousand pounds. I don't think you can take this lightly anymore. What will her next step be? Murder to get me out of her way?'

'I know. I know. You're right. There's something very wrong with her. I thought I could help her…'

'You always think you can help people.'

'…but she's just too troubled. I can't do anything.'

'People like this need medical help.'

I agreed with him. Then said, 'I'd like to try and get some more sleep now.'

He left.

I buried my face in the pillow. Oh, God. What had I done? I didn't want all this. I just wanted my life back. That quiet, old life, unrocked.

Her Majesty's Prison for Women
Yorkshire

Monday. I'm back now. They let me out on weekend release, to prepare me for my freedom. At last, freedom is coming. They haven't given me a date yet, but the Governor said sometime next month.

I'm not meant to go and see her, not ever again. And they'll tell her that if I step within a mile of her house, then she must ring the police and they'll bring me straight back here to finish my sentence.

But I think she'll be pleased to see me, once she knows what I have to say. She won't tell. Perhaps, in time, she'll give me another chance. Perhaps.

Part Four

WRECKAGE

1

Alice

I slept and woke, then slept again. Time passed, but I barely noticed, or cared. Sometimes it was light and sometimes it was dark, but Bo had done what she'd done and there was nothing else.

Now and then, I prayed for her to come back and for it to be the way it had been, just for that little, magnificent while. I reached into the space beside me, feeling for her. She wasn't there, and she wasn't there. I closed my eyes. I wept.

I woke to the sound of a sharp, repeated knock on the door.

Pulling on my dressing gown, not quite sure what time it was, I went to answer it.

Two police officers, one male and one female, stood on the step.

'Alice Dark?' the man asked.

'Yes,' I said, suddenly feeling criminal to be bleary-eyed in my dressing gown at … oh, what was the fucking time?

'We'd like to talk to you. Could you let us in?'

I stepped aside. The bed was still down, the covers unkempt, an empty wine bottle and a glass filled with cigarette butts stood on the floor by my pillow. Everything in the room reeked of decay, of someone who hadn't got her life together, not in any way.

The police officers stood there, looking around, taking it all in.

Then the man said, 'Have you got any idea why we want to talk to you?'

'I should imagine it's because of Bo Luxton.'

He nodded and eyed the books by the bed. Six of them, all by Bo Luxton. 'Now, you're not going to go to prison or anything, but we'd like you to come to the station later today. You're not under arrest right now, so you can refuse to come. But if you don't come, we can issue a warrant for your arrest.'

'I'll come,' I said.

'You're entitled to a solicitor.'

'I don't need a solicitor. It's fine.'

He raised his eyebrows. 'When can you be at the station?'

'I'm not sure what the time is now…'

'Eleven thirty.'

'Then I can come at twelve.'

He gave me directions and they saw themselves out.

For a moment, I stood in the middle of the room, feeling dazed. I couldn't be in any real trouble. Bo had asked me to move here, and Bo had left me that note (which I'd found, in the end, under the bed). I could explain everything to them and they'd realise it was nothing.

But I didn't have the emails anymore. Like some weak and pathetic puppet, at Bo's bidding I'd deleted them all. Then I'd even sent her a message and said, 'I have deleted all your emails, as you asked. I can't believe you've done that. They were my most treasured possessions, ever.'

I wondered whether Bo had lost her mind. Maybe she'd panicked when she realised what she was risking, and now she was insane. What could she have said to the police? 'I had an affair with a woman fifteen years younger than me and now I wish I hadn't. Please put her in prison.' But Bo was the one in the wrong. She was the married one. The elder one. The mother. She was the bitch in all of this.

I showered, put my blue French Connection dress on, and applied my best make-up. I wanted to compensate for what the police had seen: the shambles of my flat; me lying in bed nearly until the afternoon, six novels and a pile of papers by Bo Luxton beside me, along with a bottle of wine. It wasn't looking good, so far as respectability went.

At five to twelve, I walked round to the station and waited. The officers who'd been to my flat came out and met me, then led me through a series of windowless corridors and huge metal doors they had to unlock on the way. I'd seen all this on TV. I was one step away from prison.

Eventually, we arrived at a small reception area, where another officer stood behind a desk, filling out papers. He looked up at me. I started to smile, as I did automatically whenever I met people, then stopped. His gaze was stern, severe, angry.

He put down his pen. 'Alice Dark,' he said.

'Yes.'

'I can see from your records that you're in the worst trouble you've ever been in.'

I had nothing to say.

'You've never been in trouble with the police before.'

'No.'

'That fact is working for you in this instance. If you had anything – anything at all on your file – I would be arresting you today. But you don't, so you are going to talk to my colleagues, and after that, the most likely outcome is that you will be cautioned.'

I stared at him, silenced.

He gestured to the other officers. They unlocked the door to a small room and told me to go inside. It was shabby. Bare walls, no windows, nothing but an old table and three hard, black chairs.

'Sit down,' the man said.

The woman fiddled with a tape recorder.

I sat.

'Tape recorder running.'

'I'd like you to begin by telling us about your friendship with Bo Luxton, from when it began until today.'

I took a deep breath and started.

I spoke quickly: the course; the bond we'd shared; the emails; the visit to Grasmere after I split up with Jake; the love I suddenly felt; the love Bo felt; the visit while Gus was away – I didn't mention the sex, let them work it out for themselves; the sadness we'd both felt when I went home; the suggestion that I move to Grasmere; the move; the confusion; the note.

'Is that all of it?'

'I think so.'

'Right. Listen to this. This is Ms Luxton's statement about your friendship with her:

'"I first met Alice Dark in May 2015, when I taught on a week-long residential course for aspiring writers and Alice was one of my students. I was immediately drawn to her and her work, finding her to be very talented and also a lively, funny young woman. We got along well.

"Alice described aspects of her life to me. She appeared to be drifting somewhat and had a boyfriend she described as 'a waster'. I was concerned that when she went home, she would sink back to unproductive ways, and I wanted to help her make sure that didn't happen.

"We stayed in touch by email. After a few weeks, Alice said she had split up from her boyfriend. She seemed very, very upset. Really devastated. I invited her to my home in Grasmere to try and help her feel better.

"While she was staying, she confided in me a lot. In particular, she said that when she was a child, her mother used to beat her, and she was removed from the family home and sent to live with foster parents. She hardly saw her mother after that, not until just before she died, which was a year before we met.

"I was deeply moved by Alice's story. Again, I wanted to help her. I would have described us by this stage as very close. I had quite maternal feelings towards her, and an urge to look after her.

"However, once she had gone home, things changed. She started emailing me compulsively, about fifty messages a day. The number was overwhelming. I stopped reading most of them, but occasionally when I did read one or two, they shocked me. She appeared to be declaring a love for me that was sexual and romantic. She also told me about a past that involved drugs, alcohol and promiscuity, and which led to her having several sexually transmitted diseases. I didn't know why she would tell me such unsavoury aspects of her life.

"I became afraid of checking my emails and didn't know what to do. I did send her a message once to say that I wanted her to stop sending such frequent messages and to get on with making her life better – finding a nicer place to live, getting a job, going out and meeting new people. I said I was still prepared to be her friend, but that the quantity of messages was too much for me.

"It was around this time that I foolishly told her that my husband, Gus, was going away for work for a few days. Alice somehow mistook this for an invitation to visit me again. It was during the school summer holidays so I was very busy with my daughters and my own work; without my husband around to help, I would never have suggested she come to stay at such an inconvenient time. However, she did. Still wanting to help her, I tried to encourage her to get out of our house, walk around the countryside. Really I was trying to keep her away from me and my daughters. Fortunately, she left before my husband came home, and I hoped that would be the last I would see of her.

"However, once she returned to Brighton, her emails kept coming, and again I could not read them all. I opened one that said she planned to come and live near me, and another one that said she had emailed my publicist, pretending to be a literary critic with an interest in me, and had persuaded my publicist to send her some of the rare work from my early years.

"At this point, I decided I needed to end my friendship with her entirely, and blocked her email address, expecting that once my messages bounced back, I would move on.

"However, instead of email, she simply found another way to get in touch with me and a couple of weeks later, I had a letter saying she was moving to Grasmere and expected me to meet her at the train station. I spoke to my husband and we decided that I ought to go and make it clear that I wanted nothing more to do with her.

"I did this. When I saw her at the station, she was very different.

She used to be smartly dressed and well groomed. Now, she seemed drunk and her clothes were shabby. She smelled of alcohol. I told her I didn't want her living near me. She cried and shouted and called me a fucking bitch. I left, realising by now that Alice was a very troubled young woman. I was greatly disturbed and also quite frightened of her.

"At times in my emails, Alice had referred to my husband as 'an overbearing pillock' and said she wanted to kill him. Although I was offended by this and didn't like it, I had assumed she was joking. However, I now became concerned for the safety of myself and my family. We all stayed at home for three days, afraid to go out in case she was there.

"It was Wednesday when she came to Grasmere. On Saturday, my family and I went for lunch at a café in town. We had been there just ten minutes when Alice walked in and came to our table. The only thing I could think was that she must have been lurking outside our house all this time and then followed us when we finally had the courage to go out again.

"I told her, calmly and forcefully, to leave us alone. My daughters were deeply distressed. She went, and I hoped that would be the last I would ever hear from her.

"However, when we got home, my husband checked my emails and my Facebook messages for me. There were no emails from Alice, because I had blocked her, but on Facebook there were two messages demanding that I give her £3,000 or she would tell my husband that we'd had an affair. She said she wanted to ruin my life.

"That evening, I went to bed early. I was exhausted from the stress of everything that had happened, but my husband stayed up. He received five silent phone calls between 8 pm and 2 am. I can only assume these were from Alice.

"Alice's behaviour is having a deep and damaging impact on my family. We are afraid to leave our house, my daughters are frightened and we have reason to believe that she could be violent. We want her to move away from Grasmere and back to Brighton where she lived before. I am not a doctor, but it is my belief that Alice is suffering from some sort of mental illness for which she needs urgent treatment."'

The police officer put the papers down and stared hard at me. 'So you see, you and Bo have very different perceptions of your friendship. She doesn't want your attentions, Alice. She wants you to leave her alone.'

I shook my head, 'But she knew. She asked me. I…'

He looked hard at me again and said, 'Can you prove this?'

I shook my head. I couldn't prove it. The emails were gone. I said, 'I didn't keep her emails, but…' I wanted to suggest I bring him my iPad, so he could search the hard drive and retrieve them, but I could see he didn't believe a word I was saying. He wasn't going to listen to me, spend police resources on this. He wanted me out.

He said, 'I have seen your messages to Bo, and your letter. There is no excuse. You need to leave her alone. We're not going to arrest you today, but if you make any further contact with Bo, that will be it. You will be arrested and the case will go through the courts. Do you understand?'

I nodded, angry and ashamed. No one believed me. All I wanted now was to leave the police station. I would do anything – anything at all – to get out of this horrible, windowless room.

'We are going to give you a formal caution. You don't have to accept it, but if you do, you will be able to leave the station today and put this behind you. If you don't, then you will be arrested and the courts will be involved. Getting the courts involved is the last thing we want to do with someone who has no previous criminal record and who seems to have just made a very big mistake. I advise you strongly to accept the caution.'

I knew I could do nothing else. Some distant part of me was telling me I could fight this, I could get those emails back. But it was awful there. I just wanted to leave.

I said, 'Yes, I'll accept the caution.'

He motioned that I should follow him, back to the reception area, where I would be formally dealt with: cautioned, fingerprinted and then photographed for the police archive.

And so I went.

2

Bo

I let myself into the house after the walk home from school. Already, snow lay on the highest peaks, but it was still autumn here. Outside the kitchen window, sycamores wept their leaves and turned the dying year gold. Autumn's beauty was pensive, I thought as I hung my coat on the stand; in the soft breeze all around me, I could hear the fierce sounds of winter.

I paused for a moment when I got to the kitchen and wrote that down. I'd be able to find symbolic meaning in the observation one day, stick it in a poem (probably about maturing love – how beautiful it was, and how vulnerable the aging lovers were as time marched relentlessly onward) and let critics speak of my perceptive, subtle genius, even though artists and writers had been saying all this stuff for centuries and I just echoed those who came before, the ones who had really known it, really felt it. I didn't experience any of those things other people spoke of – those feelings that marked them out as warm and human, instead of isolated and cold as I often felt myself to be. Dead at the core. I would not be vulnerable as Gus aged.

My love was ice cold.

I went to the larder, took out yeast, oil, salt and white bread-making flour, then fixed the dough hook onto the food processor. Maggie had asked me to make mini baguettes again. I bought mini baguettes for them every week, but both girls insisted they were better when I made them myself. Now and then, when my work had reached a decent cooling point, I left it for a morning and baked instead. It was often when I was up to my elbows in flour that ideas came to me.

Now, as I mixed everything in the processor and set it slowly going, my mind drifted to Alice. I couldn't think of her these days without fear. I worried about her potential for vengeance. Alice would be vengeful, I was certain of that. She was full of angry energy, and now had enough time on her hands to think and dwell and plot. Yes, that was Alice. Angry, damaged Alice.

Angry and damaged, I told myself. Mad. Remember the emails – so many of them they wore me out to open and read. Remember the demands, the neediness.

Remember the love.

Oh, that endless, selfless love. She'd taken my breath away with her devotion. But surely there was something pathological in a love like that. Alice had practically scratched out her own heart and handed it to me on a plate, and I knew I wasn't worth taking that sort of risk for. For all my fame, I was just a middle-aged woman, dead at the core. Rotten, I suspected sometimes.

I smeared olive oil round a bowl and tipped the finished dough into it, then covered it with the PTA tea cloth I'd bought when Lola was in year two. Twenty-two self-portraits by Lola and her classmates, with names in lopsided letters underneath them, Lola Hartley being one. The girls had Gus's surname. I'd kept mine when we married. I'd thought about changing it, in rejection of my mother, but it was such a boring, conventional thing to do, and my mother was so stupid, the symbolism in the act would be lost on her. So I kept it.

Alice would never change her name, either. I was certain of that. Independent, feminist Alice.

It had been a relief for a few days, knowing she was out of my life, now. I hadn't been able to forget about her when every day the emails were flooding in, declaring love, declaring sacrifice (she'd have given up on children, for me), declaring that she was there, she would wait, she would wait as long as I needed, as long as it took.

God, it was exhausting, to be loved like that.

I turned off the food processor and left the dough to prove.

A week had passed since I'd been to the police. A week without Alice. An empty inbox, no notification on Facebook, where I'd had her marked as a best friend so I'd never miss her posts. The message would come in: 'Alice Dark updated her status', and I would hurry to read it, because always it would be something that lifted my day. After she'd left Jake, she'd written, 'I am celebrating a night alone with a tub of Häagen-Dazs. I ate some, recalled with a shudder the days when I'd have been expected to perform an erotic task with it, then with deep joy ate the rest.' I would never dream of saying something like that, but I couldn't help admiring the boldness of the person that did.

But there was nothing now. Just silence. My emails were all boring, my Facebook news lacked life.

After the incident with the police, I'd spent two afternoons hanging around the village near her flat, waiting for a glimpse of her, just to make sure she was still alive. I was almost certain that she'd still be there. For a start, she had no money to go anywhere else, but she'd also be devastated, and most likely too devastated to make any sort of decision.

I hadn't seen any sign of her. There'd been no movement of curtains, no flitting of shadows near the window, nothing at all. I thought, *Alice could be dead in there.*

The idea kept scratching at my mind. That Alice might kill herself had first occurred to me when I was typing my statement to the police. The girl was so troubled, I wondered if this would drive her over the edge – all the grief and confusion. Confusion like this could kill. I'd learnt that much from Christian.

> *'My son was fine before you got your claws into him. He wasn't ill. He's never been ill. Never been depressed or unstable. You are a manipulator. You drove him to this. You know it as well as I do, and I hope you can live with it.'*

No one had believed Lucy Winter. The police pitied her. They pitied me as well. It was chaos. A dreadful, tragic mess that my family and I now had to live with.

I passed the rest of the morning with housework and making a few notes for my next chapter, then baked the baguettes at the bottom of the Aga. When they were done, I lined a basket with a red tea cloth and packed six of them into it with some brie and grapes, and two slices of ginger cake.

Once, when Alice had been staying here and the girls were in bed, we'd spent the evening on the terrace, eating brie-and-grape baguettes and ginger cake while the sun set and the air filled with the scent of lilies, and the sky burned orange over the mountains all around them. Later, when it was dark, we'd made love right there on the grass, and both said we'd never been this happy, never loved anyone this much…

I put on my duffel coat, hung the basket over my arm and stepped outside. The air was cool and sharp, the sky heavy with wintering cloud. The afternoon lay grey as a secret.

I walked quickly down to the valley and into the village, where tourists still thronged the streets and the churchyard.

When I reached Alice's flat, I stood outside for ten minutes or so, watching. There were still no signs of life in there. I carried my basket up the steps and put it gently down in front of the door.

I didn't need to leave a note. Alice would know.

Then I walked away to collect the girls from school.

3

Alice

I had barely left the studio in the week since it happened. There was no one to see in Grasmere and nothing to do unless I wanted to walk the fells; and although Bo had told me time after time that nature could heal me, I had no strength for it. I simply lay on my back in bed, taking long, deep breaths and rubbing my fist over my chest to try and ease the ache beneath my skin. I needed all my energy just to stay alive.

My heart and mind felt beaten. Bo had ransacked them and kept the spoils for herself, like some parasite feeding on the shreds of my wellness, energised by my unravelling.

I was falling apart. I'd never known there was truth in that sort of expression before, but now I understood: People broke, and I was breaking. And it was as real and physical as shattering a limb.

If I'd had the strength to step outside myself and think about it, I would probably have been troubled by my reaction. Until now, I'd imagined myself charging through life, cool and indestructible. There was so much awfulness behind me and I'd survived it all – not just survived it but triumphed over it, squashed those traumas in my fists and said, 'Fuck you.' Until this happened, if I'd been honest, I'd have said I didn't really believe in mental sickness, only a lazy weakness of the mind.

But now I was here, barely able to move or think, barely able to do anything at all but fight to stay upright as surge after surge of wild emotion knocked into me. I had no idea how to stop it. For a while, I smoked and drank and slept through it, but the sleep was filled with images of Bo and the police, and when I woke, my mouth was a desert, my head bruised, my stomach swaying with booze.

Once, I woke up and thought, *If I stay here, I will die*. And it was like a glimpse of the future; I saw it with ice-clear certainty.

But there was nowhere to go, and I had barely any money. For the first time since I was a child, I longed for my mother.

My mother.

She wrote to me, in those sick years after she realised what she'd done. Plaintive, apologetic letters that I read and discarded. There was no way to mend that rift. It was huge and permanent. My mother could do nothing to make up for the memories I had to haul around for the rest of life, the weight of them pushing me down, making me stumble, my face in the dirt.

'Put it right,' she'd said with her dying breath, as if doing so was easy, as if finding a good man and having a couple of babies and giving them beautiful, ordinary lives were nothing more than decisions I had to make. I had made the decision long ago. A family, real and intact, was all I wanted, but it floated in the distance, as far off as a moon; sometimes it nudged its way out of the dark, slowly swelling so at times it appeared full and bright before me, within my grasp; but before I could grab it, it faded again, and everything around me went black.

'Put it right.'

'Well, mother,' I wanted to say, 'I've been doing my best, but I can't stop fucking it up.'

I started a list of all the things I was really bad at.

I began with holding down a job. I was awful at that. Awful at being bored, but mostly awful at serving other people. I hated sitting at a desk in front of a screen full of spreadsheets while all that expensive Russell Group education slowly dissolved from my mind until those years spent slogging for it – slaving away to understand literary theory and long sections of untranslatable Chaucer – wasted away, because now I was here, in a world where my capacity for critical thought counted for nothing, and all that mattered was my capacity to bring in money that would never be mine but would go to some fat, arrogant man who cracked the whip and voted Tory.

I was also a terrible cook. I'd once invited people over for dinner, handed them bowls of crisps and nuts when they came through the door, then taken myself into the kitchen, where I'd ploughed my way through a bottle of wine as I cooked, and had ended up so pissed that I had gone back to the living room, taken a seat among my hungry guests and said, 'I'm sorry. I'm too pissed. Can we just eat crisps instead?' They had all rallied round and ordered a pizza from Domino's, which we happily ate out of the box; then we'd stayed up till 3 am, smoking weed and drinking and agreeing that we just weren't the sort of people to manage a civilised dinner party, despite our combined age now being more than 147. No one had seemed to hold my failure against me, but I never attempted to host anything after that, not even a Waitrose ready meal for two.

I was terrible at staying sober and not smoking thirty a day. In fact, I was terrible at doing those things that wouldn't kill me, like exercise and healthy eating and drinking water. I couldn't open a bottle of wine without finishing it and then, usually, moving on to the next one. I couldn't go to a party without waking up the next morning beside someone I didn't know.

Relationships. I was dreadful at them. Appalling. Worse than anyone I knew. I'd spent the first twenty-three years of my life staying away from everybody, but now I was twenty-five and had behind me a long list of disastrous encounters with men who were still in love with their exes, or still in love with the one they were cheating on, or just fundamentally not in love with me. One of them had been so not in love with me that he'd battered me, and I hadn't left. I'd stayed with him, like some tired cliché of a desperate woman. When I did finally get myself together and walk away, it was meant to be my turning point. After him, I was going to get involved only with good men. My mother's words had haunted me. 'Put it right.' I would put it right. I would.

Then I had met Jake. And he *was* a good man. OK, it hadn't worked, but he had been a step in the right direction towards that dangling moon of emotional fulfilment.

And then there was Bo. I had never imagined someone like her would come along and set me back like this.

Bloody Bo. Bo who understood me, Bo who knew exactly what she was doing when she said those vicious things, when she stamped on me in all my most vulnerable spots, when she wrote that statement to the police and betrayed me so hard it was like being eleven and living through my mother's violence again. The worst thing of all was that Bo knew; she knew exactly what that betrayal would be doing to me.

I wondered how much of it she'd planned. Had this all just been a game to her? Making me fall in love; saying she'd written stories especially for me because she loved me; telling me to write to her publicist – was it all just a cool, calculated step towards destroying me?

I shook my head. I supposed I would never know.

Bo. Bloody Bo, who'd seemed so lovely, so stunningly lovely, but was in fact calculating and wicked, playing games with my mind and feelings.

So now I was here, alone in my flat, pissed, hungry and falling apart.

I needed to do something. My MA started in a week, but I didn't want to go to Lancaster anymore. If I were to have any chance of getting over this, I needed to be away from all reminders of Bo. I decided to phone Sussex, ask if they'd take me last minute, even though I'd turned them down before. I could be back in Brighton for the start of term…

But I had no money. I'd squandered the fees on … on *this.* On Bo. I would need a loan, now, and I'd need to beg my boss at the language school to take me back. He probably would. But I was so far away, here in Grasmere. Brighton now seemed like another world, a place where I'd been young; a time that was Before Bo. I knew now that Bo was the hinge that would divide my life. There would be the old me from Before Bo, and the new me – the one who would emerge from the chaos of After Bo.

There was so much to work out if I was going to make it back to Brighton, damaged and afraid. So much to organise if I was to even consider moving my MA course. I looked at my laptop, unopened on the table in the middle of the room. I wasn't sure I even had the energy in me now to write a book. Unless I wrote a book about Bo. That, I supposed, would be something into which I could channel my anger and all this wretched, wretched grief.

For now, though, I needed another drink. I'd woken up this morning with every intention to make it through twenty-four hours on nothing but brown bread and water, but it was now half past six and my resolve had failed. Being alone with my endlessly spinning thoughts frightened me. I needed to knock myself out. I looked in the fridge. There were only two beers left; they wouldn't do it.

I slung on my coat and picked up my purse from the floor. I was going to keep buying booze and fags until the money ran out and my Visa card was declined, and then I would just rot away.

I opened the front door.

On the top step were a bunch of lilies and a wicker basket covered in a gingham cloth – the kind carried by Little Red Riding Hood through the forest. Puzzled, I looked inside. Six mini baguettes, a bunch of grapes wrapped in kitchen roll, a triangular slab of brie and some cake, which I knew immediately was Bo's own, sticky with lemon icing and knobbled on the inside with crystallised pieces of ginger.

What did this mean? What the fuck was it? An apology? An expression of regret? Or was it love?

My mind started spinning again, out of control. I went over every possibility, trying to settle on a meaning that made sense. I wanted to believe it was love. I wanted to believe it was an apology and that Bo would turn up tomorrow in person, say she was sorry and ask me to forgive her. And I would. I would take her back in an instant, even though I shouldn't, even though all Bo deserved at this moment was hatred and contempt and then a gradual movement by me towards feeling nothing at all. But God, that would be so slow; it would take years, I knew that; years and years before I could hear Bo's name without anger or pain.

I left the basket and the flowers on the step and walked on to the off licence, where I bought twenty Mayfair and a four-pack of Stella. When I got home, they were still there, so I picked them up, took them inside, put the lilies in a glass and ate one of the baguettes filled with brie and grapes. The taste of it opened my memory, and took me straight back to that night in Bo's garden, when we'd sat for hours talking and eating, and watching the orange sunset smash over the fells like something holy, and I had felt the strength of this love overwhelm me, and wept with it.

I was always weeping now. Weeping, or howling.

I finished what I was eating and thought, *Bo knows*. She knew exactly what she was doing when she dropped that basket off, exactly the effect it would have on me. And I had no idea what her motives were. Perhaps she was trying to summon the courage to come up and talk to me. Or perhaps she was plotting poison. But the effects of Bo's poison were so unpredictable, I had no way to protect myself. I certainly couldn't go to the police. They'd never take me seriously. Bo had gagged me.

But then another thought occurred: Surely this offering she'd left couldn't be nasty. It had to be love. Because if it wasn't love, then Bo wasn't the beautiful, beautiful woman I had known; instead she was cruel. Nothing more than a wild cat, scratching its claws on my mind.

4

Bo

I was always thinking about the baby. Every day for twenty-five years, that red, screwed-up face had been in my mind. I followed her growth in other children, and in my own. Now and then, when we were visiting my parents on the caravan site in Woodstock, I would study them from where I sat, trying to piece together the child from their features. Would she have these eyes, those ears, that neat, white chin? I found my family inescapable. The genes were too strong, passed down whether I wanted them or not. I tried to turn away and reject them, but every time I looked in the mirror, they were there: my mother's eyes, my father's forehead, my brother's nose – all making my face a grotesque genetic mockery.

I thought I'd recognise the baby, if I ever saw her again. And then what would I do? Would I sit her down and tell her the story, hand her the pith of her pale beginnings? Would I apologise for giving her up? Or would I sit back, serene and unknowable as an angel, and say I was glad she'd had a good life and I knew her parents were wonderful?

Alice wasn't the baby. I knew that. Alice was someone else. But, unmothered and abandoned, she carried all the hallmarks of my lost baby; in her I had found the image of that child, of Willow, and because of that I had loved her sublimely, recklessly, dangerously. And now, as a result, everything was chaos. I'd made a criminal of Alice, but for what? To silence her. To stop the world from finding out that there was something inside me that kept on surfacing, a cruelty so ruthless it could slice out hearts.

My home, my daughters, my husband, my success ... There were days when it felt they amounted to nothing more than camouflage.

I leaned my head on my desk. What I'd wanted was to sweep Alice away, but she was still here, in my head, under my skin, everywhere. Alice was everywhere.

Sometimes, I wanted her to die. I thought it was the only way to get her out of me.

I picked up the mobile phone on my desk and rang my mother. The call failed. The signal on her caravan site was haphazard, and my mother only checked her messages when she had credit on her phone to hear them, which wasn't often. I pulled some paper out of a drawer and wrote her a letter instead. Email was beyond my mother. The internet was off her radar.

Mum,

I was thinking of coming down for a visit sometime next month. I have to meet with my agent in London, so could drop in for a cup of tea if you're around. How does 13th November sound to you? There are some things I would like to talk about. Do you remember the baby I had when I was fifteen? I wondered if you knew what had happened to her? I would like to trace her, if I can.

Bo.

I always ended my letters to my mother like that. Just Bo. Love was not a word I put anywhere near my family. It wasn't a word we knew, or understood. Lovelessness was genetic, I thought. Handed down the generations like cancer or madness.

5

Alice

I didn't know where I was. I'd been to rock bottom before, lots of times. I knew what it was like – the jaggedness; that feeling of weight too hard to push against; the hopelessness of finding my way up through the murk.

This was somewhere new, though. This was far beneath rock bottom, and it was dark and frightening. It felt like a place few others had ever been to, and there was no one who could guide me out.

There was nothing here. Nothing but pain.

My head was too small. It was too small to hold this. All other thoughts departed. Confusion and Bo were everywhere.

I didn't know who Bo was anymore. And I didn't know who I was, either. Because, if I was sane and normal, and if those memories of Bo saying she loved me, would move heaven and earth just to touch me, would die for me – if those memories were real, then Bo was wicked and cruel and evil. But if they were not real, if I had imagined it all, then I was mad.

Thinking about it, puzzling it over, trying to find an explanation I could settle on was exhausting.

I crawled into bed and thought, *I would rather be mad.*

The scent of lilies hurt. I wanted them to disappear. They wore me out. I was meant to admire their beauty, their scent, keep them alive. I could hardly look at them, or touch them. They were not Bo. They did not soothe.

I turned away from them. I didn't want the responsibility of flowers. I didn't care whether they lived or died.

6

Bo

I needed a project. A new book to work on. Sales of my most recent novel were slow and places at festivals becoming more scarce. My agent wanted to meet me to discuss our next steps, to make sure my plan was to construct a hit, something original and shocking that could compete with the brilliant young things coming up behind me, hogging all the space at Edinburgh, Hay, Oxford…

Low sales. They'd never happened to me before. Everything I'd ever written had flown off the shelves. I was famous everywhere. Americans loved me, Australians loved me, even the Japanese paid me to sign books in their huge, sterile shopping malls. I'd always thought I hated fame, but now I was finding I hated this more. Low sales were the start. In five years' time, I'd be forgotten. This was it. I was on my way out, aged forty.

I laid everything on the bed that I was taking with me to London for the meeting with my agent. I'd booked a hotel room in Bloomsbury for two nights. There was no way I could stay in my mother's wagon. The claustrophobia was suffocating.

I pulled my overnight bag down from the top of the wardrobe, where it lived for most of the year. Last time I'd packed it, I was going to Northumberland, where I would meet Alice. I sighed at the sight of the bag. It was a remnant from when life was simple, the life I thought I'd have back by now: neat, calm, domestic, beautiful in its easiness, nothing but writing, walking and caring for my girls.

That was the one thing I knew I was good at. I was good at looking after my daughters. Feeding them, protecting them, nurturing them … Yes, I had done all that, and I'd done it well. They were as cared for as any children were whose mothers loved them with all that raw urgency I'd read about in the baby-advice guides. Motherhood was something I took seriously. I wasn't going to hand on misery and produce cold young women. Lola and Maggie would be sane, confident, happy. They were my proof. They were all I needed. I was good at mothering. I was good at everything motherhood demanded: devotion, self-sacrifice, patience. No one who was this good at caring for people could ever be evil.

The girls were in their bedroom.

I went in and smiled at them. 'I'm going now,' I said.

They each came up and hugged me and told me they'd miss me. Maggie gave me a picture she'd drawn of rabbits. I slipped it into my handbag.

I kissed them both. 'Be good,' I said.

'Will you bring us a present?'

'I'll bring you a book.'

Maggie wrinkled her nose. 'Boring.'

I kissed her again and left. I hated leaving them.

Downstairs, I said goodbye to Gus. He barely looked up.

'I'll be back late on Friday,' I said. 'I'm calling in at my mother's on the way.'

'Your mother's?'

I shrugged. 'Duty.'

'Enjoy it.'

I left, got in the car and drove down through Windermere and out onto the M6. It was five hours to London. I turned on Radio 4 and wondered if anyone would be talking about me. They often were, but all the way through *Woman's Hour* and two programmes devoted to contemporary literature, I was not mentioned once. Other, newer writers were spoken about, the prize-winners of tomorrow, rather than of me, the washed-up winner of yesterday.

Stop it, I told myself. Just stop. It's a blip in sales. It doesn't have to mean the end of everything.

But it was. I believed in instinct, and mine was strong; I knew with absolute, deep-soul certainty that my career as a writer was coming to an end.

I cried all the way to the M4.

'Oh, Bo. There is so much love for you here.'

We were drinking wine while waiting for our meal. Vanessa, my agent, spoke sweetly, but I knew she didn't mean a word of what she said. There was no love for me. There was an understanding that I'd brought the agency significant amounts of money for fifteen years and now I was dwindling and something needed to be done about it.

She went on: 'We want to help you plan something new, so we know we're on to a winner before you even start. Now, have you got any ideas you can bring to the table?'

I hesitated. 'I'm sorry. It's been such a stressful time recently. I've had an incident with a stalker. I don't know if you know about that?'

Vanessa shook her head and frowned, concerned, 'I haven't heard anything at all about it. It sounds awful.'

'It was. I taught on this writing course – it was a few months ago now, back in May – and there was a young woman there called Alice Dark. I tell you her name because I think she'll become known before long. She was lovely, or so I thought. To cut a long story short, she started sending me love letters – emails, in fact. I told her to stop, but she wouldn't, and then she suddenly moved to live near me and made death threats against my husband – real death threats – and she tried to blackmail me too. She wouldn't leave me alone.'

Vanessa leaned forwards, nodding in sympathy. 'Bo,' she said. 'You have a story right here. I'm sure you can do something with this. Turn this into a brilliant novel. A thriller.'

'I have had that thought myself,' I admitted.

'There's a lot in here. A lot that's relevant. You know that museum of women's history? There's all that stuff there about Jack the Ripper … I don't know … You'll be able to do it better than I can, but surely you can say something meaningful about sexual predators today. Something feminist. Something … Oh, I don't know. Of course, you can't be homophobic about it. You can't be accused of saying, "Oh, women have always been so vulnerable and now all these bloody lesbians have the freedom to come out and get married, we're even *more* vulnerable…"'

'No, I definitely don't want to be accused of that.'

'But have a think about it. Plan it out and send me your ideas. I have absolute faith in you. I know you can do something magical with this, you'll be able to invest it with an emotional reality that will resonate with all your critics. I really think this could be great.'

I sipped my wine. Perhaps she was right.

7
Alice

Despair turned to rage, and rage turned back to despair, and then rage and despair joined forces against me until I thought they might kill me.

I got out of bed and paced my flat in fury. Bo had wrecked me. Deliberately and carefully, she'd hurled a grenade at my being and shattered it; and now I was barely able to catch myself up. I'd left half my mind trailing behind me. Nothing made sense. If I saw Bo now, what would I do? Would I weep and fall against her and beg her to make everything right again, or would I take that face in my hands and slap and slap and slap?

I wanted to undo time, meet Bo all over again and look out for the clues this time, find the hints in what she said, in the way she behaved, in her demeanour; I wanted to pin down a moment of nastiness amidst the gentle, angelic care, turn it over and over in my mind and say, 'This was it, the sign all along that Bo was never the person she seemed.' I sat on the floor, surrounded by six novels – six hundred thousand words, all written by Bo – looking for her in the pages. I wanted to find the depths of her psyche, the nastiness, the hell.

But there was nothing. Nothing there at all.

Fuck you, I thought. *Fuck you for doing this to me, for putting me here, in this place where I am out of my mind.*

I thought of all the ways I could get Bo back. I could phone her husband and tell him my story, because surely, after all these years of living with her, he had some idea of the woman who lurked beneath the surface? All I'd need to do was give him the other side of the tale, and hope he could see the truth in it. Or I could write an anonymous letter to her publisher and tell them. But what would they care, really? Besides, Bo would have already covered that base, already slandered me to every professional she could think of.

Or I could do what I'd already thought of, and write a book about it. A thriller. Make a story of what had happened and send it out to the world, so that Bo's shame could peer down at her from every bookshelf in the country. I'd neglected my writing recently. My head was so full of Bo, I hadn't had any energy to put into my project about the Victorian criminal underworld. But now Bo had handed me a story on a plate, just like that.

8

Bo

I drove to Woodstock the next morning, playing things over in my mind. Yes, I could construct a shocking, brilliant novel about a famous person with a troubled young stalker – a young woman confused about her sexuality and her mother. Thoughts of Alice's work had niggled at me recently. I worried that I'd inadvertently given her all the material she needed to grow up, move on from her mother and write something with real ambition and depth. The perfect revenge novel. I needed to make sure I did it first. I had all the advantages: fame, an agent, a fan base. It would take Alice years to fight her way out of obscurity.

I drove into the village just outside Woodstock and parked beneath the beech trees by the church. It was the closest I could get to my mother's caravan, and even then, there was a mile-long walk to the site. Still, it was pleasant enough. The weather was insanely mild for November, even for the south. Wild roses swung in the long grasses by the river and the sun beat with springtime warmth. The news put it down to *El Nino,* but Gus insisted it was climate change, the unsettling beginnings of worldwide catastrophe.

After half a mile or so, the wide riverside route narrowed into a path that stretched through the beech woods. A breeze stirred the year's fallen leaves at my feet, their brush against the earth crisper and drier than the gentle whisper of those still left in the trees. I walked on until I reached a rotting bridge over a drying stream and then into the clearing where my mother's caravan stood beside two ramshackle wood cabins. Everything was weather-beaten and old, but the setting was beautiful. At the edge of the clearing, near a cluster of silver birch trees, a fox laid down, opened its mouth and yawned. I wished I'd brought my camera.

My mother had been here more than two years. It was the longest she'd stayed anywhere.

I went to the steps of her caravan and rapped on the door. As I waited, I adjusted my hair. I looked good, I knew that. My jeans were expensive, my turquoise top cashmere, my coat long. I could swish in this outfit, effortlessly, and say without words, *I have left you behind.* It was a more powerful vengeance than merely cutting her out. No, I would keep on putting myself in front of my mother, saying, 'Look what I have become. Look how clever I am, how talented, how rich; and then look what you are. And know that I will never help you, however hungry you might be, however cold, however hard you beg, you will not get a penny from me.'

It gave me a feeling of deep satisfaction.

The door to the caravan opened and my mother stood there. She was skinny, I thought, undernourished. Her face showed signs of age and burden.

We didn't hug or kiss hello. My mother stepped back and opened the door wider. That was as much of a welcome as I knew I would get.

Inside was only one room. Two benches and a small table were the only furniture.

My mother offered me a can of beer from several that floated in a bucket of water on the floor. I shook my head.

'Got nothing else,' my mother said.

'That's fine. I won't stay long. Can I sit down?'

'If you like.'

I took a seat.

My mother sat opposite me and cracked open a can for herself. 'What brings you to this neck of the woods?'

'I was in town, meeting my agent about my next novel.'

'Oh, yeah. And what is it this time? Some load of intellectual crap no one can make head nor tail of, like the last one?'

'I didn't know you'd read the last one.'

'I didn't. Couldn't make it past the first fifty pages. No one wants to read that stuff, Bo – brothers and sisters writing poetry, walking up mountains and falling in love with each other. It's horrible. Write romance, for God's sake. Something people want to read at bedtime.'

'I'm going to write a thriller about my stalker.'

'That poor young man?'

'No. A woman this time.'

'What? A new one?'

I shrugged.

'Why do all these people stalk you?'

'Because I'm famous.'

'You're only a writer. It's not like a pop star or a Hollywood actress.'

'It is for them.'

'They want your money?'

'They want me to love them.'

'Fools.'

'Anyway, there's another reason I wanted to see you.'

'Yeah. You said. The baby.'

'Yes.'

'It's been years since I heard from them.'

'How long?'

'Fifteen, twenty years, maybe.'

I felt my heart droop. 'Can you remember their names?'

'Yeah. The mother called herself Rosa Ferris and the dad was Will.'

'So I could look them up?'

'You could, but I don't know why you'd want to drag through all that now. The girl's dead, Bo, don't you remember?'

'What?'

'Yes, I told you. I told you at the time. She was ill by the time they took her. She hadn't been fed since she was born. You remember how you didn't feed her? They did their best, but the poor scrap was malnourished and too weak to take the bottle. They didn't take her to the doctors soon enough – they were afraid the social would take her off them – so she was on her way out before she even got seen to.'

There it was again. A fist in the stomach, in the chest, in the heart. Fists everywhere. For a while, I could hardly breathe.

After a long moment, I said, 'You didn't tell me. I would have remembered.'

My mother dismissed my accusation with a wave of her hand. 'Oh, maybe I didn't. It was years ago, Bo. It was a kid. It died. You've got your own kids now. What does it matter what happened to that one?'

I took some deep breaths, got myself calm again. I stood up. 'You're right, mum. Thanks. Thanks for telling me again. I must have just forgotten. It's no big deal, as you say. I didn't want the child. It was hardly mine at all. I wasn't even … Well, you know. If I'd had any say in it, it would never have been conceived.'

'Don't bring all that up now. We were skint. We needed money. It was an easy way to bring some in. You'd have ended up homeless without it.'

'So you said.'

'Plenty of girls sell themselves for a bit of extra cash here and there.'

'I'm sure they do.'

'I'd have done it myself, if I'd been pretty enough. Still would. I'm poor, Bo, you have no idea. If I thought I could make even a tenner opening my legs for a man, I'd do it now.'

Without warning, I spun around and slapped my mother across the face.

Then I left.

Westbrook Library

Customer ID: **********4544

Items that you have checked out

Title: Bitter orange /
ID: 34143110451042
Due: 24 May 2022

Title: Exquisite /
ID: 34143110296371
Due: 24 May 2022

Title: The first time I saw you /
ID: 34143130047911
Due: 24 May 2022

Title: The hanging club /
ID: 34143110166897
Due: 24 May 2022

Total items: 4
Account balance: £0.00
03/05/2022 15:53
Checked out: 5
Overdue: 0
Hold requests: 0
Ready for collection: 0
Messages:
Greetings from Koha.

Items that you already have on loan

Title: The good sister /
ID: 34143110546353
Due: 24 May 2022

Thank you for using the bibliotheca SelfCheck System.
Thank you for using Westbrook Library

.

.

.

9

Alice

'She's a bitch.'

At the other end of the line, Anna spoke matter-of-factly. I supposed she was used to seeing the bad in people. It came with twelve years in the police force. People were scum. They were arseholes. Trying to find their shreds of goodness was the way to madness. If Bo was behaving like a bitch, then she was a bitch.

'Don't make excuses for her,' she said. 'We see that all the time. Battered woman syndrome. You're strong enough to let that go. It sounds to me as if she's on the narc spectrum.'

'The what?'

'Narcissist. Psychopath. People without conscience. They prey on the vulnerable, charm them and then fuck them up and leave them, but they're generally lovely to everyone else, so no one believes the victim and the victim goes mad.'

'Right,' I said.

'So the best thing you can do with this woman is get her out of your life.'

'That's it?'

'What did you want to do? Please don't tell me you want to get back with her.'

'No.'

'Revenge?'

'Yes, sometimes,' I admitted. 'I'd like her to suffer. I'd like her to suffer a lot. But then I remember dignity.'

'So decide what's more important – dignity, or revenge?'

I thought about it. 'Revenge,' I said, 'if I could do it well, without trouble. And it needs to be something better than sewing mackerel into the curtains of her bourgeois home.'

'Have you got her emails?'

'No. She told me to delete them, so I did.'

'Were you always on your PC when you read them?'

'iPad, mostly. And phone. She sent text messages when she asked me to move here.'

'You can have them retrieved. You'd have to pay for it, but it's perfectly possible.'

'And then what? Send them to her husband?'

'Exactly. And was there anything else she said in that statement that was a definite, absolute lie? Not just a twisting of the truth, but an outright lie?'

'Five silent phone calls. She said I made five silent calls to her house after I'd seen her in the café with her family. I wanted to get in touch with her husband and get him to say they didn't happen.'

'God, Alice. You are so naïve.'

'What?'

'Do you think she'd just stick that in there if the phone calls didn't happen? Of course they happened. She's a woman who covers all bases. She'd have made them herself.'

The thought of it made me felt sick. That someone could be so calculating and manipulative. Someone like Bo, who'd seemed … I left the thought unfinished. I'd had it so many times.

I said, 'What can I do?'

'Have you got her number?'

'Yes.'

'Then you can have it traced.'

'How?'

'You could ask the police, but to be honest, they're likely to refuse. Accepting a caution is basically admitting you did it, and they're not going to waste time and resources on it. You could hire a private detective. It would cost you, though.'

Fight back, I thought. Don't be passive and powerless. Fight back.

I said, 'Can't you do it?'

'I'd lose my job if they found out.'

'OK. How much do these private detectives cost?'

'I don't know exactly. A few hundred pounds, probably, to trace a call.'

'Shit.'

'Look at it this way. This madness has already cost you thousands. What's a few hundred more to straighten it up? Besides, you might get some of it back if you can prove you were framed.'

'I haven't got a few hundred pounds.'

'Have you got a credit card?'

'Yes.'

'Then use it. Seriously, you don't want that caution hanging over you for the rest of your life. It's not like a conviction, or a criminal record, but it's not good. Get the bitch found out. Once the detective has the info, send it to me, and I'll make a case for your local police force to look into it some more.'

'OK. I'll do it.'

'Make sure you do. Start the ball rolling now, as soon as we've finished talking. Look up three private detectives online and email three of them for quotes about getting a number traced.'

'Alright.'

We said goodbye and I immediately did as she suggested.

I'd phoned Anna for advice. She was never rich in sympathy, but she had knowledge of the law and the way the police worked, and they were the things I needed. I'd told her the whole story: moving to Grasmere, the police, the caution, the basket of food on the step. 'She's a bitch,' Anna had pronounced. It was clear and simple the way she said it; there were no subtleties, no shades of grey, nothing that could be excused by psychological frailty or a barbarous past. No. She was evil. The rest of her – the lovely, caring, beauty of her – was a mask, and it had slipped.

'You should never have accepted the caution,' Anna had also said. That was probably true, but I hadn't seen I had any choice. The police said they would arrest me if I didn't, and all I'd wanted at the time was to get away, for it to be over.

But now, after speaking to Anna, I felt slightly better. Forget Bo Luxton and all her talk of walking in nature and being my own mother. I would heal through revenge and justice.

Lucas Robinson, Private Detective
24b Lancaster Road, Manchester, M1

Dear Alice Dark,

Following our initial conversation on the phone, I am pleased to attach records of traced telephone calls made to 01539 472018, The Riddlepit, Nr Grasmere, Cumbria, between the hours of 8 pm on Saturday, 12th September and 2 am on Sunday, 13th September.

You will see that there is a total number of five calls made, each one traced to a mobile phone registered in the name of Ms Bo Luxton.

If I can be of any further assistance, please do not hesitate to get in touch.

Yours,

Lucas Robinson
Private Detective

I put the letter into an A4 envelope – it would have seemed such a shame to fold it up and crease it – along with the copies of all Bo's emails and text messages that I'd had retrieved. I licked the envelope closed and wrote 'Mr Augustus Hartley' on the front. My heart beat loudly. Never in my life had I done anything this deliberately destructive. But Bo deserved it. I felt no guilt.

I wasn't going to trust the post with this. I waited until I knew Bo would be out collecting the girls from school, then walked up the fellside to her house and dropped it into the mailbox at the end of her drive. To make sure I wouldn't run into her on the way home, I carried on walking all the way to Glenridding, then caught two buses home to my studio.

I was moving back to Brighton the following week. I'd emailed Jake, a sheepish, embarrassed message, telling him what had happened. 'And now I'm stuck,' I said at the end. 'I'm stuck in Grasmere with no money and all I really want to do now is come home to Brighton, start my MA and pretend it never happened. Is the offer of your floor still open? If so, I would love to take it, just until I'm back on my feet again.'

He'd replied saying yes straight away, as I'd known he would.

Everything was sorted out now, in my head. I would take out a loan for the fees, find a damp, old house to rent with other students and then leave the MA with a book ready to publish.

I'd started it yesterday: *Exquisite*.

10
Bo

The child was twenty-five years dead. All this time, I'd been following her growth in my mind, picturing her face, imagining her talents, her insecurities, her weaknesses, and yet all the while she'd been lying cold beneath the ground, her small body rotting away.

I was cross with myself for letting it get to me like this. Why should I even care? I hadn't known the child; I'd barely spent four days with her and all I'd wanted, even then, was for someone to take her away. The dawn of her short life was brutal. I could never have brought her up.

But still, to think about her every day, knowing she was having a good life, in defiance of her violent beginnings, had brought me comfort. The beautiful, fantasy child of my creation. Now and then, I let my mind wander away from the gritty truth that I could never have cared properly for that baby, and imagined instead that I'd kept her. The life I pictured for us was strong and good. I saw myself, aged fifteen, escaping with the baby to a forest somewhere and making us a home. There we lived, just the two of us, surviving only on what the Earth provided. It was a simple life, and poor, but there was love between us and so it didn't matter. I called the baby Willow and loved her so hard that she stayed with me forever. We were perfect.

But the baby was dead, and the loss of her hurt.

Pain was new to me. New and terrible. This was why I'd locked away that cracked and damaged heart. It was Alice, bloody Alice who'd opened me up and found it again, who'd made me weak and debilitated.

But how I still wanted her. I wanted to knock on her door and tell the whole dreadful story, and for Alice to love me better. Because that's what Alice would do, I knew that. If I turned up at her flat, apologised, wept and asked forgiveness, Alice would have me back again. I could make promises, wild promises to restore that exquisite love and eternalise it. We'd each write novels about it – poems, diaries. We would go on forever, Alice and me, and our love would be revered everywhere.

God, it could be so profoundly romantic, if we let it.

Alice would let it. I remembered a conversation we'd once had, when Alice had told me she had a terrible history of taking back men who'd hurt her. It made no sense, she said. She was an intelligent woman with a first-class degree, but when it came to life, she was naive. I had said, 'It's not stupid. The thing about being hurt badly is that the only person who can make you feel better is the person who hurt you, and so you keep going back and they keep making you better, but then they hurt you again, and so it goes on.' And Alice had looked at me, wide-eyed with amazement, as though I had just handed her the truth about all the pain in the world.

I thought about that now, and how I longed for Alice to make this new pain stop. Alice. Dear Alice. My darling, lost child.

I came off the M6 and drove on to Windermere, through Ambleside and finally into Grasmere. Tourists were everywhere, even now, this late in the year, flooding the valleys. I thought they were idiots. They spent all their time crowding the villages, gazing at the surrounding fells and saying they were beautiful, but with no idea of what they'd see if they'd only walk a mile upwards.

I slowed down as I approached the bakery above which was Alice's flat. Once again, there were no signs of life. Perhaps she wasn't there. Perhaps she'd left after that day in the police station.

I parked the car in the centre of the village, then got out and walked back. I stood outside for ten minutes, staring up at the window. Nothing. I looked at the flight of stone steps that led to the front door. Should I? How would Alice greet me? Would she laugh and smile and hug me? Would she cry and shout hysterically, 'Look what you have done to me'? Or would she slap my face and tell me to fuck off?

Quite possibly, knowing Alice, she would do all three.

I sighed and walked back to the car. I wasn't ready to see her; to face all that hot, exhausting emotion.

I drove to the foot of the fell and up the rough dirt track that took me to The Riddlepit and the girls. Home. I was always glad to come home again, where everything was warm and comfortable and calm. Part of the reason for its calmness was that it lacked passion, but I didn't mind that. Passion was for other people. Passion was for the weak.

But as soon as I opened the door, I sensed it. Something had changed. The atmosphere was thick and bitter, filled with bile.

The girls were fine. They charged downstairs and flung themselves at me in the hallway, barely letting me breathe, asking how Granny was, and what I'd brought them from London.

I reached into my bag and handed them each a book I'd bought from one of the second-hand shops on Charing Cross Road. *Carrie's War* for Lola and *Amazing Grace* for Maggie. They took them and humoured me by turning them over in their hands before abandoning them on the floor and returning to their games. Last week, Maggie had looked me square in the eye and said, 'Mummy, you might like books and think reading is great, but I don't.' And there it was, straight from the horse's mouth: I might be your child, but don't ever think you can mould me into a version of you. Still, I kept on trying.

Gus hadn't come to greet me. I hauled my bag into the kitchen and set it on the table. He was there, in his usual place, in the rocking chair, drinking tea and reading. He didn't look up as I walked in.

I busied myself putting water in the coffee machine. Still he didn't look at me. It was deliberate; a hard, definite effort to ignore me. His body was rigid with it.

Eventually, I stood directly in front of him and said, 'Hello, Gus.'

He raised his head slowly. He didn't smile. An air of silent fury surrounded him. It silenced me. I returned to the coffee machine, racking my brain for what could be the matter with him.

Then it caught my eye: On the table was a large brown envelope, fat with hundreds of sheets of paper inside, and on the top, as if left there deliberately for me to see, a letter, on headed paper – a private detective.

I picked it up, read it, and a cold knowledge filled me: My life was about to disintegrate.

At last, Gus spoke. 'Can you explain this to me?' he asked.

I shook my head. 'I have no idea what it is,' I said.

He stood up, came over to me and pulled the papers out of the envelope. 'Let me try and jog your memory,' he said, and started to read. '"Gus is going away next Tuesday for three nights. Come and stay. Please. Love you, adore you."'

He dropped that page and picked up another one. '"Goodnight, my sweetheart. I am picturing you lying asleep, hoping your dreams are peaceful. Love you."'

'And then the winner, Bo. The one that tops them all. "Darling, gorgeous Alice, I have a suggestion. I know you've only just moved, and I know it's a lot to ask, but … why don't you let your flat go and come and live in Grasmere? There is plenty of accommodation in the village and I'm sure you could find work to keep you going. I can help you financially if you need help…"'

He looked at me. 'What is going on?'

I did what I always did on the very rare occasions I felt cornered. I started to cry. I spoke hysterically, 'I don't know. I don't know why she would do this. I didn't send those messages, Gus. I didn't do it. She's evil. She's evil.'

He sat down. 'Is she as evil as that young man who stalked you five years ago?' he asked.

I shook my head. 'Stop it, Gus!' I cried. 'I can't bear to be reminded of that.'

'Oh, really? Well, that's tough, Bo, because I am going to remind you of it.'

I put my hands over my ears, but his words filled the room around me.

'Don't you remember Christian, the young man you used to teach, who fell in love with you and wouldn't leave you alone? Do you remember that? And he pursued you so vigorously that we went to the police and then a day later, he was dead? Do you remember that?'

'I am asking you to stop.'

'And I am telling you to listen. Do you remember he killed himself because he thought he was insane? He thought he was insane because you told him he'd imagined an affair with you, because you somehow – using God knows what techniques – made him doubt his own grip on reality? Do you remember that, Bo?'

I said nothing.

'Because I remember it. I remember it well – how you cried and wailed and said you hadn't meant for him to kill himself; you'd just wanted him to leave you alone, and everyone – every single person who heard that story – pitied the life out of you. I would like to know what really went on there, Bo. I would like you to tell me what happened.'

'Nothing! It was as I said. Don't do this, Gus. You are being unbelievably cruel.' I cried harder.

Gus went on staring at me, his face taut with disgust. In the end he said, 'We're not going to get anywhere, I can see that. You vicious, lying cow.'

'I am not lying.'

He bellowed. 'Well, what the hell is all this, then?'

'I don't know. It's Alice. She's evil. I'm sure she is. She made these up. They're fake.'

He waved the letter from the detective in front of my face. 'And what is this, then?'

I cried more and started to breathe more quickly, as though I might hyperventilate because of the terror of it all. 'I don't know. I don't know. It's a terrible trick, Gus. She's playing a terrible trick on me.'

'Tricks of this nature are vile. No wonder she was so angry with you. No wonder she demanded money from you.'

'Why won't you listen to me, Gus? You're my husband. You're meant to be on my side.'

'I am worn out with being on your side. I've had a feeling from the beginning that none of this was as it seemed, that no one ends up with two bloody stalkers in five years. You provoked this, Bo. You did everything you could to make that girl obsessed with you and then you tricked her. I have no idea why you would do this, and frankly, I don't want to know. You need to pay her back what you owe her, and you need to get yourself to that police station and tell them the truth.'

'They know the truth.'

'I am not continuing this discussion. You are going to do what I have said, or I will do it for you.'

'You're blackmailing me. You bastard.'

'Indeed I am. And I'm leaving you.'

'What?'

'You're a monster, Bo Luxton, and I no longer wish to share my life with you.'

'But you have to.'

'No, I don't. There has been nothing between us for years, and now it's over. It's done. I do not wish you to be my wife.'

He walked away.

I stood in the kitchen and wept.

11

Alice

I felt sure Bo was watching me. Three times now, I'd seen her walking around outside the flat. I knew immediately it was Bo, even before I'd seen her face. The shape of her in her duffel coat was enough. I would recognise it anywhere: the exact height of her, the curve of her shoulders, the gentle swell of her hips, the movement of her limbs as she walked. Even now, after everything, the sight of Bo made me catch my breath.

I worked hard at hating her. It should have been easy, but still there were nights when I lay awake in my bed and sobbed for the loss of her. Sometimes, I thought I would do anything it took to have her back again – back as the person I'd known; not this cold, manipulative woman who lied and tricked.

I remembered Anna's words. 'People like this prey on the vulnerable. They pretend all sorts of things, and then they reveal their true selves.' Anna would say Bo had never loved me, was faking it all along, but I couldn't bring myself to believe that. No one could mimic emotion that deep, they just couldn't. Bo's sea-change was rooted in something complicated. Those stories about her childhood, all her talk of strength and being alone…

'Don't think like that, Alice,' Anna warned.

No. I wouldn't think like this.

Brighton was calling me back. I had houses to look at next week. Shared houses, with other people. I'd had enough of living on my own. I wanted the company of others. I couldn't afford anything other than a damp room in a tumbledown house in an area where crime rates were high and people were poor, but I didn't mind. It was life.

I looked at the screen in front of me. *Exquisite*. It was flying from my fingers. I'd already written ten thousand words.

Bo, I knew, had told everyone about me. She'd made it clear in her statement to the police, telling them about my message to her publicist. She hoped to spread the news around the book world that Alice Dark was a stalking madwoman.

Well, Alice Dark was not a stalking madwoman. Alice Dark was a woman of sound mind, and she was fighting back. My story was going out in the world. And Bo Luxton, the famous author that everyone loved, could fuck herself.

12
Bo

So the house was going on the market and Gus was leaving me. I was brisk and matter-of-fact about it. There were things that needed sorting out. Custody of the girls and money. I'd need more money. I was going to come out of this with half of all we had. Half – when in fact for the last fifteen years, my earnings had been so much higher than his, and when I'd done all the childcare, all the school runs, all the birthday parties as well. His contribution to our life together was nothing more than occasionally feeding the cat, and he only did that to stop it mewling at him.

I was not going to become a woman that someone had left. Oh, no. I was leaving him; I would make sure of that.

'Have you seen my keys?' he asked, barging into the study without knocking and spilling a bottle of water onto the floor.

'No.'

'I left them on the side, where I always leave them, and they're not there.'

'I haven't got them.'

He went out again.

We'd agreed to tell the girls that afternoon that we were separating. I said I'd do it on my own, but Gus said it was something we had to do together. 'They need to hear it from both of us, so they know it's definitely happening, that we're both agreed on it and their lives aren't going to be ruined by it. It's really important.'

I suspected he didn't trust me. He was worried I'd tell them it was all his doing, tell them he'd had an affair. Tell them he was an ageing bastard. Still, they'd find that out for themselves soon enough.

I could hear him stomping around somewhere in the house, still hunting for his lost keys.

For two more hours, I sat at my desk, mapping out my new novel, *Stalked.* I would make sure my version of the story was the only one the world would know. I needed to get it out before Alice did, or she'd ruin me.

Gus didn't make it to his appointment. His keys didn't turn up, and I wasn't going to lend him my car, or offer to take him myself. If he wanted to end our marriage, then he had to swallow the downside of independence.

I finished my work, then emailed the New Writers' Foundation to let them know I was available for teaching next year. It was a pain, having to spend a week away, but it was a thousand pounds in the bag, and at the moment, a thousand pounds wasn't to be taken lightly.

In the afternoon, we called the girls into the living room. Gus had decided we would tell them, and then afterwards I was going to take them to Lancaster, to see *Cinderella* at the Grand Theatre. Show them that life was still good, that nothing would really change. They'd just live in two smaller houses instead of this one big one. That was all. The only perceptible difference.

The girls sat down on the sofa. They appeared to sense that something serious was happening, because they didn't fight or argue or whinge. They just sat there, straight-backed and silent, waiting for the blast.

I said, 'We wanted to talk to you, to tell you that some things are going to change.'

Then Gus said, in his calm therapist's voice, so replete with compassion and understanding that I could barely hear it without wanting to slap him, 'And change can be frightening at first, can't it? But we want to help you understand that this will all be OK. It's not bad, just different, but it will take some time to get used to the change.'

Lola said, 'You're getting divorced.'

Gus looked taken aback.

Lola continued, 'That's the only thing it can be.'

I nodded. 'Yes, you're right. We're separating. We will have to sell this house and buy two smaller houses, one for Daddy and one for me.'

Maggie said, 'Which one will we live in?'

'Well…'

Gus said, 'You can live in whichever one you like, whenever you like. The houses will both be in Grasmere and you'll have a bedroom in each one.'

Lola said, 'Alright. We can decide all of that stuff later, then.'

I felt as if I was watching my older daughter take sudden, giant strides to maturity, years before she ought to.

Maggie cried. I moved to comfort her, but before I was able to, Lola took my place. 'It's alright, Mags,' she was saying. 'It'll be fine…'

I watched, and as I watched I saw the rift open. Lola and Maggie stood on one side, Gus and me on the other. The girls were uniting, child survivors of their parents' war.

I drove the girls to Lancaster for the matinée performance, then afterwards took them for dinner at Pizza Express. I was bored and irritable. A whole afternoon on my own with them always left me like this. But I had to get used to it. This was to be my life now. A single mother, on my own with two children, steering them alone through childhood and the endless drama of the teenage years.

I had so many reasons for regret. I regretted it all. I wished there was something I could do to make it up to them.

To make it up to Alice.

13
Alice

There was no food in the flat and I needed to eat. I stood at the window and looked out for several minutes, checking for Bo. The thought of her out there, lurking among the trees and the shadows, frightened me. Nearly a week had passed since I'd dropped that envelope into her mailbox. She would not be hovering outside, waiting to spring a surprise proposal for a lesbian marriage, that much was certain.

I put on my coat and jogged to the shop, where I filled my basket with fruit and vegetables and brown rice. All those things Bo had said I must eat in order to keep body and mind working together. 'Remember that good nutrition is vital for spirituality as well as physicality. Don't forget the two are linked,' she'd said. At the time, I thought Bo was profoundly insightful. Now, I thought she was a wanker. But even so, I did what she said. I was putting myself back together, piece by piece.

I paid at the self-service checkout. For weeks now, I'd avoided cashiers, in case my card was declined and I'd have to face the shame of putting everything back on the shelves. At least if it was refused at self-service, I could just drop the basket and run.

But again, it was accepted. On the way home, I risked a trip to the off licence to buy some cigarettes. Again, my card worked. I stopped off at the cash point and checked my balance, something I usually avoided doing.

The illuminated text came up on the screen: £3002.67 credit.

Good God.

I went into the bank and asked for a statement. There it was, clear as anything: 16 Nov 15. Paid in, Mr Augustus Hartley and Ms Bo Luxton – £3000.

An admission. An acknowledgement by one or other of them that they accepted what I'd said. Vindication. I had money again. And freedom.

I walked home, lighter than I'd felt since coming up here. A weight had been lifted from my shoulders. My life, my future, was becoming affordable now, not something I was attempting on nothing but a wing and a prayer.

I was still lost in those thoughts as I rounded the bend to the main street where the bakery stood with my flat above it; so I didn't notice her straight away, not until the figure stepped out in front of me, smiled and said, 'Hello, Alice.'

Bo.

For a moment, I stood still and speechless and stared at her. Then I walked on, up the stone steps to the door.

Bo stood at the bottom. 'Please, Alice. I would like to talk to you. I'd like to explain.'

I turned back to face her, 'I have nothing to say to you.'

That wasn't true. I had plenty to say to her.

'I understand why you don't want to speak to me. I do. But please give me five minutes and I'll explain it all.'

I couldn't help it. I was curious. I was more than curious. I was eager – desperate, perhaps – to hear what Bo had to say.

Let me not weaken, I thought. *Let her not cast that spell over me and reduce me to a powerless wreck. I am alright now. I am OK.*

I opened the door, stepped inside and held it wide for her. Bo tripped delicately up the steps and I was torn between wanting to knock her back down them and wanting to beg her to stay, to come back and let things be as they'd been before.

14

Bo

I walked in and looked around. The flat was small but charming, and Alice had put some pictures on the wall and a rug in front of the old fireplace. I said, 'You've got it looking lovely in here.'

Alice spoke crisply. 'Thanks.'

I pulled a chair away from the table at the side of the room. 'Can I sit down?'

Alice nodded and took the seat opposite me. 'What are you doing here?' she asked.

I sighed. 'I don't blame you for being angry.'

'Right.'

'I want to apologise.'

'What for?'

I looked at her blankly.

'Tell me what you're apologising for.'

'For…' I gestured widely. 'For everything.' I wasn't going to spell it out, that was certain. 'Things were very difficult, Alice,' I went on. You've met Gus, my husband, so you've seen what he can be like.' Here, I looked at her, wanting acknowledgement.

Alice nodded.

'He's aggressive and controlling. And jealous. He's always been jealous, of everyone in my life. He won't speak to my friends, he resents all my success, and he…' I let my voice trail off for a moment before continuing, '…he thinks I'm going to run off with every man I meet.'

Alice was listening.

'Just before you left Brighton, he found his way into my emails. He read everything you'd sent and he…'

She was hanging on every word.

I took a deep breath before I continued. 'You were right, that week I didn't get in touch with you, when you worried that he'd hurt me.' I looked at Alice. 'He did hurt me.' I shook my head, as if I couldn't continue.

'Bo, I'm sorry.'

'He couldn't cope with the shame of it, the blow to his ego. You know – his wife running off with another woman. He would never have coped, never have lived that down. He was worried word would get out somehow, and so he forced me. He forced me to say you'd stalked me, and that you were crazy. He wanted you silenced, so no one would ever find out.'

Alice let her breath out all at once. 'And the phone calls?' she asked. 'Where do they fit in?'

I said, 'I don't know. To be honest, I think they were just a coincidence. I think one of the girls got hold of my phone that night and accidentally called us.'

Alice nodded.

'But anyway, it has been like this for many years between Gus and me. I learnt to live with it and protect myself because he wasn't usually violent, just mentally abusive, and I am good at coping with that. But after this – now he has hurt me and made me inflict so much damage on you – I have finally decided enough is enough and I've told him I'm leaving. We're putting the house on the market. A few rooms need decorating first, but it should be for sale in a few weeks. I don't know how long it will all take. These things have a habit of dragging on … But Alice, I want to make this up to you. I want to prove how sorry I am.'

'OK,' she said.

I looked at her and smiled sadly. 'I think you don't believe me,' I said.

'It's not that. I do believe you. But I was just starting to recover from what happened. I've made plans…'

I looked at her with interest. 'Really? What plans?'

'I'm going back to Brighton, to start an MA in creative writing.'

I clapped my hands. 'Oh, Alice. That's wonderful! Good for you.'

'And I was planning to move at the weekend. Saturday. I don't want to stay here in Grasmere.'

'Then don't. You know I would never stand in your way. You must do whatever you need to do, and I can wait. We can take it slowly. Much more slowly than before. It was all such a rush last time, such a wonderful whirlwind. We could try again, and keep our senses this time.'

Alice said, 'I'm sorry you went through all that.'

'Me, too. But I'm sorrier for what you went through.'

I reached over and took her hand.

Alice let me.

15

Alice

I made myself remember. I took a notebook and wrote it all down, everything that had happened. The lies, the viciousness, the police. These were not the actions of someone in love. They were the actions of someone who loved no one. What would Anna say? I asked myself. Or what would I say if this were happening to one of my friends? I knew exactly. 'Get away. Run.'

Bo had been here again this morning. I was on my way out to buy milk for the coffee that was fuelling my work, and there on the doorstep was a bunch of white roses, with twigs full of white berries scattered among them, and a book: *Creative Writing.*

Poor narcissistic Bo, trying to prove her love. The love she wasn't capable of. The happiness that lay always out of her grasp.

I picked up the roses and brought them inside. The berries seeped. I took a breath, then wrapped them in newspaper and folded them into the bin. Bo was seductive. She was tempting, but I knew she was horseshit.

The rift was wide and unmendable. My mother had gone to her grave without my forgiveness, and Bo would, too. There was no need to forgive and forget. I would never forgive the unforgivable.

16

Bo

I was working and working in a frenzy. All night, I went on, writing and writing and writing. I hardly slept. This was it, I thought, this was how it used to be, in the old days when ideas had flown from my hands like birds and soared into the skies.

I was writing the book as a collection of short stories, told in random order. It was a structure that was meant to reflect the terror and confusion of being stalked, of having your life broken by someone obsessed with you. The stories were gothic, creepy, a hybrid of styles, thrilling to read. Thrilling and frightening and devastating.

I'd finished five so far and sent them to Vanessa, who gushed and gushed. 'I love them,' she wrote. 'Bo, these are brilliant. I am going to email some editors now and start whipping up a buzz around them.'

Yesterday, she'd phoned and said the buzz was happening. A major editor had read the samples and wanted an exclusive on the finished book. She wanted to be the first to get the real thing in her hands and make a decision about it. 'Fingers crossed, Bo,' Vanessa wrote. 'Fingers crossed.'

My computer pinged – an incoming message.

It was Alice: 'Bo, I'm leaving Grasmere and I'd like to see you before I go. I'll be off on Tuesday, but will be home from now until then if you want to come over. A.'

I eyed the message carefully. This wasn't what I'd expected. There was no *darling*, no *beautiful Bo*, no *love you endlessly*. There wasn't even a kiss.

There was just the news that she was leaving.
I wrote back, 'Darling, why?'
But no answer came.

17

Alice

My bag was packed. I was ready to go. Tomorrow. I was going back to Brighton, to sleep on Jake's floor until I'd found a room of my own. My last hurrah. A final fling with youth.

This studio held nothing precious. No special memories, nothing meaningful except that this was the place where I'd aged. I'd lost my mind and got it back again, and now I was re-emerging. I hadn't shed my skin. I'd shed my core, replaced it and now I was unrecognisable.

A knock at the door.

I opened it. Bo, of course, standing before me in blue jeans, a pink v-neck and boots. I knew I was meant to want her. I was meant to reach out for her, and, without words, the two of us would kiss and tumble into bed and love would be there between us again, tangible and deep.

'Hi,' I said.

Bo came in and looked around. 'You're really going?' she asked.

I nodded.

'And what about us? How will we stay in touch? What do you want to do, sweetheart?'

Her tender concern fell like rain.

I said, 'There is no "us" now. I was tempted. I really was. But I can't forgive you for what you did.'

Bo looked hurt and bemused. 'But I explained all that. I thought you understood. My husband. He…' her voice trailed off and she started to cry.

I did not budge. 'I know what you said, but I'm afraid I don't believe you. The phone calls…'

'I told you about the bloody phone calls!'

'I don't believe you,' I said again.

Bo stopped crying and looked at me, silent, her blue eyes fixed upon me.

I shuddered. I thought, I am in the presence of evil.

18

Both

The blows flew.

It wouldn't stop. Fists in my face. A plague of fists, a storm of feet.
The boot going in,
the boot going in,
the boot going in again and again
until darkness fell.

Afterwards, I held her against me; the warmth of her breath on my neck; the warmth of her body; staring down at her, holding her gaze, her eyes glazed. Gone.

'My beloved,' I whispered. 'My beloved.'

The dark moved slowly over us and deepened. We hid inside it, bright stars, our light collapsing.

She rested her head on my shoulder. I kissed her forehead, and did not move after that, or even stir as she slept on.

No words passed between us.

19

Alice

My eyes moved slowly. The lids were heavy and stuck together, and would not open far.

A voice said, 'Alice? Alice, sweetheart, can you hear me?'

It was warm and familiar and filled with tender care, and I thought it must be my mother, though some dim awareness told me it couldn't be. It couldn't be.

The person soothed my face with water.

'You've been very hurt, Alice, but you're alright now. I'm here. I'm taking care of you. We'll get you to hospital. It will all be alright. Everything is fine now. Everything's fine.'

It was my face. Wrecked. Black, swollen eyes; grazed cheeks; thick lips; a chipped front tooth.

'What happened to me?' I whispered.

The voice that spoke was the one I'd heard earlier: Bo's.

'A young man did it. But don't worry. Don't worry. It will heal. It will heal, and you are beautiful still.'

I lay back against the pillows and closed my eyes again.

I had no idea what was going on.

My senses returned in flashes. The feelings came back first – anxiety, heartache, fear. It reminded me of those mornings in Brighton, when I used to wake with terrible hangovers and a pervading sense of shame, but only ever had the vaguest suspicion of what the shame was about. I'd have to spend hours then, piecing together exactly what had happened, what I'd done and what the consequences were going to be for everyone.

Now, I woke up and felt the ache of a broken heart, and was anxious and afraid of something indefinable. I turned my head and saw the beautiful woman beside me and knew that it was Bo and that I'd loved her and everything had turned terrible between us.

I reached out my arm and took Bo's hand in mine. 'Thank you for staying with me,' I whispered.

Bo said, 'What do you remember, Alice?'

I said, 'I remember you.'

I did remember her. I remembered her as clearly as the sun. Bo. Beautiful, beautiful Bo.

Bo, who had come back to me, was caring for me with the tenderness of a mother, who was telling me over and over that she loved me.

Yes. I remembered her.

I closed my eyes. My mind drifted and sank.

Bo was still there when I woke again, gazing at me with tearful concern.

I said, 'We fell out.'

Bo nodded. 'Yes, we did, but it's OK now. Everything is OK.'

But it wasn't. When we'd fallen out, the world had rocked and everything on it died.

I said, 'You can go home. You don't have to stay.'

Bo said, 'I want to stay. Dear, sweet Alice. You have been through so much.'

I thought, I have been through you.

20

Bo

A nurse came to change Alice's dressings and clean her wounds. I watched her work with the quick, nimble fingers of a seamstress. A flourish of gauze, the smell of antiseptic, the sticking of plaster and it was done.

I said, 'Will she be OK?'

'She's been quite lucky. The man who did this wasn't strong. The CT scan showed up a couple of small fractures to the skull and cheeks, but nothing that will cause permanent damage.'

'And her memory?'

'It will come back.'

'She says she remembers nothing.'

'The police will help her. They have methods.'

The nurse turned her back and busied herself with her notes. I moved closer to the bedside and took Alice's hand in mine again. I ran my fingers through her hair and stroked her face around the dressed wounds.

For once, I felt out of my depth. I didn't know how this worked. I wasn't a scientist or a doctor. All I knew was how to charm people. The doctors, the nurses, the police … they would see how good I was, how caring, how kind. I planned to stay here, planned to sit by Alice's side every day until the doctors let her go home. I was going to talk to her, keep on telling her, over and over, about the young man I'd seen coming out of her flat. I would help her remember.

The nurse left.

Alice opened her eyes. 'What happened?' she asked.

I said, 'Sweetheart, you were attacked. Yesterday morning. But you will be alright, my love. You will be alright.'

'Who?'

Gently, I stroked Alice's face. 'We don't know, not exactly, but I saw him. When the police come, I'll give a description, and your memory will come back. It will come back, sweetheart, and you'll describe him, too, and they'll find him. They'll find him.'

Alice said, 'Where were you?'

I spoke with tender concern. 'Are you ready to hear all this now? You've been through so much…'

'I'm ready. I want to hear it.'

'I came to visit you. Do you remember? You said you were leaving Grasmere and I wanted to convince you to stay. I love you so much, Alice. So much.'

Alice was silent.

I went on. 'But you insisted. You said you were going to Brighton, and I could see your mind was made up and so I went. I went to the café opposite your flat because I wanted to be calm and unflustered when I got home to my girls. While I was sitting there, I saw a young man jogging down the road towards where you lived. He stopped and looked around, then checked a piece of paper he took out of his pocket. Then he ran up the steps to your front door very quickly. I thought perhaps he was your new boyfriend, and that was why you didn't want to see me anymore.'

Alice smiled.

'Shall I go on?'

'Yes.'

'I drank my coffee, and then after a while – ten minutes or so – the young man came running out again, looking very flustered and red-faced, and I noticed his clothes were torn, as though he'd been in a fight. I watched him scarper – that's how I would describe his movements, he was certainly fleeing from something – and then I got up to leave, but something made me turn back. The young man had given me a very uncomfortable feeling, and I wanted to check that you were OK. Are you sure you're ready for the rest of this, sweetheart? I don't want to shock you.'

'I've been shocked,' Alice whispered. 'I'm already shocked.'

'So I went up to your flat and found the door wide open. I walked inside and that was when I saw you.' I took a deep breath before continuing, and when I spoke, my voice was barely a whisper. 'You were lying on the floor, and at first I thought you … At first I thought you were dead.'

'Oh, Bo…'

'I kneeled down on the floor beside you and took your pulse and saw that you were still alive, but injured. There was blood on your face. A lot of blood. So I called the ambulance. While we were waiting, I put you in the recovery position and sat with you and talked to you. Then, when the paramedics came, I travelled with you to the hospital so that you'd have a loving face beside you when you woke up.'

'Thank you,' Alice whispered, and took my hand.

21
Alice

A doctor came to see me. She brought scan photos of my skull, my face, my neck.

She spoke breezily, 'The good news is that the person who did this was not strong. You have a small fracture to your skull and some fractures to your cheeks, all of which will cause a lot of pain but heal without intervention. There's some minor bleeding around the brain. All the rest is superficial. The bruising and swelling will disappear in a few weeks and you should, I think, make a full recovery, with little to no permanent scarring.'

'Thank you.'

'The police will be here later to talk to you and try and take a statement about what happened.'

'I don't know what happened.'

'They will help you remember.'

Bo was still there when the police arrived, still holding my hand, still wiping my face, still caressing the skin around the plasters.

The male officer, who was new to me and not the one from before, said, 'It's important that we speak to Alice alone.'

Bo looked reluctant to leave. 'Alice?' she said 'Is that alright?'

I nodded.

Bo said, 'I won't go far.'

The police officers looked kindly at her as she went. They sat down on chairs beside the bed.

The female officer spoke. 'Now, Alice,' she said. 'I know this is difficult for you, but do you have any memories at all of what happened this morning? Anything at all that will help us. We want to find the person who did this to you.'

I said, 'It was her. It was Bo Luxton.'

22
Bo

I left when the police arrived and thought it best not to go back. It had taken all my nerve to stay here today. I was wearing Alice's trainers, which I'd found tied to her backpack while I was waiting for the ambulance. I'd kicked off my boots and hurriedly put them on. They were tight on my feet and uncomfortable, but I didn't care. The boots had to go. I'd rummaged in Alice's drawers for a carrier bag and wrapped them up in it, carrying it casually under my arm while the paramedics lifted her into the back of the ambulance. Later, I dumped them in a bin in the hospital car park.

Now, I stood outside my body and watched myself moving in panic. Slow down, I thought. Think.

But there wasn't time. Alice's injuries weren't as bad as I'd thought. Alice was not dying. She'd never been dying. And her memory would come back – that young, razor-sharp memory…

God, if I had known she wasn't dying, I never would have called the ambulance. I did it so the police would place me beyond suspicion. I hadn't meant to lose it like that…

I wanted to get away, but where could I go now? The girls needed to be here in Grasmere, where their lives were, and they needed me here, too. I couldn't just scoop them up, take them somewhere else and say, 'Your mother lost her temper. We have to hide.'

Everything had to be as it ever had been. Carry on as normal, I told myself. It was the only way to stop the world from swaying.

I caught a taxi back to Grasmere. The driver dropped me in the centre of the village and I walked the rest of the way, up the fell to The Riddlepit. It was sharp and windy, the mountains and the lake purpled with evening. Two stars hung above me, one larger than the other, and they flickered in and out, light as insects.

I thought, *I would like to catch one of these, if I can*, but as I walked up the fell they disappeared, and I looked out at the empty sky and wept.

It was past nine by the time I got home.

'Where the hell have you been?' Gus demanded.

I sighed deeply and took off my coat. 'Out,' I said.

'You can't just go out for twelve hours and not tell me.'

'I can. We're separated.'

'We haven't discussed what we're doing with the girls. You didn't ask me if I had plans, if it was fine for you to just swan off and leave them with me.'

'I didn't swan off.'

'You didn't tell me.'

'I went to hospital.'

He rolled his eyes. 'Of course you did.'

'I did, actually.'

'Is it terminal?'

'What?'

'Whatever you went to hospital for.'

'No.'

'That's convenient.'

'A friend of mine was beaten up.'

'Which friend?'

'Alice.'

'Oh, Jesus Christ, Bo. When will this ever stop?'

The rest of the evening passed quickly. I went upstairs and checked on the girls. They were worn out, sleeping in their bunk beds. I ran myself a bath. I let myself sink into it and closed my eyes. Images of the day drifted back to me: Alice in her flat, telling me she was leaving; that gentle snatching of power and rage. It was rage like nothing I'd ever known before.

I hadn't meant for it to be like this. All I'd wanted was for Alice to come back to me, to love me like she'd done before. And she said no. She said no and my heart broke and I didn't mean to, but I turned on her.

I had lost it. I'd done myself in.

I wanted to undo the day, go back to the beginning and start it again, and this time I wouldn't go to Alice's. I would stay at home, play Monopoly with the girls, read them books, make cakes, walk over the fell to the tarns. I'd live the whole day, peacefully, happily, moving slowly back to that life I'd had before, simple and normal and quiet. Then I thought, *If I could really wind back time, I'd go back to that old life and change its direction and never even meet Alice at all.* And then I got so absorbed in winding back my life to the time I wanted, the time I wanted to freeze, that I found myself in the wagon with my brother one night, that night before the first man came, and that was the time I settled on, that was the time I froze, because that was the night I died and my long, inside rot began.

23

Alice

The swelling went down quickly, but my head still ached and my memory was murky water. But now and then, when I was resting and least expected it, an image broke to the surface – Bo, arriving at my door, expensively dressed and elegant – but before I could reach down and grab it, the waters muddied again and the memory was gone.

But I knew it was Bo who'd done this. The day had come back to me, in botched fragments. I remembered that face close to mine, and the things she was hissing in my ear: 'You will pay for what you've done to my family, Alice Dark. I am going to hurt you so hard you'll spend the rest of your life regretting it. I am going to wreck your pretty face and your clever head. You can forget university. When I'm finished with you, you'll be in a home where people are paid to feed you through a straw and wipe your pert little arse.'

It was enough. I didn't want to remember more than that.

I said, 'Can I stop it coming back?'

The doctor shook her head. 'I'm afraid not, Alice, but we can arrange some psychotherapy for you, with a therapist who deals in post-traumatic stress. He can help you manage the flashbacks.'

I shrugged. Maybe, I thought.

The police brought my bag from where it had been in my flat, packed and ready to go.

I said, 'My trainers have gone.'

'We'll find them,' the officer said.

'It doesn't matter.'

He said, 'We've got enough evidence. We're going to arrest Bo Luxton today.'

'OK.'

'I'll let you know what happens. When are you going home?'

'The doctors said it will be this week. Maybe tomorrow.'

'Do you have someone you can stay with?'

I said, 'I'm going to Brighton, to sleep on my ex-boyfriend's floor until I find a place of my own.'

The police officer smiled wanly. 'Are you sure you're up to that?'

'It's not for long.'

He nodded, then said goodbye and left. I took my laptop out of the bag, sat on the bed and fired it up. I opened the document: *Exquisite.* For days now, I'd been trying to plan it out, so I knew what I was working towards, but I'd had no sense of an ending. Where was this going? Until now, I'd had no idea. But Bo had handed it to me, in her fist full of pure, white pearls.

24

Bo

Saturday morning. I was whipping up pancake batter for the girls' breakfast when the knock on the door finally came. I'd been expecting it. I smiled at Lola and Maggie, who were waiting for me to toss the first pancake into the air and catch it. The sight of it always left them awestruck and laughing. They were so easily entertained.

I dusted down my apron with my hands. 'Wait a moment,' I said. 'It's probably the postman with a parcel.'

Gus was still in bed. I opened the door to the two police officers I knew I'd see there.

I looked at them quizzically. 'Hello,' I said kindly. 'How can I help you?'

'Are you Mrs Bo Luxton?'

Ms, I thought, but now probably wasn't the time to correct them. 'Yes, that's me.'

One of the officers showed me his badge. 'We are arresting you on suspicion of causing bodily harm to Alice Dark. You do not need to say anything…'

I said nothing. Even now – even though I knew this was going to happen; had known for two days that it was inevitable – it came as a shock.

'Do you need to inform anyone?'

'My daughters,' I said, and returned briefly to the kitchen. 'I'm just popping out for a moment, girls,' I said. 'Go and jump on Daddy to wake him up, and he'll come down and finish making your breakfast.'

The girls moaned about my absence for a bit, then did as I'd suggested.

I took off my apron, slung my coat over my shoulders and went back to the hall to the policemen.

Their car was parked on the driveway beside the house. One of them opened the door for me and I climbed inside.

As the officers put on their seat belts, I looked up at Gus's bedroom window and saw him there, watching. He shook his head. I'd lost his sympathy long ago.

I was in a corner now, I knew that. There was nothing I could do to stop this, or erase whatever evidence they had. All I could be was obedient, charming and lovely. I would get myself off with fame, beauty and kindness. I'd make it impossible for me to be guilty.

At the station, they told me I was entitled to a solicitor. I said no. Innocent people could defend themselves, I thought.

They led me to an interview room. I wondered if this was where Alice had come, that day she'd been cautioned for stalking. Had she sat in this chair, talked about me and sobbed?

I looked at each officer in turn, confident but deferential. That was the way to be. Confident in my innocence, but always polite and cooperative.

'Can you tell us where you were at 10:30 am on Thursday, 10th December?'

I thought about it for a while, then took a deep breath and retold the story I'd told Alice at the hospital.

The officer nodded. He said, 'Alice has informed us that her assailant was you.'

I gasped. 'I can't believe it. I can't believe she would do that.'

He went on. 'We have seen the evidence she sent you – the traced phone calls that you claimed she had made to your home when she was "stalking" as you called it. But the calls go back to your own phone number. Why is that?'

'I have explained this to Alice before. I don't know how this happened. All I can think is that my children must have got hold of my mobile phone that night and phoned us.'

'Five times until 2 am?'

'It's possible.'

'Let me put something to you, Mrs Luxton. And listen carefully. You were feeling stalked by Alice Dark. You claimed that she pursued you and sent you messages, and then moved to Grasmere to be near you, but you had done nothing to encourage this at all. You then claimed that she made five silent phone calls to your home phone number and threats against your husband. All of this, based on the evidence we saw, looked like the truth. So we hauled Alice into the station and we cautioned her. Alice then went away and thought about this, because she believed she was innocent and wanted a way of proving it. So being a savvy young lady, she paid to have old emails and texts retrieved from her iPad and for a private detective to trace the phone calls. The phone calls went back to your number, and the messages from you are asking her to live in Grasmere so the two of you can be together…'

'I…'

'And then Alice, feeling angry with you and wanting revenge, sent all these things to your husband. Your husband raised the issue of your previously having had a stalker who killed himself. He also said he was going to leave you. So the two of you are selling your house and you've told your daughters. You, Mrs Luxton, have been feeling very upset about all this, about having your cover blown. And so you went round to Alice's house and the sight of her getting ready to leave Grasmere – the sight of her, moving on with her life, unharmed by you, despite everything – made you so furious you couldn't help yourself. You laid into her.'

'No…'

'And then you were frightened. You were frightened you might have killed her and knew what that would mean, so you wanted to keep one step ahead. You phoned an ambulance and concocted a story about how you had witnessed a young man go to Alice's flat and come away with blood on his hands, and you decided the best thing to do was present yourself as someone who cared about Alice, someone who really cared deeply about her, despite everything. So you took a deep breath and you went with her to the hospital and sat by her bedside until the police came and her memory came back. And then you lost your nerve and you scarpered. Is that right?'

'I'm sorry. You've made a mistake.'

The other officer reached under the table and brought out a Tesco carrier bag, which he put down in front of me. I thought for a minute they were my boots, the ones I'd dumped in the hospital car park. But they weren't. They were Alice's trainers.

'What can you tell me about these?'

'I have never seen them before.'

'Never?'

'Never.'

'Then what were they doing in your wardrobe, Mrs Luxton?'

'I'm sorry?'

'We found them in your wardrobe when we searched your home yesterday. You were out, but your husband was in and he gave us access. We found these trainers – the very trainers that Alice said yesterday had disappeared – in your wardrobe.'

'I don't know how they got there.'

'You don't think that, perhaps, after you'd kicked Alice in the head and fractured her skull, you thought you'd better change your shoes before the police got there, and so you took the first pair you could find?'

'No.' I was losing this now. I knew it. I began to cry. 'I don't know why Alice would do this,' I said. 'The girl is evil, she is truly evil. I have nothing I can defend myself with because she has covered all her tracks and all I can do is speak the truth and hope you will believe me.'

The officer looked unimpressed. 'You can save that for court, Mrs Luxton.'

25

Alice

I was waiting for my taxi to the station. I still looked a wreck, but better than I'd done before. My tooth had been fixed and the swelling around my eyes and lips had gone, but the bruising was there, large and purple. I looked like a woman who'd been in a fight, and it was oddly humiliating, to go out in public like this.

But still. I was here. I was alive. Actually, I thought, I was more than alive. I was great.

That morning in hospital, I'd unpacked my bag and taken out the collection of Bo's novels. I'd started tearing them up, but it was a long process and, once the destructive, therapeutic element had worn off, it was also incredibly boring, so I just threw them in the recycling instead. They'd made a loud thud as they hit the bottom of the bin. A satisfying sound. Like Bo's head against a wall.

Yesterday, they'd arrested and charged her, and released her on bail. Now, I just had to wait for the trial.

'Oh, she'll get herself a good defence lawyer,' the detective said, 'you can be sure of that, but the evidence is irrefutable. She'll be going down for this.'

I'd nodded. It didn't give me the feeling of satisfaction I'd been expecting.

I was calm now, barely a shred of anger left in me. Wrung out, perhaps. No energy left to feel anything at all. And Bo … Well, Bo was mad. There was nothing, really, to feel good about.

Except that I was getting away from her. I was walking away now, open-eyed and in charge. I'd seen Bo Luxton for what she was – cruel, manipulative and deeply sad – and I would never go back there again.

'Don't pity her,' Anna warned. 'She doesn't need pity.' And I knew now she was right. It didn't matter what made Bo like this, the fact was she was like it, and she was bad, and I needed to get away.

The taxi pulled up in front of me. I picked up my bag and stepped inside

Her Majesty's Prison for Women
Yorkshire

I am being released soon, back into the world of big skies and mountains and seas. I have been sick for outside, for the world beyond these gates, for fresh air and the smell of autumn fires.

And for my girls.

My girls don't visit me here. They think I'm ill, and that I've gone away to be made well, which isn't far from the truth. I write to them every week. Sometimes, they write back, and their letters arrive in plain white envelopes, addressed in Gus's black scrawl. They tell me about school, their friends, new sweets they've tried. Often, they say they miss me, but overall they're upbeat. They tell me nothing bad, though I'm sure bad things have happened in the time I've been gone.

They're still living in Grasmere with Gus. He bought a cottage in the village centre, probably to make the school run easier. I've given it some thought and know I can't go back there. There, I am known. Gus said he'd keep it secret, for the girls' sake, but it was in the local paper and I am bound to be a point of intrigue.

Instead, I've decided to go to London. I can be anonymous there. Perhaps I'll change my name, write more books, be new and unknown and brilliant. Just like Alice.

Alice. I looked her up on the internet last week, just to see what she was up to. She's having a book published: Exquisite. *I've ordered it from Amazon. It's about me. I suppose that was inevitable, but I have my own story too.*

I will track her down. We need to put this right.

Part Five

JUSTICE

1

Alice

They charged her with causing ABH and said the trial would be at a Crown Court, where sentences were more severe than if she'd only appeared before magistrates. The backlog at the Crown Court was a year long. She wouldn't be tried before next Christmas. They gave her bail, on condition that she didn't come near me.

I had no choice but to try and put it out of my mind and move forwards with my life. I went to stay with Jake and started my MA. There were sixteen people in my group, plus three tutors and an occasional visiting editor. All of them thought I was onto something with my book. I had to submit a chapter every week and the whole class would read it in advance and then discuss it at the workshop, pulling it apart, criticising it, offering their suggestions for improvement. There was a buzz about it, a feeling of excitement; and always that unanswered question lingering in the air: 'Is this a true story? Did it happen to you?'

I didn't tell anyone about Bo. I didn't speak about her at all, but always she was there, a wound in my heart and mind. I had no idea how long it would take to heal. I suspected it could be a lifetime, that Bo wasn't something that could just be put in the past and forgotten, but that she'd become part of the furnishings of my mind, forever affecting the way I moved in the world.

Perhaps, in time, it would be good.

On the last day of term, one of the younger men from the course asked me to join him for lunch. His name was Max; he was writing a children's book. In a different time, a different life, I would have found him attractive, but not now. I didn't think I'd ever find anyone attractive again. Only Jake was safe at the moment. Dear, lovely Jake, who'd offered me a space on his floor and then let me stay when his housemate moved out. Dear Jake, the man who would never go anywhere in life but who had a good, rich and generous heart. For me now, that was all that could ever matter.

Max took me to the café in the basement of the library. It was always quiet – only staff and research students ever went there, and filled it with an atmosphere of scholarly calm that made me feel like an imposter. I wasn't an academic or even very clever. I was just writing a thriller.

Max sat opposite me. He said, 'I really admire your book.'

'Thanks.'

'It's a brave subject.'

I shrugged.

He went on: 'There's a rawness to it that makes me think this happened to you.'

I kept my tone casual. 'I think everyone's work is influenced by things that happened to them.'

He nodded. Then he said, 'Would you like to come for dinner with me one evening? I'd love to talk more to you.'

I shook my head. 'I'm sorry,' I said, and smiled. 'I'm off the market.'

He eyed me quizzically, 'Really?'

'Really.'

'Not forever, surely?'

I wiped my lips with my napkin. 'Yes,' I said. 'Forever.'

No one was going to come near me. I was barricading my heart against mutiny. Never again would anyone break me with curse, or fist, or threat of love.

For a year, I wrote the book and rewrote the book until I could write it no more. I sent it out to literary agents. There was rejection – they told us on the MA to expect it – but there was also interest and I was taken on by someone who wanted to sell it to publishers.

She sold it.

2

Bo

Christmas. The trial was approaching and everything lay in ruins: my marriage, my home, my children, my career. After it happened, word had been leaked to the press, and then of course it flew round the book trade: Bo Luxton had been arrested and charged with causing ABH. She'd framed an innocent young woman. Also, she'd cheated on her husband with a lesbian.

It was all out there, the whole sordid story of my private life, and there was nothing I could do to fix it.

Vanessa's final email was brisk and cold. 'Dear Bo, It gives me no pleasure to say that, in the light of recent events, the publisher has decided to postpone your forthcoming novel, *Stalked,* until further notice. I also think it would be wise for you to find someone else to represent you in future. Wishing you all the best, Vanessa.'

Everyone was distancing themselves from me. Everyone. Not a single London publisher was going to print my most magnificent and powerful novel yet. They were running from me, the woman facing trial for violence.

I'd never known how important a clear name was. And my name was sullied now, forever, and wouldn't die with me. It would go down in the literary history books, the biographies. I could see it already: 'For years, Bo Luxton had a carefully constructed image in which she presented herself to the world as someone who cherished her private life above all else. She kept herself apart from the more glamorous side of the publishing world and devoted her time to teaching and her family. She gave the impression that she was a great mentor, one who sought out emerging talent and brought it into the light. However, behind this angelic mask lurked an altogether darker being, one who was capable of great acts of mental cruelty and even violence.'

I closed my eyes at the thought of it, of people – the world, the future – thinking badly of me. It made my stomach sway and swell until I thought I might be sick. I could not be remembered like this. I just couldn't.

For the first time, I felt completely helpless.

The girls didn't live with me now. Two days after the arrest, Gus sat opposite me in the kitchen, looked straight at me and said, 'I am going to apply for full custody.'

I said, 'You can't.'

'I can. I always thought you were a great mother, Bo. It was the one thing I felt sure of, despite everything else. I've always been suspicious of you and hated how secretive you are, but I had faith that you could look after the girls, that you were the mother I wanted my children to have. But now…' He let his voice trail off and held out his hands as if admitting defeat or helplessness '…I don't know who you are. You beat a woman and fractured her skull. I can't let you look after my children. Not now, not after this.'

'What are you trying to do to me, Gus?'

'I'm not trying to do anything to you. I am thinking only of what's best for the children and how to keep them safe.'

'You know I would never hurt them.'

He shook his head. 'I don't know that. How can I know that?'

'I'm their mother. You can't take them away from me.'

'It's for the judge to decide.'

I hated the way he did this. He was always so calm when it came to important discussions. As soon as anything became heated, he walked away and ended it.

I said, 'I won't let you take them away from me, Gus. I'm getting custody.'

'Unless a miracle happens for you, you're on the brink of going to prison, Bo. I think it's unlikely the judge will rule in your favour on this one.'

Oh, the smugness. The bloody arrogance and smugness of him. But he was right. I didn't want to go to court over it, to be humiliated in public and lose my girls.

I let him take them.

I hired a top barrister. He said I had two options: I could plead not guilty and try to get off; or I could plead guilty and present a defence, or at least some mitigating circumstances. I decided to go for guilty. The evidence against me was overwhelming and it was more honourable to admit the guilt. My reputation could be restored if I presented myself as vulnerable, desperate, broken…

The mitigating circumstances were love and chaos. I'd made a dreadful mistake that had almost cost me my family. I was heartbroken and I was also still deeply in love with Alice but had to pretend I wasn't to save us – me, my husband and my girls. But then Gus told me he was going to leave, so my family was going to fall apart anyway, and I wanted to try again with Alice, the love I'd had to sacrifice before. She rejected me, and all the stress and heartache of the previous months came out. For a minute I lost control. Then I realised what I'd done and called an ambulance.

I wasn't bad. Just deeply distressed. I was hardly responsible.

The weekend before the trial, the girls came to stay with me. On Saturday, we played Uno and did some baking, then I made a flask of hot chocolate and we all wrapped ourselves up in hats and gloves and carried the sledge over the fells to Helvellyn, where fresh snow had fallen in the night.

We stayed there for hours, striding up the lower slopes of the fell and then sliding back down it, the white faces of the mountains holding us inside the scene.

I watched them, and memorised it.

By the time we left, snow was falling heavily, and the walk home was long and hard and cold. Winter had begun its slow descent down the mountains and I knew that, by January, everywhere would be bitter and dark.

I held each girl's hand in mine as we trudged steadily on.

At home, I made vegetable soup, which we ate with crusty rolls I'd baked myself.

I bathed the girls and afterwards said, 'Come and sleep in my bed tonight.'

So they did and we sat up late, the three of us, reading old storybooks and poems. And when the girls laid down to sleep, I kissed each one and looked at them for as long as I could, and thought that, if I gazed at them hard enough, then a picture of me would be painted on their memories. I smiled tenderly.

While they were sleeping, I went downstairs and started cooking. Mini baguettes, tomato soup, cheese scones, meringues. I filled the fridge and the cupboards with all the things they loved.

At midnight, I went to bed but I didn't sleep. Before they woke, I got up and took myself for a walk round Grasmere's mountain edges, where frost lit the morning and the lake lay hard as mirrors. I shivered. The sky sagged, burdened with snow and I knew I wouldn't see it again for a long time.

They were still sleeping when I went home.

Dear Lola and Maggie,
1. *Know that you are loved.*
2. *Make mistakes. It's OK.*
3. *Eat well.*
4. *Be kind. Always*

Mum xx

Part Six

RENEWAL

Exquisite

Alice

The judge sentenced her to eighteen months in prison. She put forwards her plea for mitigating circumstances. I sat and listened to her, and had no idea what to think.

Anna watched the trial from the public gallery. Afterwards, she said, 'That woman is a manipulator.'

'You're probably right.'

'Don't believe a word of it, Alice. Not a word. She's dangerous. Deeply, dangerously manipulative. I saw her working the judge there, trying to present herself as the victim in all this. It's horseshit.'

But she was so convincing. I wondered if she believed it herself.

My book was published nine months after the trial. I had a launch party at a bookshop in Brighton. Friends, students and tutors from my MA all came, and the local press. For that night, I allowed myself to be proud. I'd made something good spring out of the awful, mind-wrecking experience of loving Bo Luxton.

I could only imagine, when I wrote her chapters, what had been going on in her head. I based her story on things she said at the trial and things she said to me; but really, there was no knowing whether anything I wrote was real. Bo Luxton was an enigma, impossible to grasp.

At the launch, we all drank champagne and ate book-shaped cakes. Afterwards, I stood and read the first chapter out loud, then everyone bought copies and I sat at a table and signed them.

I sat there for half an hour, scrawling my name in fifteen, twenty, thirty books. I took no notice of the door, where ordinary customers came and went. I didn't watch who was going in and out. I didn't notice anything at all, not until a familiar voice said sweetly, 'Congratulations, darling. I can't believe the lengths you have gone to, the lies you've told, just for a book deal.'

I looked up.

She was there, smiling at me, as if nothing bad had ever passed between us.

Acknowledgements

Thank you first of all to my nine brilliant beauties: Susannah Rickards, Essie Fox, Caroline Green, Geraldine Ryan, Emma Darwin, Julie-Anne Griffiths, Ruth Warburton, Rosy Thornton and Emma Haughton – for reading, feedback, advice and all the meaningful and frivolous chatter I couldn't live without.

Thank you to my Hexham friends for reading drafts, having my children over for tea during the writing of crucial chapters and for making the school yard a uniquely cool place to hang out: Fi White, Hannah Reynolds, Emma Haynes, Genevieve Crosby, Jo Allan, Ruth Smith-Berry, Katherine Calder, Deb Copland and Nichola Palmer.

Thank you to Muzna Rahman for reading and encouraging from the start, and to Catherine Redpath for enthusiasm.

Thank you to Claudia Cruttwell, who read the Novel that Never Was with diligence and commitment, and didn't tell me I was an idiot when I announced my new direction.

Thank you to my agent, Hattie Grunewald, and everyone at Blake Friedmann who has worked on this book with passion and excitement. And to my editor, the wonder that is Karen Sullivan.

Finally, thank you to Clay, Bonnie and Sam, who force the writing life into second place, where it belongs.

You are all forces for good in a wicked world.

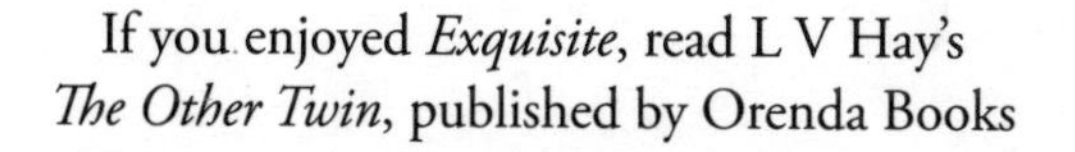

If you enjoyed *Exquisite*, read L V Hay's
The Other Twin, published by Orenda Books

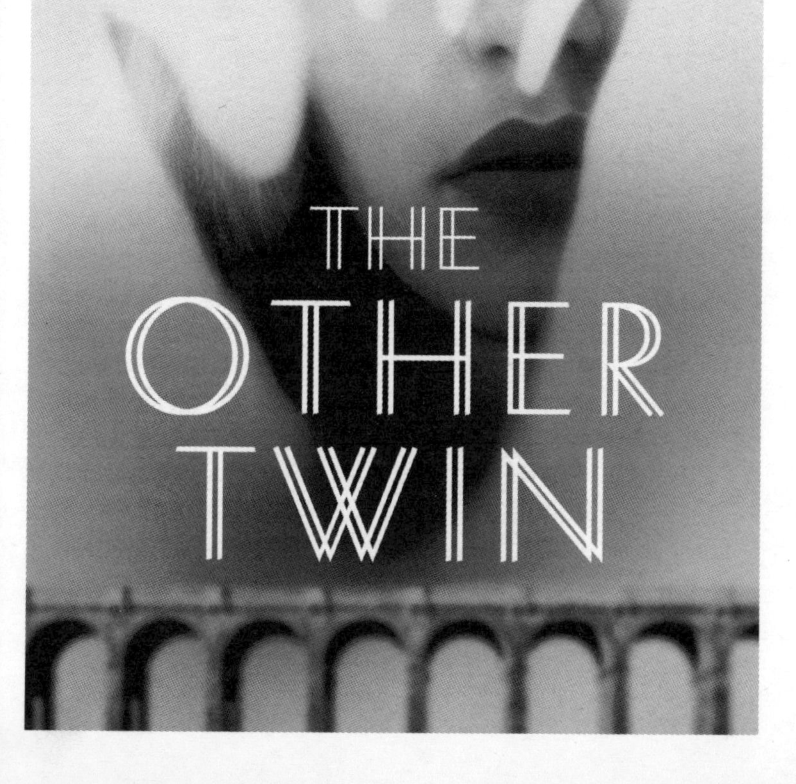